ANGELES MASTRETTA

MEXICAN BOLERO

TRANSLATED BY ANN WRIGHT

VIKING

VIKING

Published by the Penguin Group
27 Wrights Lane, London w8 5tz, England
Viking Penguin Inc., 40 West 23rd Street, New York, New York 10010, USA
Penguin Books Australia Ltd, Ringwood, Victoria, Australia
Penguin Books Canada Ltd, 2801 John Street, Markham, Ontario, Canada l3r 1b4
Penguin Books (NZ) Ltd, 182–190 Wairau Road, Auckland 10, New Zealand

Penguin Books Ltd, Registered Offices: Harmondsworth, Middlesex, England

First published in Mexico as *Arráncame la vida* by Ediciones Océano, 1986
This translation first published in Great Britain by Viking 1989
1 3 5 7 9 10 8 6 4 2

Printed in Great Britain by Richard Clay Ltd, Bungay, Suffolk
Filmset in 11 on 13½pt Monophoto Baskerville

A CIP catalogue record for this book is available from the British Library

ISBN 0–670–82885–2

CONTENTS

This book is for Hector, my accomplice,
and Mateo the boycotter.
Also for my mother and my girlfriends, including Veronica.
It obviously belongs to Catalina and her father,
who wrote it with me.

HISTORICAL NOTES

The Mexican Revolution, which overthrew the thirty-year dictatorship of Porfirio Díaz in 1911, was the first major revolution of the twentieth century. The first elected President Francisco Madero was, however, under attack from the start – from Victoriano Huerta and Felix Díaz on the right and Emiliano Zapata and Pancho Villa on the left. He was assassinated in 1913. The subsequent factional in-fighting dragged the Revolution on until 1917, when most of Mexico was controlled by Generals Venustiano Carranza and Alvaro Obregón. Carranza was elected President and a new nationalist constitution featuring civil liberties, anti-clericalism and agrarian reform based on communal landholding was approved. By this time one million people had been killed and a new political élite of revolutionary generals had emerged.

Six more years of jockeying for position among the generals followed. Villa and Zapata resorted to guerrilla warfare. Obregón criticized Carranza's failure to implement the constitution and when Carranza tried to block Obregón's way to the Presidency, he was murdered. Obregón was elected in 1920 and four years later, in the first peaceful transfer of political power, he handed over the Presidency to his Sonoran ally Plutarco Elías Calles. Conflict between the government and the church hierarchy still raged, however. The four-year Cristero Rebellion of peasant communities opposed to the secular state was finally suppressed in 1929 (the year Catalina and Andrés are married). In that same year Calles effectively retained power through a protégé President after Obregón was elected but assassinated before taking office. Calles united the main actors in the revolution – generals, peasant and labour leaders – in the National Revolutionary Party (PRN) which, under different names, has nominated all successful presidential candidates and ruled Mexico to this day.

During the 1920s and 1930s the retired revolutionary generals consolidated their power and made personal fortunes through political patronage. Corruption and violent land appropriations among these caciques – provincial strongmen – were common.

In 1934 the 'people's champion', Lázaro Cárdenas, was elected President. He broke the power of the Sonoran dynasty begun by Obregón and carried out a 'Six-Year Plan' of social reform and economic progress. This included nationalization of the US and British oil companies in 1938. He reorganized the PRN under the name Mexican Revolutionary Party (PRM) and it tightened its grip on politics by further extension of patronage, and by dominating the CROM and CTM, the major trade-union confederations.

Manuel Avila Camacho was elected in 1940 (the year Catalina moves to Mexico City and meets Carlos Vives) and Juan Andreu Almazán, his unsuccessful opponent, threatened to rebel but did not. Camacho's election marked the end of the first chapter of post-revolutionary Mexico. From then on modernization, industrialization and a return to cash-crop agriculture became the bywords. Camacho reconciled the government with the Church and the USA and began to demilitarize politics. The old generals gradually lost their influence in the PRM to professionals and technocrats. In 1946 (the year Andrés Ascencio dies) the new President, Miguel Alemán, swung Mexico to the right through closer ties to the USA and by encouraging foreign investment. He changed the ruling party's name again – to the Institutional Revolutionary Party (PRI) – and the Mexican state became entirely monolithic with the 'official party' and the civil service indistinguishable from each other.

Ann Wright

CHRONOLOGY

1911   Thirty-year dictatorship of Porfirio Díaz over-thrown. Francisco Madero elected President. Emiliano Zapata rebels and demands land reform in 'Plan de Ayala'.

1912   Madero under attack from left and right. Puts down rebellions of Pascual Orozco and Felix Díaz. Pancho Villa supports him.

1913   Madero overthrown then assassinated by Victoriano Huerta. Venustiano Carranza begins Constitutionalist Revolution against Huerta in the north, supported by Villa and Alvaro Obregón.

1914   Huerta defeated and flees into exile. Provisional government under Carranza. Obregón supports him but Villa rebels and forms alliance with Zapata.

1915   Villa defeated but still carries out guerrilla raids. Carranza government recognized by United States.

1917   New nationalist Constitution promulgated. Subsoil wealth declared property of the nation. Carranza becomes constitutional President.

1918   The Mexican Regional Workers' Federation (CROM) is formed at a national labour congress.

1919   Zapata retreats to the mountains, is ambushed and killed.

1920   Carranza tries to block Obregón's candidacy for the Presidency and is killed. Provisional President Adolfo de la Huerta calls elections and Obregón is elected. Literacy and education programme and agrarian reform finally begin.

1923   USA recognizes Obregón's government. Villa assassinated.

1924   Election of Plutarco Elías Calles. Like Obregón and de la Huerta, he is from the state of Sonora.

1926   Ongoing conflict between the government and the church results in the Cristero Rebellion.

1927   Constitution amended to allow Obregón's election and term to be extended to six years.

1928   Obregón re-elected but assassinated before taking office.

1929   Pascual Ortiz Rubio elected President but Calles remains as recognized 'boss'. He forms National Revolutionary Party (PRN) uniting the main actors in the Revolutions – generals, workers and peasant leaders. Cristero rebellion suppressed and government re-opens churches.

1931   New wave of clerical persecution begins.

1932   Ortíz Rubio resigns for 'health reasons'. Abelardo Rodríguez chosen to complete the term.

1934   Lázaro Cárdenas elected to carry out a new 'Six-Year Plan' of reform and economic progress. By the end of his term 50 per cent of Mexico's crop land is cultivated by communal villages.

1935   Cárdenas encourages formation of labour unions

and agrarian organizations. Emphasis on social welfare programmes.

1936   Cárdenas breaks the power of the Sonoran dynasty founded by Obregón and restores vast powers to the Presidency. Calles is deported. End of religious persecutions. Welcomes refugees from Spanish Civil War.

1938   Cérdenas decrees expropriation of major oil companies in accordance with the 1917 Constitution. State oil company Pemex formed. PRN reorganized under the name of the Mexican Revolutionary Party (PRM).

1940   Manuel Avila Camacho elected President. Juan Andreu Almazán, the unsuccessful opponent, threatens to rebel but does not. Gradual demilitarization of politics.

1942   Mexico joins Allies in war against the Axis powers.

1946   Miguel Alemán elected. Swing to the right with closer links to the USA. Emphasis on industrialization, foreign investment. Neglect of communal agriculture. PRM reorganized to give wider representation to professionals and civil servants. Becomes the Institutional Revolutionary Party (PRI).

GLOSSARY

ATOLE Drink made out of maize dough cooked with water, sugar, salt and milk

CAMPECHANA Type of croissant

CEMPAZÚCHIL Orange flowers that blossom in November. Called the 'flower of the dead' and used for decoration on the Day of the Dead

CHALUPAS Small pancake with chilli, beans and cheese

CHARRO Rural Mexican dressed in typical Mexican costume for festivals, fiestas, parades on horseback

CHILEATOLE Maize drink with chilli

CHILES EN NOGADA Stuffed chillis with a thick white sauce of almonds and pomegranates

COMPADRE/COMADRE Term used for very close friends, godparents of children, witnesses at weddings, etc. Implies almost a family relationship

CORRIDO Folk song based on legends or current events. There are many famous corridos of the Mexican Revolution

EPAZOTE Mint-like herb

FRONTÓN Wall game not unlike fives

MARIACHI Band of musicians in typical Mexican costumes. Composed of trumpets, violins, guitars and voices

MARIMBA Percussion instrument composed of wooden resonators, on the same principle as the xylophone

MOLE   Chocolate-based sauce with chilli, spices, plaintain and peanuts

MUÉGANO   Small caramel-covered biscuits

PAMBAZOS   Sandwich with potato and sausage, fried in chilli sauce

PIÑATA   Decorated paper parcel with sweets, biscuits and toys inside. Can be large or small. Large ones are beaten until they burst by children with sticks

PIPIÁN   Nut-based sauce with sesame seeds and chilli

PIRÚ   Tree with very thin leaves and red berries

POZOLE   Consommé made of pork and vegetable base

TAMAL   Mixture of maize dough, minced meat and chilli, wrapped in maize leaves and steamed

TINGA   Meat dish made with flaked meat and lots of onions

CTM   Confederación de Trabajadores Mexicanos – Mexican Federation of Labour

CROM   Confederación Regional de Obreros Mexicanos – Mexican Regional Workers' Federation, formed in 1918

CNC   Confederación Nacional Campesina – National Federation of Peasants

PRN   Partido Revolucionario Nacional – National Revolutionary Party (the party which has provided all presidents since its formation)

PRM   Partido de la Revolución Mexicana – Party of the Mexican Revolution (formed from the PRN in 1938)

PRI   Partido Revolucionario Institucional – Institutional Revolutionary Party (formed from PRM in 1942)

MEXICAN BOLERO

CHAPTER ONE

Many things happened in Mexico that year. Andrés and I
got married, for one.

I met him in a café in the colonnades. Where else?
Everything in Puebla, from engagements to murders,
happened in the colonnades.

He was over thirty and I was not even fifteen. I was with
my sisters and their boyfriends when we saw him come up.
He introduced himself and sat down to talk to us. I liked
him. He had large hands and lips that inspired fear when
pressed together and confidence when they laughed. It was
as though he had two mouths. His hair became ruffled as
he talked and tumbled over his forehead as insistently as
the habitual gesture with which he pushed it back. He
wasn't what you'd call handsome. His eyes were too small
and his nose too big, but I had never seen anyone with eyes
so alive, nor known anyone so sure of himself.

Suddenly he put his hand on my shoulder and said,
'They're such idiots, aren't they?'

I looked around, not knowing what to say.

'Who?' I asked.

'Say yes, your face says you agree,' he said, laughing.

I said yes, but again asked who.

He had green eyes and, winking one of them, said,
'Puebla people, sweetie. Who else?'

Of course I agreed. To me, Puebla people paraded around as though they had owned the title deeds to Puebla for centuries. Not like us, the daughters of a farmer who had stopped milking cows because he had learned to make cheese, and not him, Andrés Ascencio, who had become a general due to luck and his own cunning and no thanks at all to being born with an aristocratic surname.

He walked home with us and visited us often after that, dividing his favours between me and the rest of the family, including my parents, who were as amused and flattered as I was. Andrés told them stories in which he always came out on top. There wasn't a battle he hadn't won, or a corpse he hadn't killed for betraying the Revolution, the commander-in-chief or whoever happened to be to hand.

He won us all over. Even my elder sisters – Teresa, who began by dubbing him a lascivious old man, and Bárbara, who was scared stiff of him – ended up having as much fun with him as Pía, the youngest. He bought my brothers off by taking them for spins in his car.

Sometimes he'd bring flowers for me and American chewing-gum for them. The flowers never impressed me, but I did feel important arranging them while he smoked a cigar and talked to my father about the trials and tribulations of country life, or the leaders of the Revolution, and the favours they all owed him.

Afterwards I'd sit listening to them, proffering opinions with a conviction only my closeness to my father and my total ignorance allowed.

When he left I'd walk him to the door and let him kiss me for a moment as though we were being spied on. Then I'd run off after my brothers and sisters.

We began to hear rumours. Andrés Ascencio had many women, one in Zacatlán, another in Cholula, one in the La

Luz district, others in Mexico City. He deceived young girls, he was a criminal, he was crazy, we would be sorry.

We *were* sorry, but only years later.

At the time, Papa made jokes about the dark rings under my eyes and I'd smother him in kisses. I liked kissing Papa and feeling eight years old again, a hole in my sock, down-at-heel shoes and a bow on each plait on Sundays. I liked imagining it was Sunday and we could still go and fetch the donkey (on its day off from carrying the milk) and ride into the alfalfa fields. From my hiding place I'd call: 'Come and find me, Papa.' I'd hear his footsteps near me and his voice, 'Where's my little girl? Where's my little girl?' until he'd finally stumble over me: 'Here she is,' and he'd flop down beside me, holding my legs and laughing.

'She can't escape now, a frog has caught her and wants her to give him a kiss.'

And it was true, a frog did catch me. I was fifteen and dying for something to happen to me. That's why I agreed when Andrés suggested I went to Tecolutla with him for a few days. I'd never seen the sea. He told me it was black at night and transparent at midday. I wanted to see it. I just left a note, saying,

Dear Mama and Papa, Don't worry, I've gone to see the sea.

In fact, I went to get the biggest shock of my life. I'd seen stallions and bulls mount mares and cows, but a man's erect prick was something else. I let Andrés touch me without moving my hands or making a sound, stiff as a cardboard cutout, until he asked me what I was afraid of.

'Nothing,' I said.

'Why are you looking at me like that then?'

'I'm not at all sure it will fit,' I replied.

'Of course it will, old girl, just loosen up,' he said and

slapped my backside. 'See how stiff you are. You can't do anything like that. Relax. Nobody'll eat you if you don't want to.'

He touched me all over again, no longer in a hurry. I liked it.

'You see, I don't bite, Señorita,' he said formally, as though I were a goddess. 'Look, you're all wet,' he commented in the same tone my mother used when congratulating herself on a stew. Then he put it in, moved around, breathed heavily and cried out as if forgetting I was underneath, rigid again, well and truly rigid.

'You don't feel anything, why don't you feel anything?' he asked afterwards.

'I do feel, but I didn't understand the end bit.'

'Well, the end is the important bit,' he said to the sky. 'Ah, these old wives! When will they learn?'

And he went to sleep.

I was awake all night, I was on fire. I paced the room. A liquid ran down my legs. I touched it. It wasn't mine, he had spilled it into me. At dawn I took my fears to sleep. When he felt me get into bed he just stretched out an arm and pulled me onto him. We woke up with our bodies entwined.

'Why don't you teach me?' I asked him.

'What?'

'Well, to feel.'

'That's not taught, it's learned,' he replied.

So I decided to learn. I concentrated on loosening up, so much so that I seemed quite simple-minded at times. Andrés talked and talked as we walked along the beach; I swung my arms, exercised my mouth until my jaw nearly dropped off, pulled my belly in and out, flexed my buttocks.

What did the general talk about? I don't remember

exactly, but it was always something to do with his political ambitions. He talked to me as though he were talking to a brick wall, without expecting an answer or asking my opinion, requiring only an audience. In those days he was planning to replace General Pallares as Governor of Puebla. He called him a fool, but worried about him as though he weren't.

'He can't be such a fool if you're so concerned about him,' I said one afternoon. We were watching the sunset.

'Of course he's a fool. What business is it of yours, anyway? Who asked your opinion?'

'You've been talking about the same old thing for four days, time enough for me to have an opinion.'

'Hark at the lady. She doesn't know how babies are made, yet she already wants to boss generals around. I'm getting to like her,' he said.

When the week was over he delivered me home with the same aplomb he'd taken me, then he disappeared for a month. My parents received me back without question or comment. Their future wasn't too certain and they had six children, so they were just pleased the sea was so beautiful and the general had been kind enough to take me to see it.

'Why doesn't Don Andrés come?' Papa asked after about fifteen days.

'He's busy planning to unseat General Pallares,' I said. Instead of thinking about him I'd become obsessed with 'feeling'.

I didn't go to school. Not many girls did after primary school, but I had done a few extra years because the Salesian nuns had given me a grant to study in their clandestine secondary school. They were forbidden to teach, so I didn't get a diploma or anything, but I enjoyed it. I was grateful for everything. I learned the names of the tribes of Israel, the names of the chiefs and descendants of each tribe, the names of all the cities and all the men and women who appeared in the Holy Bible. I learned that Benito Juárez was a Freemason and had come back from the other world and tugged at a priest's soutane to remind him not to bother saying Mass for him, that he'd been in hell for some time.

At any rate, I finished school with passable handwriting, some notions of grammar, very few of arithmetic, none at all of history and several cross-stitched tablecloths.

Now that I was at home all day, Mama put all her energies into turning me into an excellent housewife, but I always refused to mend socks or pick the bad bits out of the beans. I had lots of time to think, and I began to despair.

One afternoon I went to see the gypsy in the La Luz district, who was supposed to be an expert on love. There was a queue of people waiting. When it was finally my turn, she sat before me and asked me what I wanted to know. I told her very seriously, 'I want to feel.'

She looked at me for a while. I looked at her too. She was a fat, jolly woman, with white breasts half hanging out of her low-necked blouse; she wore coloured bangles on both arms, and gold earrings dangled from her ears down her cheeks. 'Nobody comes here for that,' she said. 'Your mother won't be here complaining afterwards, will she?'

'Don't *you* feel either?' I asked.

For an answer she began to undress. In seconds she'd undone her skirt, taken off her blouse, and was naked, since she wore neither knickers, undies nor bra.

'We have a little thing here,' she said, putting her hand between her legs. 'That's what we feel with. It's called the bell, but it probably has lots of other names. When you're with someone, try to remember that this spot is the centre of your body, that all good things come from there;

remember that it's what you think, hear and look with, forget you've got a head and arms, put everything there. You'll be surprised what you feel.'

She was dressed again in a trice and pushed me towards the door.

'Off you go now. I'm not charging you because I only charge for lies and what I've told you is the truth.' She made a cross with two fingers and kissed it.

I went home secure in the knowledge that I knew a secret that was impossible to share. I waited until the lights were off and Teresa and Bárbara seemed fast asleep. I put my hand on the bell and moved it. Everything important was there, that's where I saw, heard and thought. I had no head, arms, feet or belly-button. My legs went stiff, as though they wanted to escape my body. Ah yes, everything was there.

'What's the matter, Cati? Why are you breathing so hard?' asked Teresa, waking up. The next day she went round telling everyone I had woken her up with some weird noises, as though I were drowning. My mother was worried and even wanted to take me to the doctor. That's how the Lady of the Camelias' tuberculosis had begun.

To this day I sometimes regret not having had a church wedding. I would have liked walking down a red carpet to the altar on my father's arm, with the organ playing the wedding march, and everyone looking at me.

I always laugh at weddings. I know that in the end all that spectacle turns into the everyday boredom of sleeping and waking next to the same old pot-belly. But the music and the procession, presided over by the bride, still makes me more jealous than amused.

My wedding wasn't like that. I'd have liked my sisters as bridesmaids in pink, silly and sentimental, decked out in organdie and lace, Papa in black and my mother in a long dress. I'd have liked a dress with wide sleeves and a high neck and a train stretching out behind me down the altar steps.

It wouldn't have changed my life, but I could have toyed with the memory as other women do. I could just imagine myself walking back down the aisle, leaning on Andrés and waving from my newly acquired position of nobility, from the privileged status people bestow on a bride when she comes back from the altar.

I'd have liked to be married in the cathedral, the aisle would have been even longer. But I didn't have a proper wedding. Andrés convinced me that it was all silly nonsense and that he couldn't jeopardize his political career. He had fought with Jiménez in the war against the clergy, he was loyal to the commander-in-chief, so on no account was he going to get married in church. A civil wedding, yes, the law had to be respected, though the best thing, he said, would have been a military marriage ceremony. He almost had his way, because we were married very much like soldiers.

He came to our house one morning.

'Are your parents in?' he asked.

Yes they were, it was Sunday. Where would they be if not at home, the same as every Sunday?

'Tell them I've come for you, we're getting married.'

'Who?' I asked.

'Me and you,' he said. 'But the others have to come too.'

'You haven't even asked me if I want to marry you,' I said. 'Who d'you think you are?'

'What do you mean who do I think I am? Andrés Ascencio, of course. Stop grumbling and get in the car.'

He went into the house, exchanged a few words with Papa, and came out with the whole family behind him.

Mamá was crying. I was pleased because it lent a touch of ceremony to the occasion. Mothers always cry when their daughters get married.

'Why are you crying, Mama?'

'Because I have a premonition, my child.'

Mama was always having premonitions.

We arrived at the registry office. Waiting for us there were some Arab friends of Andrés, his bosom pal Rodolfo with his wife Sofía, who looked at me with disgust. I imagined my legs and my eyes probably upset her, because her legs were thin and she had tiny eyes. Her husband *was* Under-Secretary for War, though.

The judge was a little squat man, bald and solemn.

''Morning, Cabañas,' said Andrés.

'Good morning, General, delighted to have you here. Everything is ready.'

He took out an enormous book and stood behind a desk. I was still consoling Mama when Andrés pulled me to his side, facing the judge. I remember Judge Cabañas's face, red and flushed like an alcoholic. He had thick lips and talked as though his mouth were full of peanuts.

'We are gathered together to celebrate the marriage of General Andrés Ascencio and Señorita Catalina Guzmán. In my capacity as representative of the law, the only law required to establish a family, I ask you, Catalina, do you accept General Andrés Ascencio as your lawful wedded husband?'

'All right,' I said.

'You have to say "yes",' said the judge.

'Yes,' I said.

'General Andrés Ascencio, do you take Señorita Catalina Guzmán for your lawful wedded wife?'

'Yes,' said Andrés. 'I do, I promise her the respect the strong owe the weak, and all those other things too, so you can save yourself the speech. Where do we sign? Here's the pen, Catalina.'

I didn't have a proper signature – I'd never had to sign anything – so I just printed my name the way the nuns had taught me: Catalina Guzmán.

'Put de Ascencio, Señora,' said Andrés over my shoulder.

Then he did a quick squiggle which in time I learned to recognize and even to imitate.

'Did you put de Guzmán?' I asked.

'No, dear, that's not how things are. I protect you, not you me. You're my family now, you are mine,' he said.

'Yours?'

'Where are the witnesses?' called Andrés, who seemed to have taken over Cabañas's job. 'You, Yúnez, sign here. And you, Rodolfo. What else did I bring you for?'

When it was my parents' turn to sign, I asked Andrés where his parents were. It hadn't occurred to me before then that he might have some.

'I've only got my mother, and she's ill,' he said in a voice which I heard for the first time that morning and which only came out of his throat when he talked of her. 'That's why my *compadres* Rodolfo and Sofía came. So that I'd have some family, too.'

'If Rodolfo signs, my brothers and sisters should sign too,' I said.

'You're crazy, they're just kids.'

'But I want them to sign. If Rodolfo signs, I want them to sign. They're my friends,' I said.

'Let them sign then. Let the kids sign too, Cabañas,' said Andrés.

I'll never forget my brothers and sisters coming forward to sign. We hadn't been in Tonanzintla long enough for them to lose their country-bumpkin look. Bárbara was sure I'd gone mad and opened her eyes wide. Teresa didn't want to join in. Marcos and Daniel were very serious as they signed, hair slicked down in front and sticking up at the back. They did their hair as if they were having a front-view photo taken, and never mind the rest. We'd put a bow in Pía's hair almost as big as she was. Her eyes just reached the top of the desk and from then on upwards there was nothing but an enormous red-and-white spotted silk ribbon.

'Don't ever say your family doesn't give itself airs,' said Andrés tickling my waist. I didn't realize it at the time, but now I'm sure he said it for my father's benefit. Over the years I learned that Andrés never said anything without good reason, and that he would have enjoyed threatening my father. The previous afternoon he had talked to him. He'd said he wanted to marry me, and if my father wasn't happy about it he had ways of convincing him, good and bad.

'The good ones then, General. It will be an honour,' my father had said, unable to refuse.

Years later, when his daughter Lilia wanted to get married, Andrés told me: 'Think I'm going to behave with my daughters like your father did with you? Not on your life. I won't have any bastard carting off my daughter from one day to the next. My daughter's suitor will have to ask for her hand in good time, so I can investigate the cretin who wants to fuck her. I'm not just giving my offspring away. Whoever wants her will have to beg for her and show what he's got to offer. If there's a deal to be done, I'll do it; if not, to hell with him. And they'll get married in church, damn it, now that Jiménez has made a balls-up of his quarrel with the Church.'

Pía couldn't sign her name, so she painted a balloon with eyes. The judge patted her bow and took a deep breath to show his patience was wearing thin. Luckily that was the end of it. Rodolfo and Chofi signed quickly, the pair of fatties were dying of hunger.

We went to the colonnades for breakfast. Andrés ordered coffee all round, chocolate all round, *tamales* all round.

'I want orange juice,' I said.

'You'll have coffee and chocolate like everyone else. Don't disrupt things,' scolded Andrés.

'But I always have juice for breakfast.'

'What you need is a war. From now on you'll learn to have breakfast without juice. Who gave you the idea there'll always be juice?'

'Papa, tell him I have juice in the mornings.'

'Bring the girl an orange juice,' my father said in such a defiant tone that the waiter shot off to get it.

'All right. Have your juice like a *gringa*. Whoever heard of a peasant waking up to orange juice in this country? Don't think you'll always get what you want. Life with a soldier isn't easy. Get that into your head once and for all. And you, Don Marcos, remember she's not your little girl any more and I give the orders at this table.'

There was a long silence, broken only by the sound of Chofi biting into a freshly baked *campechana*.

'Hey!' said Andrés, 'Why so quiet? This is a party! Your sister is married, kids, aren't you going to give her a send-off?'

'What, here?' said Teresa, who had a deeply ingrained sense of the ridiculous. 'You're crazy.'

'What did you say?' asked Andrés.

'Lots of luck! Be happy!' yelled Bárbara, throwing rice over us. 'Lots of luck, Cati,' she said as she stuck the rice in my hair and kneaded it into my skull as she caressed me. 'Lots of luck,' she kept saying as she hugged and kissed me until we both began to cry.

CHAPTER TWO

We were never just an ordinary couple. As newlyweds we went everywhere together. Even to gatherings of men only. Andrés would arrive with me and stand chatting, his arm around me. And his friends nearly always came to our house on 9th North. It was a big house, too big for the two of us, in the centre of town, near the main square, my parents' house and the shops.

I went everywhere on foot and was never alone.

In the mornings we'd go riding. We'd take Andrés's Ford to the Plaza del Charro, where our horses were kept. The day after our wedding he bought me a roan mare I baptized Nightmare. His was a stallion called Al Capone.

Andrés got up as soon as it was light, giving orders as though I were his regiment. He didn't stay in bed a single second after his eyes were open. Then he'd do physical jerks round the bed, pontificating about the importance of exercise. I'd lie still, covering my eyes and thinking of the sea and laughing mouths. Sometimes I'd stay there so long that Andrés would come back from the bathroom where he shut himself in with the newspapers and screech: 'Come on, you lazy cow. What're you up to, acting as if you were thinking? I'll wait for you downstairs; I'll count to 300, then I'm going.'

I'd get out of my nightie and into my trousers like a

sleepwalker, doing my hair with my hands, passing the mirror buttoning my blouse and brushing the sleep from my eyes. Then I'd run downstairs with my boots in my hand, open the door and there he'd be, '. . . 298, 299. You didn't have time to put your boots on again. You're slow, old girl,' he'd say from the car, revving up.

I'd stick my head through the window, kiss him and ruffle his hair before jumping down and running round to get in beside him.

The Plaza del Charro was some way out of town. The sun would already be warm when the stable lad brought our horses. Andrés would leap on to his horse unaided, but first he'd help me up on to Nightmare and pat her neck.

The countryside stretched out before us. We'd ride over it as though it were our own ranch. It never occurred to me that we'd need all the ranches we eventually owned. This was enough for me.

Sometimes Al Capone would take off for God knows where. Andrés would give him his head and let him run. At first I didn't know that horses copied each other and I was scared when Nightmare bolted off after him as though I'd asked her to. I couldn't hang on without banging my backside against the saddle at every step. I got huge bruises all over. When I showed them to my general in the afternoons he nearly died laughing.

'Because you bang your buttocks on the saddle. Press down in the stirrups when you gallop.'

I'd listen to his instructions as though he were God.

He'd always be surprising me with something, and he found my ignorance funny.

'You can't ride, can't cook, you couldn't fuck. What were you doing for the first fifteen years of your life?' he asked.

*

He always came home at mealtimes. I started taking cookery lessons with José and Clarita Muñoz and became expert at stews. I beat cake mixtures by hand, as though I were brushing my hair. I learned to make *mole, chiles en nogada, chalupas, chileátole, pipián, tinga*. Lots of things.

There were twelve of us in the ten o'clock class on Tuesdays and Thursdays. I was the only married woman.

After José Muñoz dictated the recipes, his sister Clara would lay all the ingredients on the table and share out the various tasks.

We worked in pairs, and the day we did *mole* I was with Pepa Rugarcía, who was about to be married. As we stirred the sesame seeds with wooden spoons she asked me, 'Is it true there's a moment when you have to close your eyes and say an Ave Maria?'

I laughed. We went on turning over sesame seeds and agreed to talk about it in the afternoon. Mónica Espinosa was frying pumpkin seeds on the stove next to us and invited herself to the gathering.

When everything was fried, we had to grind it.

'No gadgets,' said Clarita Muñoz. 'Times are hard, so it's best to learn to use the mortar and pestle.'

We took turns. One by one we stood over the mortar and moved our arms up and down on the chillis, peanuts, almonds and seeds. But we only managed to half crush them. Clarita let us feel total idiots for a while, then began grinding with her thin little arms, moving her waist and back, in a frantic desire to crush the ingredients to a pulp. She was tiny but strong. As she ground she went red, but didn't sweat.

'See that? Did you see?' she said when she finished. Mónica began to clap and we all followed suit. Clarita went over to a tea-towel hanging on a hook by the sink and wiped her hands.

'How can you even think of getting married? I hope you're not as useless at everything else.'

We finished at three in the afternoon, with our aprons splattered with red spots. We had *mole* up to our eyebrows. The turkey was divided into fourteen and we each took away a sample dish.

Andrés was waiting for me when I got home, as hungry as a stray dog.

I showed him the *mole*, decorated it with sesame seeds, and we sat down to eat it with *tortillas* and beer. We didn't talk. But in mid-bite we'd signal to each other and go on eating. When he'd cleaned his plate so thoroughly you could see the blue pattern of the Talavera pottery, he said he didn't believe I'd made the dish.

'We made it between us.'

'The Muñozes made it between them, you mean,' he said.

He kissed me and went out again. I went to meet Pepa and Mónica in the colonnades. They were already there when I arrived. Mónica was crying because Pepa had assured her that if a boy gave you a French kiss you'd get pregnant.

'Adrián gave me one yesterday when Mama wasn't looking,' she said between sobs.

I took them to the gypsy in La Luz. They certainly weren't going to believe anything I said. When I'd asked them if they knew what a man's prick was for, Pepa had said, 'Isn't it for peeing?'

We went to the gypsy and she explained to them, rubbed them with an egg and made them chew a few parsley stalks. Then she read our palms.

She assured Pepa and Mónica that they would be happy, that one would have six children and the other four, that

Mónica's husband would be sickly and Pepa's would never be as intelligent as she was.

'But he's rich,' said Mónica.

'Very rich, my child, and nobody can take that away from him.'

When I held out my hand, she stroked the middle of my palm and stared at it.

'Ay, my child, what strange things you have here.'

'Tell me,' I asked.

'Another day. It's very late now, I'm too tired. You asked me to teach these two. Well, I did. Off you go now.'

'Tell her,' begged Pepa and Mónica while I kept out the hand she'd dropped. So she looked at it again, rubbed it again.

'Ah, young lady, you've got a lot of men here,' she said. 'You've also got a lot of troubles. Come another day. I'm probably not seeing very well today. I get like that sometimes.' She let go of my hand and we went off to get a sandwich at Meche's.

'I'd like a hand as interesting as yours,' said Pepa as we walked along 3rd West to her house.

That night, lying beside my general, I stroked his stomach.

I love him now, I thought; who knows later on? He answered me with a snore.

About a week later we invited a friend to taste the *muéganos* I made at the Muñozes'. We were having coffee when some soldiers arrived with an order for Andrés's arrest. It was for murder, and was signed by the governor.

Andrés read it without a murmur. I began to cry.

'What d'you mean they're taking you? Where to? You haven't killed anyone.'

'Don't worry, I'll be back shortly,' he said, and asked his friend to stay with me.

'I'm going to ask for an explanation. It's bound to be a mistake.'

He patted my head and left.

When he'd closed the door I began to cry again. His arrest was more humiliating than a kick in the face. How could I face my friends? What would I tell my parents? Who would I sleep with? Who would wake me in the mornings?

The only thing I could think of was to rush over to the Church of Santiago. I'd heard they'd got a new Virgin who could perform all kinds of miracles. I regretted all the times I'd missed Mass, and all the first Fridays of the month I hadn't observed.

Santiago was a dark church with saints on the walls and a resplendent gold altar. There above me was a Virgin, her baby touching her heart with his hand.

The rosary was said at six. I leaned forward so the Virgin could see me better. The church was full and I was afraid my problem would be lost in the crowd. At six on the dot the priest arrived at the altar with his enormous rosary between his fingers. He was young, had big eyes and thinning hair. His voice rang out so loudly it could be heard all over the church.

'The mysteries we are going to contemplate are joyful mysteries. The first, the Annunciation. Ourfatherwhichartinheaven . . .' he began.

I answered the Our Fathers, Ave Marias and other prayers with a fervour I hadn't even experienced at school. Deep inside me I repeated, 'Look after him, Virgin Mary. Bring him back to me, Virgin Mary.'

At the end of each mystery the organ in the choir played the first notes of a well-known hymn, then the priest lifted his voice and the congregation sang after him.

After the litany, two altar boys appeared with censers

and began waving them backwards and forwards towards the Virgin. The place filled with silvery smoke.

'Our Lady of the Sacred Heart, pray for us, pray for us,' we all sang. Down the main aisle several women crawled on their knees towards the altar, their arms spread out in crosses. Two of them were crying.

I thought I should go with them, but I was too embarrassed. If I had to go that far to get Andrés out, he most certainly would not be coming back.

I redoubled my pleas. I spoke quietly looking at the Virgin, so serene, so sure of her crown and all who looked up at her from below.

She didn't see us, her eyelids were lowered, she was ageless and without worries.

Suddenly the organ stopped playing, the priest, spreading his arms and making the sign of the cross with each hand, said, 'Grant us, Our Lady of the Sacred Heart, the ineffable power which your Divine Son gave us with his adored heart. Recognizing your virtues, we beseech your protection, O Celestial Guardian of the Heart of Jesus!' I don't know how it went on, but the moment came when each person had to ask the favour they'd come for.

A vast murmur invaded the church. From all around came the noise of hundreds of voices. I murmured too.

'Let Andrés come back, don't let them lock him up, don't leave me all alone.'

'Do not abandon us,' the voices followed the priest as he spoke. Arms spread out in crosses filled the church.

The congregation surged towards the altar, pressing me against it. The organ played *Farewell, Gentle Mother*. We all sang. 'Our hearts beat for you. Farewell, a thousand times, farewell.' Then suddenly shouts came from the back of the church.

'Long live Christ the King! Long live Christ the King!'

Several policemen came down the aisle and pushed their way towards the altar. Though dizzy from the crowd and the incense, I heard one of them say to the priest, 'Come with us. You know the reason, so don't make a fuss.'

The organ played on.

'Please allow me to finish,' said the priest. 'I'll give the blessing with the Eucharist, then I'll accompany you wherever you wish.'

The man allowed him to get up from his kneeling position and he walked towards the sanctuary as if he were not afraid. I assumed it was confidence in his Virgin. He opened the sanctuary and took out the enormous host. An altar boy brought him the monstrance of gold and red stones. He opened it, put the host in the middle and turned towards us. We all made the sign of the cross, and the organ continued playing until the priest went down the steps into the vestry. I followed him. I only got as far as the door but I saw him take off his stole and put on a hat. That was enough for me to lose all my confidence in the Virgin of the Sacred Heart.

That night I went to bed trembling with fear and cold, but at least I didn't go to my parents' house. I talked for a while to Chema, a friend of ours who had been around, investigating. Andrés was accused of murdering a man who had forged diplomas which were then sold to army instructors. They said he'd killed him because he had had the original idea and was in charge of the whole operation, and that when the Secretary of State for War discovered the apocryphal titles and went after the forgers, Andrés was afraid and did away with the man who knew most about him.

Chema said it was impossible, my husband wouldn't go round killing for the sake of it and besides he wasn't interested in puny deals like that. The problem was that

Governor Pallares detested him and wanted him out of the way.

I didn't understand why he hated him if he had beaten him. He was the one in power. Why infuriate Andrés, who was already livid at having lost?

The following day the papers published his photo behind bars; I didn't dare leave the house. I was sure no one in my cookery class would talk to me, but it was my turn to bring the ingredients for the *chiles en nogada* and I couldn't not go. I arrived at 10.30 with a sleepy face and a basketful of peaches, apples, plantains, sultanas, almonds, pomegranates and peppers.

The Muñoz family kitchen was enormous. There was room for the twenty of us without anyone knocking elbows. When I arrived, the others were already there.

'We're waiting for you,' said Clarita.

'But I . . .'

'No excuses. The world depends on women for food; it's a job, not a game. Start chopping that fruit. Let's see now, girls, who's going to help her?'

Only Mónica, Pepa and Lucía Maurer came forward. The rest watched me from behind the table. They would have liked to say that Andrés was a murderer and they weren't mixing with his wife, but that wasn't how things were done in Puebla. None of them were friendly, but none spoke their minds, either.

Mónica stood next to me with her knife and slowly cut up a plantain as she asked why they had taken the general away and if I knew the real story. Luci Maurer put her hand on my shoulder and began peeling the apples she took from my basket. Pepa couldn't stop biting her nails, but in between bites she told Mónica off for asking so many questions and, when she'd got her to stop her interrogation, she said, 'Were you afraid in the night?'

23

'A bit,' I answered, slicing peaches.

When we left the Muñoz's house, I hesitated in the middle of the street with my dish of chillis garnished with parsley and pomegranate. My friends were picked up at two on the dot.

'Pay no attention,' said Mónica as she got into the car in which her mother was waiting.

I walked home. I opened the door with the gigantic key I always carried in my bag.

'Andrés!' I shouted. No one answered. I put the dish of chillis on the floor and kept shouting: 'Andrés! Andrés!' No one answered. I sat cross-legged and cried into the sauce. With my back to the door I was gazing through huge teardrops at how green my garden had grown when the bolt rumbled back exactly the way Andrés did it.

'Aha, crying for your *charro*, are you?' he said. I got up and touched him. The afternoon sun struck the window panes and the patio. I took off my shoes and began unbuttoning my dress. I put my hands under his shirt and pulled him on to the grass in the garden. There I reassured myself that they hadn't cut off his prick. Then I remembered the *chiles en nogada* and ran to fetch them. We stuffed them hurriedly into our mouths.

'Why did they take you away, why did they bring you back?' I asked.

'Because they're bastards and fools,' said Andrés.

The papers next day reported that the priest from the Church of Santiago had been given a two-year prison sentence for organizing a demonstration against the laws regulating worship, and General Andrés Ascencio had been released with due apologies, having proved himself totally and irrevocably innocent of the murder of the diploma forger.

I didn't want to go back to my cookery class. When Andrés asked me why I wasn't going any more, I eventually told him about the glares and the sneers I'd had to put up with. He pulled me to him and slapped my backside.

'You're quite something, you know,' he said. 'Just wait until I give the orders round here.'

CHAPTER THREE

It was a long wait. For four years Andrés came and went as he pleased, treating me sometimes like a burden, sometimes like a thing you buy and keep in a drawer and sometimes as the love of his life. I never knew what mood he'd wake up in; if he'd want me out riding with him, if he'd be taking me to the bullfight on Sunday or if he wouldn't come home for weeks.

I was possessed by a passion that had nothing to do with me, a desire for things I didn't understand. I was á kid. Sometimes I'd be sad, and then suddenly ecstatic for the same reasons. I was becoming the kind of woman who swings from grief to riotous laughter with nothing in between, always hoping for something to happen, anything, except for morning after morning of the same. I hated tranquillity, it frightened me.

My sad moments often coincided with my time of the month. It wasn't something I could tell the general, of course, because men aren't interested in that kind of thing. Although I wasn't ashamed of my period, not like my mother, who never talked about it and taught me to wash the bloodstained towels when nobody was looking.

In Puebla, women called their periods Pepe Flores. 'I'd love to have a Pepe Flores or something,' I'd say, 'anything but this awful boredom.' When I was sad I thought of Pepe

Flores, of how I'd have liked him to be mine, how I'd like to go to the sea with him for the five days he visited me every month.

The house on 9th North had a very tall ash tree, two jacarandas and a *pirú*. Behind them, in a corner, was a little room of adobe covered with bougainvillaea. Its only window framed a piece of sky which changed with the weather. I used to sit on the floor with my knees drawn up, thinking of nothing.

Mónica had told me that drinking anise was good for relieving that sharp pain in your legs, your waist and whatever you have beneath that skin covered in hair. I drank anise until I came out in spots and talked to myself or anyone who would listen. It gave me Dutch courage, and everything I couldn't reproach my general with directly I let fly to the four winds.

Andrés was in charge of military operations in the State of Puebla at the time. That meant that all the officers in the region answered to him. I think that was when he became a public danger and when he met Heiss and all his other associates and protégés. He earned a great deal of money. Heiss was a loudmouthed *gringo* who sold buttons and medicine. He had wangled himself the post of US Honorary Consul in Mexico and had arranged to have himself kidnapped in Carranza's time. With the money his government paid for him to rescue himself, he bought a pin factory on 5th South. He was a great wheeler-dealer. His eyes would sparkle as he planned his deals. He used not to change his gaberdine trousers for weeks, yet got rich under the very noses of the inhabitants of Puebla who saw him arrive a poor man and ended up calling him Don Miguel. They said he was very intelligent and he fascinated them. But in fact he was a scoundrel.

I knew nothing about him in those days, I knew nothing about anyone. Andrés treated me like a little doll whom he talked nonsense to, fucked three times a week and kept happy by tickling her back and parading her round the main square on Sundays. After they arrested him that afternoon I began asking more about his work and his business deals. He didn't like telling me. He always said he didn't live with me to talk business, and that if I wanted money I only had to ask him. Sometimes I convinced myself he was right. What did I care where he got the money to pay for the house, the chocolates and all the little things I fancied?

I concentrated on filling my time. I'd go and visit my friends and spend the afternoons helping them with their embroidery and making biscuits. We'd read the novels of Pérez y Pérez together. I still remember Pepa weeping buckets over Anita de Montemar while Mónica and I roared with laughter at such childish sentimentality. We helped her sew her trousseau. She was marrying an ugly, taciturn Spaniard – heaven knows why she chose him for a husband. We were very rude about him behind her back, but never dared tell her she should exchange him for the tall young man who sometimes made her laugh as they came out of Mass. Anyway, she married the Spaniard, who turned out to be madly jealous. So much so that he had the floor of their balcony removed so that she couldn't stand on it and look out.

The day of Pepa's wedding, for which I bought a dress of pale green chiffon and Andrés gave me a long pearl necklace, I woke up exhausted and didn't want to stir from my bed.

Andrés got up to do his physical jerks and I watched him as he went into the bathroom listing all the things he had to do that day. I snuggled under the covers pretending

I was going to the moon like I used to when I was a little girl. I was in the moon when he came back.

'Is it your time of the month? Why else have you woken up looking like a dying dog? Let me look at you,' he said. 'You've got cow eyes. Are you expecting?'

He said it with such pride in his voice and a gesture of such satisfaction that I was embarrassed. I felt myself blush, pulled the covers over my head and wriggled to the bottom of the bed.

'What's the matter?' he asked. 'Don't you want to give me a baby?'

I heard his voice through the covers and touched my swollen breasts as I did the calculations I usually never bothered about. I hadn't seen Pepe Flores for three months.

We went to the wedding. I spent the whole time thinking how awful it would be to be a mother – that's why I don't remember much about the celebrations. I only remember Pepa coming out of the church with the flowers round her head holding a veil that reached to the hem of her long dress. She was lovely. Mónica and I said so as we watched her come out, and held hands to contain our emotion.

'I'm going to have a baby,' I told her to the sound of the wedding march.

'That's wonderful,' she cried, and started kissing me right there in the church.

CHAPTER FOUR

I was seventeen when Verania was born. The nine months I carried her were a nightmare. I'd watched this bump grow in front of me, but I couldn't bring myself to be a tender mother. The first calamity was giving up horses and waisted dresses, the second was being fed up to the back teeth with so much discomfort. I hated complaining and I hated the sensation of being continually possessed by something strange. When she began to move like a fish swimming deep in my belly, I thought she would suddenly pop out followed by rivers of blood until I died. Andrés was responsible for all these woes, yet he couldn't even bear hearing about them.

'Women love making themselves important with this maternity lark,' he would say. 'I thought you'd be different; you grew up watching animals carrying their offspring and giving birth without all this to-do. And you're young to boot. Just don't think about it, you'll forget the discomfort, you'll see.'

He'd lost his bid to become the candidate for governor, so he was at a loose end. Travelling caught his fancy and he took me to the USA by car.

I was tired the whole time. I slept with the sun in my eyes even when the car leapt about on long, dirt-track roads.

'I don't know why I brought you, Cati,' he'd say. 'I should have invited some other woman. You haven't admired the scenery, you haven't sung to me, you haven't laughed. You've been a total fraud.'

I was a fraud for the whole of my pregnancy. Andrés didn't touch me, so as not to harm the baby he said, and this made me very nervous. I couldn't think straight, I'd forget things, I'd start one conversation and finish another, and only heard half of what was said to me. Besides, I was absolutely terrified of the actual birth. I thought it would leave me a total idiot. Andrés went away more often. He no longer took me to the bullfights in Mexico City. He left the house alone, but I was sure some other woman was waiting round the corner. Someone presentable, without a bun in her belly or huge bags under her eyes. He was right. I wouldn't have taken myself anywhere either. Especially not to the bullfights, where the women were so beautiful and their waists so slender.

I was left brooding, stroking my tummy, sleeping. I went out only to go and eat at my parents' house.

One lunchtime I was crossing the main square, blowing a little windmill I'd bought for Pía, when I bumped belly and all into Pablo, my old friend from school. Pablo's parents were from Chipilo, his grandparents from Piedmont in Italy. So he was blond, with deep-set eyes.

'You're looking very pretty!' he said.

'Go on with you,' I answered.

'I mean it. I always knew you'd be pretty when you were pregnant.'

In short, I didn't go to my parents' house.

Pablo delivered milk in a little mule cart. He left Chipilo in the early mornings. He invited me for a ride and we went out into the countryside. He treated me like a queen. Nobody was as caring towards the prospective baby as he was. Not even me, although I wasn't a good example of total devotion. That afternoon we played in the grass like children. I even forgot my belly, I even began to think it would be good to desire nothing more than that easy zest for life. I delighted in the rough material of his trousers, his unruly hair and his hands. Pablo took it upon himself to relieve me of the anxieties of my last three months of pregnancy, and I to relieve him of the virginity he still hadn't left in any brothel.

He was the only good thing about being pregnant with Verania. We played in the hay until the Sunday before the birth. From there he took me to my parents' house, because I felt Verania was on her way. My general came home days later with twenty bunches of red roses and some chocolates.

The baby was a month old and my nipples all wrinkled and swollen when Andrés arrived with the two children from his first marriage.

Virginia was a few months older than I. Octavio was born in October 1915, and so was a few months younger. They stood in the doorway of my room. Their father introduced us and the three of us looked at each other in silence. I knew nothing about Andrés's life, least of all that he had children my own age.

'These are my eldest children,' he said. 'They've been living with my mother in Zacatlán. But I don't want them in a small town any more. They'll go to school here and live with us.'

I moved my head up and down and, showing them the baby, said, 'This is your sister. Her name is Verania.'

Octavio came to look at her. He asked why she had such a strange name and I told him it was my father's mother's name.

'Your grandmother?' he asked, and began stroking Verania's cheek.

He had dark, trusting eyes. He laughed like Andrés in his charming mood and seemed ready to be my friend. I couldn't say the same about his sister. She stayed in the doorway beside her father, silent, and wouldn't look me in the eye. She was ugly, rather fat, with sad eyes and thin lips. She had small breasts, heavy hips, no buttocks and far too much stomach. I felt sorry for her.

She and Octavio moved in with us and suddenly we were a family. I even thought it would be nice to have company when Andrés was not there.

That night I exhausted him with questions. Where did these children spring from? Were there any more?

These two for the time being. He'd met their mother early in 1914 when he'd gone to Mexico City with General Macías, a little old man who was governor of Puebla following the resignation of the constitutional governor after Huerta had murdered Madero. I hadn't known much about what had happened in those years, but Andrés gave me a sweeping account the night his children arrived.

Macías was from Zacatlán, a muleteer like old man Ascencio. He'd fought the French in Puebla and joined Porfirio Díaz's army. At Díaz's side he became important and rich. When the Revolution broke out he went back to Zacatlán, where he had a farm and felt protected. Andrés began working for him, supervising the farmhands. The son of a friend, he gradually gained his confidence. When Huerta offered Macías the governorship, the old man grabbed it with glee, and took his assistant with him to Puebla. After ten months of so-called governing, he fell ill. He wanted to go to Mexico City for treatment and put himself into the hands of Andrés, who by now had made himself indispensable because he was so organized and looked after the general with dog-like devotion. Andrés knew where he had put his glasses when he lost them, as he often did, he looked after his clothes and even paid some of his bills. The general was ill for three weeks and, not unexpectedly, died at the beginning of January 1914. Andrés was left alone in Mexico City, not knowing what the hell was going on, with no work and two silver coins, a present from old Macías.

But he liked the city. He found work in a dairy in Mixcoac and stayed to see what would happen next. After all, he was eighteen and had no desire to go back to a small town.

In Mixcoac he met Eulalia. She had arrived with Madero's troops. Her father, Refugio Núñez, was an ordinary foot soldier, but enthusiastic with it. Eulalia was constantly recalling the day they had entered Mexico City and thousands of people cheered them as they got off the train and walked to the main square. Señor Madero went into the Government Palace while she and her father stayed outside, cheering with the crowd.

Eulalia's father worked at the dairy too, he both hated and hoped, and had passed on to his daughter the sombre smile of defeat and the conviction that the Revolution would soon rescue them from poverty. In the meantime they milked cows and delivered milk in a little cart driven by Andrés and drawn by an ancient horse. Eulalia didn't have to help with the delivery, her duties finished with the milking, but she liked going round the district of Juárez with Andrés, knocking at the big houses where maids in dark uniforms would come out, or from time to time very white women in silk dressing gowns and expressions on their faces which said the world was falling apart. She showed Andrés the houses that a year earlier had been demolished by the rebel cannons which had ousted Madero. Andrés still understood very little, but he became a *Maderista* for the girl's sake. Eulalia, he said, had Octavio's

34

eyes, was small and strong and made him a present of her virginity one morning coming home from the milk round.

I wanted to know everything. Strangely enough, he told me.

They spent their days together, from dawn when they got up to do the milking to dusk when they sat drinking coffee and listening to her father tell how Emiliano Zapata had captured Chilpancingo, how the revolutionaries in the north were approaching Torreón, how the traitor Huerta had made Don Porfirio a general and had sent the medal to Paris.

Heaven knows how Eulalia's father always knew everything. When some *gringo* sailors were arrested in Tampico for looting near the Iturbide Bridge, he predicted the disembarcation of *gringo* troops in Veracruz. Before Zacatecas was captured by Villa, he foresaw several days of bloody fighting and more than 4,000 dead.

Since he guessed everything, he also knew that Eulalia was going to have Andrés's baby, and after his inevitable pessimism he began mixing prophesies about the war with his grandchild's future. Eulalia accepted the changes in her body and that it would slowly stretch with the baby, but she still got up at dawn for the milking and went with Andrés on his round in the cart.

One morning in mid-July Don Refugio woke up and announced the defeat of the traitor. No sooner had he said it than the Chamber of Deputies accepted the resignation of Victoriano Huerta. From then on he predicted the fall of Puebla, Querétero, Saltillo, Tampico, Pachuca, Manzanillo, Córdoba, Jalapa, Chiapas, Tabasco, Campeche and Yucatán.

'General Obregón is arriving today,' he said on 15 August. The three of them went to the main square to welcome him.

Young Ascencio liked Álvaro Obregón. He thought that

if one day he entered the fight he would go in on Obregón's side. He looked like a winner.

'That's because you haven't seen Zapata,' Eulalia told him.

'No, but I know the faces of the Indians round those parts,' retorted Andrés.

They didn't quarrel. He talked of her as an equal. I never heard him talk about another woman like that.

When Venustiano Carranza reached Mexico City and called a Convention of governors and serving generals for 1 October, Don Refugio predicted that Villa and Zapata would not support the old man. Again he was right.

The Convention was transferred to Aguascalientes. Villa and Zapata went to that. At the end of October the Ayala Plan was approved. Don Refugio began drinking as soon as he imagined it would be possible and when the news was confirmed he'd been drunk for three days. He said over and over again, 'I told you, children. "Land and Liberty" has won.'

'You can say what you like, but they shouldn't have quarrelled with General Carranza,' said Andrés.

Eulalia stroked her stomach and prepared coffee. She liked hearing her father talk with her man.

At the beginning of November, Carranza left Mexico City and from the city of Córdoba disowned the Ayala Plan. In Aguascalientes they went on meeting as though nothing had happened, appointed a provisional President of the Republic, and went on contesting towns with Carranza's troops.

On the 23rd, the *gringos* handed Veracruz over to General Carranza and, on the night of the 24th, troops of the Southern Division entered Mexico City.

On 6 December, Eulalia woke up with labour pains. Her father decided that before anything else they had to go down to Reforma to see Villa and Zapata lead the Convention Army. A column of 50,000 followed them. The parade began at ten in the morning and finished at four in the afternoon. Eulalia gave birth to a little girl right there in the middle of the street. Her father helped the baby out, cleaned her and wrapped her in Eulalia's shawl, while Andrés watched, looking a total fool.

'Ay, Virgin!' was all Eulalia could say between pushes. She said it so often that when they got home and while Don Refugio was washing the baby, Andrés decided they'd call her Virgin. When they went to christen her, the priest said they couldn't call her that and recommended Virginia, which sounded similar. They agreed.

Eight days after the birth, Eulalia went back to the dairy with the baby at her breast and an even more brilliant smile than the year before. She had a daughter, a man and she'd seen Emiliano Zapata ride by. What more could she want?

Andrés on the other hand was fed up with poverty and routine. He wanted to be rich, he wanted to be a leader, to ride in parades, not to watch them. He was sick of milking and delivering and listened to Don Refugio's predictions as if they were a series of curses.

The Conventionalists and the Constitutionalists were fighting all over the country. One day one side would capture a town, the next day the other side would rescue it, one day one law would hold sway, the next another, for some the capital was Mexico City, for others it was Veracruz. But Andrés figured out that while the Constitutionalists always had the same leader, there were too many Conventionalists and they would never agree.

'The trouble is you don't believe in democracy,' said his father-in-law.

'I've always had a nose for things, Don Refugio,' said

Andrés. 'I don't believe in that democracy. Lieutenant Segovia was right when he said, "Unguided democracy is not democracy".'

January began with the Conventionalists governing Mexico City, but by the end of the month Álvaro Obregón had occupied the city again and during the Constitutionalist government there was a gale which brought down the street lamps and left the city in darkness. Many trees were uprooted and the roof of the hut where Andrés, Eulalia and Don Refugio lived went flying off at midnight, leaving them exposed to the cold. Eulalia thought it hilarious being left without a roof and Don Refugio began a speech on the injustices of poverty, which one day the Revolution would do away with. Young Ascencio spent the night cursing and vowed to do anything rather than be dependent and poor.

He began working afternoons as an assistant to a Spanish priest who had his church in Mixcoac. Unfortunately the job didn't last long because Obregón imposed a tax of 500,000 pesos on the clergy in Mexico City and, since they couldn't pay, all the priests were taken to the barracks. Andrés accompanied Father José, who was very rich, and heard him swear on the Virgin of Covadonga that he hadn't a penny. Obregón decreed that the Mexican priests remain in prison but freed the foreigners on condition they left the country. Father José didn't waste a minute saying goodbye to his flock and set off for Veracruz with a trunk full of gold. At least that's what it seemed like to Andrés, who had to carry it to the station.

Things went from bad to worse. Even the cows gave less milk; they were thin and underfed. Eulalia and Andrés scoured the city for bread and charcoal. Often they didn't find any and when they did they couldn't afford it.

In March, to the delight of Don Refugio and his daughter, Obregón fled during the night and the Southern

Army occupied the city again. In their wake came the president of the Convention and the majority of the delegates.

Although the hopes of Eulalia and her father grew, they did not manage to infect Andrés. And, to cap it all, Eulalia was pregnant again. The dairy paid them irregularly, but deducted on the dot all the times they were absent. Andrés began to hate his wife's illusions. He would have liked to leave. Almost twenty years afterwards he still couldn't explain why he hadn't.

Eulalia was sure that the gentlemen of the Convention really did not know the hardship ordinary people were suffering, so when she heard they were organizing people to attend one of their sessions with empty baskets, asking for maize, she didn't think twice about going along. Andrés didn't want to go, but when he saw her in the doorway with the baby on her back and her face shining, he followed her.

'Maize! Bread!' shouted the crowd, holding aloft empty baskets and hungry children. While his wife shouted with the others, Andrés cursed and raged, sure that they would achieve nothing like that.

A Convention representative told the crowd that they would buy basic necessities to the tune of 5 million pesos.

'Didn't I tell you, we'll have more than enough food,' announced Eulalia the next day as she went out with her basket to see what she could glean at the sale of cheap maize the president had ordered in the yard of the Escuela de Minería. He watched her leave carrying her little girl, her belly already protruding, thin and hollow-eyed, with the luxury of her relentless smile. He thought his wife was going mad and sat on the floor smoking a cigarette butt.

Night fell and Eulalia did not return, so he went to look for her. When he reached the Escuela de Minería he found soldiers collecting up lost shoes and baskets, and not a single grain of maize to be seen. Ten thousand people had been there to get it. There had been pitched battles over handfuls of maize, people had trodden on one another, crushed each other. Two hundred people had fainted, some because they'd almost suffocated, others because of sunstroke. Red Cross ambulances had taken them away.

Andrés went to the old Red Cross hospital for Eulalia. He found her lying on a stretcher, her baby covered in scratches, and with her eternal smile. When she saw him she said nothing, just opened her hand to reveal a handful of maize. He looked at her, horrified, and she opened the other.

'Here's some more,' she said.

Not long afterwards the dairy paid them ten pesos and, feeling rich, they went to the market in San Juan to buy food. It was twelve o'clock when they arrived. The doors of almost all the shops were closed. A host of women had gathered in front of the bakery, shouting and pushing.

'Let's go there,' said Eulalia, already on her way. And she began pushing with all the strength in her thin body.

Suddenly the doors gave way and the women charged into the bakery, as excited as they were hungry, and fell on the bread, fighting for it, filling their baskets. Andrés watched the total chaos. He saw the Spanish baker try to stop the women taking bread without paying, fighting with them, taking the bread out of their baskets again. He saw him leave the counter, hanging on to the plaits of a woman who had emptied a tin of rolls into her basket.

Andrés didn't find much money in the wooden cash box on the floor, but he quickly took what there was and looked around for Eulalia in the midst of the shawls and flailing arms of women taking bites out of their prizes. He got to the door and called her. She raised an arm and showed him a loaf she was chewing and a smile full of crumbs. She pushed her way towards him and he began to run, pulling her along after him.

'Didn't you get anything?' asked Eulalia, not understanding why they'd left the party in full swing. He didn't answer. He just let her grumble into her aniseed loaf as they rode home to the dairy. She told him he wasn't going to get a single mouthful for being so useless and cowardly.

Don Refugio had stayed behind with the baby and was rocking the cradle, which was tied to the roof with a whip. Eulalia went in happily and held her basket out to the old prophet. Andrés watched them embrace laughing and thought of keeping the money for unhappier days. But Eulalia went on criticizing him, so he pulled out of his pocket all the coins he'd managed to grab.

'Lots of one-peso coins,' cried Eulalia, hurling them into the air.

She wanted to buy a shawl that very afternoon and made Andrés buy a shirt for himself and another for Don Refugio. She found a bonnet with shiny satin ribbons for the baby and the rest they spent on sugar, coffee and rice. Andrés fought hard to keep fifteen pesos.

'Five more than we had this morning,' said Eulalia, before going to sleep.

They woke to the sound of cannons so near they thought of not going to milk the eight emaciated cows left in the dairy. But Eulalia wanted to dunk one of her loaves in the bucket of fresh milk and left even earlier than usual, before hearing her father's warnings.

The cannon fire went on all day. Andrés and Eulalia went down to Juárez with the little milk they had, but no one opened their doors. There were no trams or cars, the shops were closed and hardly a soul dared venture out.

In the afternoon the last of the Convention troops left and the next morning the first of the Constitutionalist forces entered the city. More followed two days later and with them came a new military commander, a new chief of police and another city governor.

Eulalia went to buy butter with a one-peso note and was told in the shop that it was no longer valid. She went home furious with Andrés for not having wanted to spend it all. She was so angry she tried to burn what they had left, but her father predicted the return of the Conventionalists and retrieved the notes that had begun browning in the pan.

She was growing pale and sad. Andrés said it was the pregnancy, but Don Refugio said she hadn't been like that the year before.

'They say each child is made differently,' Eulalia replied as they argued.

Five days later, the Conventionalists retook the city. As soon as Eulalia heard the news she took her notes to the shop. She bought two kilos of rice, one of flour, two of maize, one of sugar, one of coffee and even a packet of cigarettes. When the Constitutionalists returned and Don Refugio predicted they were back for good, Eulalia regarded her precarious store with pride.

Carranza had been in the city for a month and his government had even been recognized by the USA when Eulalia gave birth to a son. He had Andrés's pale eyes and her persistent, precocious smile. Don Refugio was euphoric. He could find no better omen for the prosperous future he was striving for. He named him Octavio before anyone could say anything.

Virginia was hardly a year old, but she passed into second place overnight. Her mother and grandfather were too busy with the miracle of a new-born son, and her father barely saw her first few steps so busy was he pondering how to escape quickly and permanently from poverty.

After milking he'd go out in the cart alone and drive through the city. It had begun to look orderly and even pleasant to him.

One day the owner of the dairy asked him to go to a new office called the Price Regulation Department and ask what the new price of milk was to be; he didn't want to be giving it away cheaply.

Through the information window, as though he were a ghost, Andrés saw Rodolfo, his boyhood friend from Zacatlán. He had arrived in Mexico City with the Eastern Army. Although he'd never seen any fighting, he was a sergeant; he was a paymaster and paymasters needed rank to command respect. He was two years older than Andrés. Andrés had always thought his friend a bit of a fool, but when he saw him wearing clean clothes and as fat as when their mothers used to feed them, he had second thoughts. They hadn't seen each other for over four years, but said hallo as though it were the previous day, and arranged to meet for a meal.

Andrés came home to the hut in Mixcoac very late. When his wife reproached him for not having said how late he'd be, he told her about his friend-turned-sergeant and assured her he'd soon have a well-paid job.

Don Refugio twisted the ends of his moustache.

'You see, I was right. This man will get on well with the northerners. At least there's something in all this which doesn't upset me.'

'Let's make him Octavio's godfather,' said Andrés.

Eulalia flashed her eternal smile at him and lay down on the bed next to her son.

'She says she's feeling tired,' Don Refugio told him. 'And for her to say that, she must be going to die.'

43

Unfortunately, Don Refugio's prediction was right that time as well. The typhoid epidemic which had been stalking the city for some months came into the hut in Mixcoac and took Eulalia away.

In eight days her smile slowly disappeared, she hardly talked, her body was red-hot and gave off a repugnant smell. Nobody ever recovered from typhoid. Eulalia knew that and didn't want to make those last days any harder for them. She just looked at them gratefully and smiled now and again.

'Good luck,' she said to Andrés as she lapsed into her last day of fever and silence.

CHAPTER FIVE

I believed this whole dramatic and moving story for several years. I venerated the memory of Eulalia, I wanted a smile like hers, and time and time again with all my heart I envied her the simple faithful lover my general was with her. Until the day Andrés managed to get himself named candidate for the governorship of Puebla, and the opposition sent us a leaflet that accused him of working for Victoriano Huerta when he betrayed Madero's government.

'So all that about the milking wasn't true,' I said, handing him thc lcaflet as he came in.

'If you'd rather believe my enemies than me, there's no more to be said,' he replied.

I spent hours gazing out at the garden with the incriminating paper in my hands, thinking and thinking, until he came and stood in front of my armchair, legs level with my eyes, eyes way over my head.

'So? Don't you want to be the governor's lady?'

I looked at him, we laughed, I said yes and forgot my attempt to create an honourable past for him. Yes, I would like to be the governor's lady. I'd been surrounded by cooking, breast-feeding and nappies for five years. I was bored. After Verania had come Sergio. When he cried his first cry and I felt the stone I'd been carrying in my belly had been lifted, I swore it would be the last time. I became an obsessive mother and Andrés paid me little attention. He was chief of military operations, hated the governor and was in cahoots with Heiss. That would have been enough to keep him busy, but he also went to Mexico City very often to visit his *compadre* Rodolfo who had been made an under-secretary. One day, to the total delight of both of them, his boss, General Aguirre, was named presidential candidate.

Andrés went with him on his tour of the country. He spent so much time away that Octavio couldn't even notify him when Virginia disappeared. She went out one afternoon to buy some thread and didn't come back. We informed the police, searched for her for several days, but we never found out what happened to her. On his return, her father accepted her disappearance as an inevitable death.

I didn't know he had other daughters until the governorship came up. That's when he thought the image of a good father important and introduced me to four more: Marta, fifteen, Marcela, thirteen, Lilia and Adriana, ten.

Adriana and Lilia were twins, daughters of a novice nun in the Capuchin convent in Tlalpan, to which Andrés had gone with the army to close it down during the religious persecution. I adored Lilia straight away. She had chestnut-brown hair and enormous eyes which were into everything. When she first saw me, she asked me if I were her father's wife. I said yes, and she called me Mama from then on. Adriana, on the other hand, was an introverted little girl who found it very difficult to hold her own among the rest of us.

Verania was four at the time and Sergio, whom we called Checo, was three. Octavio included, we had seven children when we moved to the house in the hills of Loreto.

It was on the hill but not on the main road; you had to turn off and go through some tiny streets until you came to a very long hedge which ran right round the block. Behind the hedge and the garden was the house. It had three floors, fourteen bedrooms, a central patio and several reception rooms. I can't bear to think about the trouble I had furnishing the whole thing.

I was just hanging the last picture when some 200 workers from the CROM knocked on the door to congratulate us. That was just the beginning; after that everyone came, from peasants to *mariachis*, not to mention Heiss and a group of Spanish textile manufacturers. The house turned into a fiesta without so much as a by-your-leave. I had to supervise a team of waiters and dogsbodies whom Andrés's assistants installed in my kitchen. The feast started at breakfast-time with tables set out all round the garden. In two weeks I'd gone from a peaceful mother of two babies to having to give orders to an army of forty servants and administer the money needed to feed between fifty and 300 people a day. The children had some country nursemaids foisted upon them who were more childish than they were, and I hardly had time to see them, what with one problem and another. Luckily my sister Bárbara came to live with me and was elegantly called my personal secretary.

The Puebla parliament gave women the vote that year, but only Carmen Serdán and a few other schoolteachers rejoiced. Nevertheless, not a single speech of Andrés's failed to mention how important it was that women play a part in the political and revolutionary struggle. One day apparently, in Cholula, several women cornered him and asked how they could help support the Revolution and in reply he told them that General Aguirre in all his wisdom had already said that Mexican women should unite to defend the rights of workers and peasants and equality in marital relationships, etc., etc. From then on I never believed a single speech he made. Worse still, three days later he spoke with ardent passion about the experience of communal land-owning and that very same afternoon he drank a toast with Heiss to celebrate the deal that gave him back the farms expropriated under the Nationalization Law. He told so many lies that once at a meeting in the bullring, people got justifiably angry and set fire to it. A lot of people were injured. Only Juan Soriano's paper reported it.

That tragedy put paid to public meetings in the city and we set off on the campaign trail round the state. We carted everyone – children, nannies, cooks – from town to town, listening to peasants demanding land, claiming justice, begging for miracles. They wanted all manner of things, from sewing-machines, tiles for their roofs, donkeys, loans, seeds, schools, to a cure for a child with poliomyelitis. I enjoyed the campaign. I liked going through dusty towns like San Marcos, and even more up to Coetzalan through the mountains. I'd never seen such vegetation, hillside after hillside smothered in plants, even the rocks covered, cliffs dropping downwards in an interminable curtain of green. In Coetzalan the women wore long white dresses and plaited their hair with silk ribbons and wound them round their heads. It was incomprehensible how they walked among puddles and stones in the forest without muddying even the hems of their skirts. They were small women, not much taller than Lilia was at twelve, and carried enormous baskets and several children at one and the same time. There were only a few people there when we arrived and we were told the peasants didn't like the Party and were afraid of elections because there was always shooting and people killed. So they were apprehensive about the candidate's arrival and couldn't care less about seeing him.

Andrés was furious with the campaign organizers who arrived in each town a couple of days ahead of us. He called them idiots and, banging the ground with his whip, threatened to kill them if they didn't get a crowd together in the square.

I got out of the bus with the children because they wanted to walk through the cobbled streets, look at the church and buy a chilli orange in the market. I followed them to get away from Andrés's shouting.

Octavio acted as guide. He wanted to impress his sisters, he thought they were so pretty and couldn't get used to the idea that someone like Marcela was actually related to him. The slightest pretext and he'd take her hand, help her over the cobbles; he was like her boyfriend. Watching the girls walk along I thought how lovely Marcela would look in the costume the Indian women wore. I arranged for us all to dress like them. Doña Remigia, the wife of the Party delegate, helped us with the clothes. The skirts were hers and her sisters, so were the ribbons. Even little Verania was given a white embroidered blouse. We went back to the square where Andrés was about to start his speech for the few spectators there were. Walking was difficult and so was holding our heads straight with all those ribbons. We looked strange, but the people liked it. They began following us as we crossed the market and by the time we reached the square we had brought General Ascencio three times more audience than his henchmen had managed to gather. We stood next to him and he began his speech by saying, 'People of Coetzalan. This is my family, a family just like yours, simple and united. Our families are the most precious things we have and I promise you that my government will work to give them the future they deserve . . .' And he went on in that vein. We listened in silence, only Checo kept taking his hat on and off and ran round our legs. Octavio seized his chance and put his arm round Marcela's waist and kept it there until the speech about the unity of the family was over.

From Coetzalan we went down to Zacatlán, Andrés's home town. The Delpuente and the Fernández families, who had owned the town before the Revolution and had seen Andrés leave it poor and bitter, now had to swallow seeing him come back to govern them.

The afternoon we arrived a man had been having a shave at the barber's and someone had asked him if he was smartening himself up to welcome General Ascencio.

'General, my foot!' replied the man. 'He'll always be a muleteer's son to me. I don't kowtow to riff-raff.'

He didn't come to the dinner the town's prominent figures gave for us. My general asked after him and regretted he couldn't be with us. As we left, someone told us he had been killed by a drunk that very morning.

Apart from that, Zacatlán was in the mood for a fiesta. There were fireworks and dancing all night. Andrés courted me as if he meant it and thanked me for what happened in Coetzalan. He was happy.

Even his mother, whom I'd seen three times and who was always cross, was delighted. She danced dance after dance as if her son had given her back her dignity and pleasure.

Doña Herminia was a thin woman with sunken eyes and a jutting chin. Her hair was white and thin and swept back in a rather unattractive bun. She had always been poor, but when her son became important it took her no time at all to get used to the good life.

She never wanted to leave Zacatlán though, and Andrés bought her a house in the main square. It had a stone façade and wrought-iron balconies, which the former owner had brought from France. Each couple and each grandchild had a bedroom there, heaven knows why because since Doña Herminia wasn't exactly welcoming, her grandchildren didn't visit her often, let alone her sons, who were too busy going round making themselves important. Andrés liked spending short periods in Zacatlán. He would stay in the stone house so that his Mama could look after him and give him what she hadn't given him or allowed him when he was a child. It was better if I didn't go and spoil the romance. Besides, I never liked Zacatlán; it was always raining and made me depressed.

We didn't miss a single village. Andrés was the first candidate for governor to run a campaign like this. He had no choice. Aguirre was the first presidential candidate to tour the country.

I enjoyed the campaign. Despite his now very arbitrary behaviour, the general was still close to us, still a normal person. I mean he'd talk without losing the drift of the conversation, he'd suddenly kiss one of his daughters and every night before bed he'd ask me how he'd done, if I thought the people liked him, if he'd been a success, if I were prepared to support him when he was governor.

Once he tried copying General Aguirre's habit of spending hours and hours listening to peasants. He went to Teziutlán, another town in the mountains. They erected a platform and the Indians filed by with their problems; they needed oxen, someone had stolen the land the Revolution had given them, the Revolution hadn't given them any, they didn't want their children to grow up in the same conditions they had. They recounted their lives and asked for things as if he were God. Andrés couldn't stand this torture for more than a day. The next morning, from the bathroom, he cursed General Aguirre's stupid customs, and asked me if I didn't think it better for everyone to develop their own style. Of course I said yes. The meetings went back to being short again, the one in Tehuacán lasted barely an hour. Afterwards we went swimming at El Riego, a farm with thermal waters where General Aguirre sometimes spent his holidays.

Election day finally arrived. I went with Andrés to vote. The next day there was a picture of us in the paper, hand in hand beside the ballot box. Since there was no one else to vote for, the elections passed off peacefully, though you couldn't say there was a massive turnout. That Sunday the streets were half empty, people went to Mass early and then stayed at home. The only ones who voted were workers from the CTM, state employees and one or two other confused souls – no one else. It had to be done, of course, for Andrés to take over at City Hall legitimately.

The inhabitants of Puebla now say that they didn't know what was in store for them and that's why they didn't lift a finger to stop it, but I don't think they would have done much anyway. They were only concerned about their own petty little lives; someone could have fallen down dead on top of them and they'd have pretended not to notice.

The early days in government were fun. Everything was new, I had a retinue of women whose husbands worked with Andrés. Checo played at being a mini-governor and the girls went to all the dances to show off. Our general saw we were enjoying it and I think he was pleased. Perhaps that's why he took us to the inauguration of the San Roque lunatic asylum, where madwomen were locked up. After cutting the ribbon and making his speech, he had a *marimba* group brought in and organized a dance. The mad ladies were very elegant in their new rose-coloured smocks and were delighted with the music. Andrés danced with a very pretty one who was there because she was an alcoholic. She hadn't had a drink for quite some time, so there she was, perfectly lucid among women who had reverted to childhood, were convinced someone was persecuting them or lurched from euphoria to depression. The governor danced with all of them, and with me, who didn't feel at all out of place; I even thought it would be a nice place for a rest.

Suddenly Andrés asked the *marimba* to stop and introduced me as the president of the Public Welfare Committee. San Roque would be under my jurisdiction, so would the orphanage and various state hospitals.

I began to tremble. What with the children and the servants I already felt weighed down by an army of people who needed instructions from me in order to move a finger, and now, suddenly, lunatics, orphans, hospitals. I spent the night begging Andrés to let me off these duties. He said he couldn't. I was his wife and that's what wives were for. 'Don't think it's all fucking and singing, you know.'

The next day I went to the orphanage. That was the fancy name for a squalid, neglected little hospital. The children ran around the yard half-naked, with runny noses and months-old layers of dirt. They were looked after by women who could barely remember their own names and couldn't tell the difference between naughty kids and retarded ones. They were all mixed up together. The babies slept in a row of iron cots on mattresses peed on a thousand times. There were new-born babies among them and a few wet-nurses had been hired to feed them twice a day with what was left in their wizened breasts.

I got rid of them. Them and the four witches who looked after the children.

A doctor who seemed very well informed felt obliged to

protest. 'Those babies could die if they drink cow's milk,' he said.

'They're better dead than here,' I replied.

Who could possibly restrain my charitable zeal? My husband, of course. That afternoon he told me I was exaggerating, there was not a penny extra for the hospice or the hospitals, and the lunatic ladies already had enough, what with a roof over their heads.

'But I've been there, they have no beds.'

'Those women have only ever slept on the floor,' he answered. 'You don't think any of the women there are rich, do you? The rich ones are roaming free.'

'And with you,' I retorted.

That morning I'd gone to New Century to collect a dress for Verania and the salesgirl asked me how I'd liked the Chinese silk coat the general had bought for me the previous day. 'Lovely,' I said, watching the horrified face of the owner, who always knew where Andrés Ascencio's purchases went. The coat had been sent to a lady in Cholula. I didn't intend to tackle him about it, but I couldn't stop myself. In any case, he pretended he didn't know what I was talking about and left it at that.

I suggested to his daughters that they help me organize balls, parties, raffles, anything to raise money for the Public Welfare Committee. They agreed. All kinds of ideas were put forward, from a première with Fred Astaire to a ball at Government House. For a while, I hadn't time to think about the mad, the sick and the orphaned, I was so busy organizing parties. In the end I think we even forgot what they were in aid of.

It was only because my sister Bárbara did her job as my secretary so well that we did in fact deliver T-shirts and shorts to the children, beds to the loony ladies and sheets to the hospital. San Roque was very clean when we arrived, the women stood in line to thank us. Their rose-coloured smocks were fading and in the daylight their faces were uglier. The young girl who had led the dancing with Andrés was still there. Another one told me that her brother had had her locked away so he could steal her inheritance. I told them to stay close to us. When the celebration was over I just walked out with them, no papers, no nothing.

That night there was a ceremony at the state college to celebrate its upgrading to university. Andrés had been obsessed by the idea from the start of his campaign and had only been governor for a few months when he managed the change in status. The head of the college was to stay on as rector of the university, and in gratitude he made Andrés the chancellor. There was criticism in the papers and people were horrified, but Andrés didn't care. He dressed up in cap and gown and made us all doll up in evening dresses.

We hadn't time to decide what to do with the ex-loony ladies, so we took them to the festivities. I lent a dress to one of them and Marta lent one to the other.

During the toast I introduced the pretty one to the rector, who took her on as his private secretary, and the disinherited heiress to the state chief justice who made it his business to see that justice was done. I think the brother was disinherited instead, because a month later I received a silver tea-set with a note from Señorita Imelda Basurto and in brackets she had added, 'the disinherited heiress'. Underneath it said, 'With my eternal thanks for your fight for justice'.

At first people used to come to the house to ask for my help with the governor. I listened and Bárbara took notes. At night I'd take my list of petitions, read it quickly to the general and accept his instructions; this one, go and see Godínez, that one, come to my office, nothing can be done about that one, give that one something from the petty cash and so on.

My first big disappointment was when a very cultured gentleman came to tell me that the city's archives were going to be sold to a paper factory. The whole of the city's archives at three cents a kilo. It was my first question to Andrés that night. He didn't even want to discuss it. He merely said they were only useless papers, what Puebla needed was a future, there was no room for all that past. The place which had housed the archives was now needed to make more classrooms for the university. Besides, it was too late because Díaz Pumarino, the city treasurer, had already sold it, and what's more, he was giving me the money for the hospice.

The next day came the embarrassing task of explaining my failure to Señor Cordero. In the event, the money from the sale didn't even go to the hospice because the *Charro*'s Association visited Andrés the day he had it on his desk and he presented it to them as a personal donation, together with the cheque from the state government.

With that my failures began, and things went from bad to worse. One day a very distraught lady came to see me. Her husband, a respected doctor, owned the house where he lived with his family – a very attractive house on 18th East. According to this lady, my general had taken a fancy to it and summoned her husband with a view to buying it. When the man said it wasn't for sale, that it was all he had to leave his children, Andrés said he hoped he would come to his senses, because he wouldn't like to have to buy it from his widow. With this threat hanging over him, the doctor agreed to sell and gave him a price. Andrés heard him say, 'so many million pesos', then took from a drawer a form giving the value put on the house for tax purposes. It was half the asking price. Andrés paid him the half and saw him out, giving him three days to vacate. The wife came to see me next day. That night I told Andrés.

'She's not only slow, she's a busybody to boot. Tell her you know nothing about it.'

'But is it true? What do you want the house for?'

'None of your business,' he said and went to sleep.

The next day I woke up Octavio with the story.

'Why don't you stop seeing all these people and do something more pleasant?' he said.

I went on explaining. I told him about the house again, thinking he hadn't understood because he was still sleepy.

'Ay, Cati, don't tell me you don't know that everything is bought like that.' He sat up in bed and stretched. Then he gave a long, noisy yawn.

'Can I come in?' asked Marcela, pushing the door.

She wore trousers and a shirt I remembered seeing on Octavio.

'Not up yet?' she asked, coming towards him with her hands behind her back. 'You're so lazy!' She threw a glass of water over him.

'Cheeky devil!' he shouted as he tried to force the glass out of her hand, and their bodies entwined. The fight turned to hugs and laughter. They were so happy I was envious.

'Thanks anyway, Tavo,' I said, walking towards the door.

'Thanks to you, Cati,' he replied when he saw me go and shut the door.

CHAPTER SIX

The first time I saw Andrés absolutely furious with Juan Soriano, editor of the weekly newspaper *Forward*, was over the bullring affair. The second was when he reported that anti-Revolutionaries had crept into the state government: Manuel García, a top-ranking official, was the one who had denounced the Serdán family; Ernesto Hernández, a government inspector in Puebla, had been a member of something called the Social Defence Force set up by Victoriano Huerta; Saúl Suárez, a tax-collector in Teziutlán, had personally fired on Venustiano Carranza in Tlaxcalantongo; and the governor himself had been in La Ciudadela at the time of the *coup d'état* in which Madero had been assassinated.

'That bastard's got it coming to him,' he said between his teeth. He put down the paper and got up from the breakfast table.

I heard him repeat it many times. But Soriano went on publishing his paper, having coffee in the colonnades and strolling round the cathedral square with his wife on Sundays. Everybody knew he went from his house to his office on foot, bought bread from the Fleur de Lis in the evenings and liked to take a solitary walk after dinner.

I read his newspaper in secret. When Andrés threw it down and stormed out cursing, I would pick it up and read it avidly. Sometimes I couldn't even understand why he was angry.

Perhaps it was because it didn't carry reports of his inaugural ceremonies, or when it did they were like the one when he inaugurated the Teatro Principal: a photo of him cutting the ribbon, and another photo of the plaque commemorating the theatre's renovation under the governorship of General Andrés Ascencio, with a caption underneath inquiring why the city council did not appear in the photo since it had paid for the work carried out.

When President Aguirre nationalized the oil industry, the only newspaper in Puebla to show any enthusiasm was *Forward*. Andrés was livid, he thought it was stupid to quarrel with powerful countries just to expropriate what he called a heap of junk. Nevertheless, when Señora Aguirre called on women from all social classes to help finance the oil debt by donating money, jewellery or whatever they had, Andrés made me join the Ladies Committee presided over by Doña Lupe.

He arrived one afternoon with a pile of boxes.

'Take these and tell her you are parting with your daughters' dowry,' he said.

There were all sorts of things, bracelets, earrings, precious stones, watches, necklaces, a gem collection as big as mine. I went to Mexico City with his daughters and the boxes. We arrived at the Bellas Artes. It was packed with peasant women carrying chickens, women going up to a table on the stage with dirty money-boxes full of coppers and even American ladies criticizing the oil companies and publicly handing over thousands of pesos.

The girls and I took our boxes to the table and offered them to the First Lady like true heroines. To complete the spectacle, when the time came I was genuinely moved and donated the pearls I was wearing.

Forward published a photo of me taking off my earrings beside Señora Aguirre's table. I thanked Don Juan Soriano, and Andrés scolded me.

Time went by slowly. I began to feel that I had been wiping kids' noses and embracing little old men with my tender-hearted mother-of-Puebla look for centuries. And all the while I heard from my sisters, or from Pepa and Mónica, that the whole town was talking about the governor's 500 crimes and fifty mistresses.

They would suddenly say, 'Look, there's one,' or, 'That's the house he bought for another,' and I would just take note. The ones who only caught his fancy for a few hours, or gave in to him temporarily to escape his threats, did not figure in my list. But I was intrigued by those who loved him, and even had children by him. I envied them because they only knew the intelligent, charming side of Andrés, they were always well-dressed and made-up when he came to see them, and he never noticed their bad moods or bad breath in the early morning.

I would have liked to be Andrés's mistress. I would have liked to wait for him in silk robes and shiny slippers, spend his money on whatever I fancied, sleep until late morning, break free from the Public Welfare Committee and the mask of the First Lady. Besides, everybody likes or pities mistresses, no one considers them accomplices. I, on the other hand, was the official accomplice.

Who would believe that I only ever heard rumours, that for years I never knew if they were true or just fantasy? I couldn't believe that Andrés had his enemies killed and dumped them in that mixture of pitch and gravel they used to asphalt the roads. But the saying went that the streets of Puebla were designed by the angels and paved with the minced bodies of the governor's enemies.

I preferred not to know what Andrés did. I was the mother of his children, the lady of his house, his wife, his maid, his habit, his joke. Who knows what I was, but whatever it was I had to go on being it – however much I sometimes wanted to escape to a country where I didn't exist, where my name wasn't associated with his, where people sought me out or despised me for myself, without mixing me up in their love or hatred for him.

One day I left the house and took a bus to Oaxaca. I wanted to go far away, I even imagined I'd earn my own living, but I regretted it before we'd reached the first town. The bus filled up with peasants, baskets, chickens, kids who all cried at the same time; and a sour smell, a mixture of rancid tortillas and squashed bodies, pervaded the air. I didn't like my new life. I got off as soon as I could and caught the next bus home. I didn't walk through the town for fear people would recognize me.

Coming into my house again made me so happy. Verania and Checo were playing in the garden; I hugged them as though I'd been kidnapped and returned home.

'What's the matter with you?' asked Verania, who didn't much care for my sudden sporadic effusiveness.

The next day I wanted to cry and crawl into a hole again. I didn't want to be me, I wanted to be anyone who didn't have a politician for a husband, who didn't have seven children with his name, sired by him, *his*, not mine, but handed over to me during the day, every day, merely so that he could suddenly appear and congratulate himself because Lilia was becoming so pretty, Marcela so amusing, Adriana growing up so fast, Marta doing her hair so stylishly, or because Verania had the Ascencio sparkle in her eyes.

Someone else, that's what I wanted to be. To live in a

house, not a vast fortress with rooms to spare, a house you couldn't walk round without falling into some ambush or other because Andrés had even planted rose bushes in the surrounding fields. There were hundreds of traps like that for those not used to them, set in case it occurred to someone to attack him during the night. It was so far from anywhere you could only go out on horseback or by car. And only Andrés was allowed out at night, we were always under the surveillance of a group of taciturn men who weren't allowed to speak to us except to say, 'I'm sorry, you can't go any further.'

I began to get obsessions. I thought it was my duty to anticipate people's desires. Whenever I had guests, I spent days thinking about their stomachs, whether they preferred their meat rare or well done, if they could eat chilli in the evening or hated spaghetti with parsley. Worst of all, when they came they ate it without so much as saying if they liked it or not, or interrupting their conversation long enough for me to say, 'Start before it gets cold.'

For most people I was part of the furniture, someone you paid as much attention to as you would a chair that sat at table and smiled. That's why dinners depressed me. Ten minutes before the guests arrived I wanted to cry, but held back my tears so that my mascara wouldn't run and make me look like a witch into the bargain. Because that's what counts, Andrés would say. What counts is being pretty, sweet, impeccable. What if the guests arrived and found the lady of the house sobbing with her head under a chair?

But it was hard for me to hide my boredom from all those men who held their wives by the elbow as though they were coffee-cup handles. They, on the other hand, looked delighted, keen to eat a good meal and tell by the menu how well liked they were.

I nearly always forgot something. However much Andrés

lectured me on how to handle the servants and make each one do what he was supposed to, when the guests arrived, Matilde the cook would remember there were no lemons, not enough tortillas to go round or that our fridge couldn't make ice for so many people. At times like these I could have happily strangled the guests, especially ones like Marilú Izunza with her blonde mane.

That particular dinner was one of the worst. I woke up that morning hating the colour of my hair, the bags under my eyes and my height. I wanted to look different, to see if I could be different, and I asked Blondie to cut my hair in any style she fancied.

And there I was, shaven and shorn, with her behind me telling me it was the latest fashion, that women didn't wear their hair cut evenly now, that I had looked like Christ with my eternal shoulder-length locks, that long hair was for young girls and I was an important lady. She showed me magazines and then plastered me with make-up, but she still didn't manage to convince me. I cried and cursed the moment I'd decided to change the way I looked.

I went to my parents' house to seek comfort. Papa was in the kitchen waiting for his percolator to spurt a stream of black coffee into the little metal cup it had incorporated inside it. It was an Italian coffee-pot. He stood in front of it every morning waiting for his espresso as though he were at the bar of a café in Rome. As the black stream began dripping and the aroma invaded the house, he would begin his tribute to his authentic Italian coffee.

'But it's from Córdoba, Papa,' I'd say every time he began his lecture.

'All right, Córdoba, but no one in the whole of Mexico makes coffee like mine; here they grind the coffee thickly and let it boil. It's impossible to drink. American coffee they call it. Only Americans could say it was good, because the American palate is ruined. Their main dish is minced meat in sweet tomato sauce. Can you imagine anything more disgusting? Just smell this, and keep your ignorant mouth shut.'

When I went into the kitchen without my hair and with the screen-goddess make-up job Blondie had done on me, Papa stopped contemplating his coffee and gave a wolf-whistle. Then he began singing, 'I loved you for your hair, now you're bald I don't love you any more.'

I hugged him. I clung to him for a while, evoking the smell of the fields and smelling the coffee. It felt so good there, I started to cry.

'Come on, it was only a joke,' he said. 'I would love you even if they shaved your head.'

'The problem is, I'm having people to dinner tonight.'

'So, what's new about that? There are dinners every night at your house. It's nothing to cry about. You're a great cook, it's something you inherited. Look at your hands, you've got peasant hands, the hands of a woman who knows how to work. My mother had to do everything herself, you've got an army of servants. Everything will be fine. Who's coming this time?'

'Nobody important. Some industrialists from Atlixco. But they'll see my hair and their wives will laugh at me.'

'Since when have you cared what people say? You're like your mother. You can't please everyone. Not if you're bald, not even with your hair down to your knees. The thing is to feel happy.'

'That's just it, I'm not happy,' I said, hugging him.

'What's bothering you? Haven't you got everything you want? Don't cry. Look how lovely the sky is. Look how easy it is living in a country with no winter. Smell this coffee. Come here, my love, let me make you a cup with a lot of sugar, come and tell Papa all about it.'

Of course, I didn't tell him about it. He didn't want me to tell him, that's why he talked to me as though I were a little girl who shouldn't grow up and we stood there, arms round each other, looking at the volcanoes, grateful for them being there and us being alive to look at them. He kissed me a lot, put his hand up my blouse and drew lines down my back until I calmed down and started to laugh.

'Better now, precious?' he said. 'Do you want to be my girlfriend?'

'Of course,' I said, 'your girlfriend but not your wife. Because if we got married you'd want me to organize dinners for your friends.'

That night Marilú came to my house with a fur that amply demonstrated how her husband shared things. She was the daughter of one of those Spanish families – father tradesman, son gentleman, grandson pauper. Her father was the grandson. He hadn't a penny, but he was sure of his social standing and was able to pass it on wholesale to his daughter. Armed with this capital, Marilú did Julián Amed the favour of marrying him. Julián was one of those Arabs who sold material in La Victoria market, waylaying people who'd come to buy vegetables and with his interminable patter forcing them to buy at least a yard of sky-blue silk. At night when the market was closed, he'd get a group of compatriots together to play cards, and from there, after several big wins (in one of which he killed the loser who didn't want to pay up, and kept his property), he had enough to set up a textile factory. He was already very rich by the time he convinced Marilú that his money and the Izunza social standing would produce wonderful children and a model family. She, then a little blonde, pale and thin from hunger disguised behind the huge dining-room furniture inherited from her grandfather, accepted after feigning

65

a certain reticence. No sooner had she married than her social status rose to the level of her husband's pocket and she became unbearable. At every opportunity she'd drop appreciative remarks like: 'I do so admire you for living with a politician. You always have to pretend, and it's so hard not to be frank. I couldn't do it. Julián is always scolding me because I speak my mind, but I tell him, what do you have to lose, you're a businessman, you don't have to kowtow to anyone, you got where you are today because you worked for it, you're not a politician. Besides, we Izunza are frank and you knew that when you married me.'

That night I was in no mood for putting up with Marilú. My cook Matilde, fed up with dinners, was furious because I mentioned that the meat wasn't moist enough. Checo was crying in his room because I hadn't waited until he was asleep, Andrés had spent the afternoon eulogizing Heiss and to cap it all Blondie had left me practically bald. The moment was not ripe for listening to Marilú but she, sitting in the middle of the drawing room in her fox fur, as though there were no fire blazing away, was telling the other women how she had sacked a maid who'd been with her for ten years because she found her trying to abort herself with a broom handle.

'Frankly, I was horrified. And all because she ignored my advice. I told her to be careful with the factory workers, one is as irresponsible as the next, they only want to see who will fall for their line. I told her so when I saw her plaiting her hair stylishly and offering to take messages to the factory. I told her, don't go getting ideas, you're better off staying here with me, I treat you well, you can look after my children as if they were your own, why get mixed up with men, they'll only keep you poor and mess you around. But she took no notice. She went off whoring because that's what they're like, those people, and then afterwards, yes, lots of tears, lots of, "Sorry, Señora," lots of, "But he deceived me." I wasn't having any of it, though. I told her straight, "Look, I'll be kind because you've worked for me for a long time, I'll keep you until the baby's about to be born, I won't pay you because you won't be able to do your work properly, just look after the children and I'll be satisfied, but when your time comes you'll have to go to town because I haven't time to help you and I don't want my children to know what's going on." What more could she have asked for? Well, she wanted to get rid of the baby. You can't imagine how upset I was, she looked such a nice girl too, I often left my children with her. Just think what she might have done, she might have murdered them as well!'

'One's children are one's own business,' I said.

'Ay, Catalina, the things you say! You can tell you're a politician's wife. Why did you cut your hair?' she said shaking her blonde mane. 'What did your father say? It's important to you what he thinks, isn't it? He was having dinner at our house the other day and did nothing but talk about you.'

'My father had dinner at your house?' I asked, shocked.

'Of course, he's representing the governor in certain business deals with Julián. Didn't he tell you he was going to be rich?'

I hated the idea of my father representing Andrés and having anything at all to do with Marilú's husband.

'I didn't know,' I said, like an idiot.

'He probably wants to surprise you. Don't say I told you,' she said with a quick glance at the others, who were looking delighted with this piece of gossip.

'Don't worry,' I said. 'Have you recently dyed your hair blonder?'

'I don't dye it. We went to the beach and the sun bleached it.'

'I don't like the beach,' said Luisita Rivas. 'You have to take your clothes off and go in dirty, salty water which everyone swims in. The sea is disgusting.'

'Ah no, Luisita. I'm sorry, but I think the sea is lovely,' said another woman.

I took advantage of the change of subject to go and look for Andrés.

He was in the middle of the circle men make when they want to talk standing up, whisky glasses in hand, dropping ash everywhere. Andrés smoked cigars, and when I came up he was biting the end off one before lighting it.

'Can you spare me a minute?' I said.

'Is it urgent?' he asked. He was holding court and hated letting the moment pass.

'Yes, it's just a small matter, but urgent.'

'Let me attend to the lady's small matter,' he said. 'Excuse me, gentlemen.'

I held his arm as though we were going for a long walk. I took him out of the living room, through the dining room and would have gone on had he not stopped me.

'Well, what is it?'

'I don't want you to mix Papa up in your affairs. Let him live his life his own way. He hasn't died of starvation yet, don't mess him around,' I said.

'Is that what you interrupted me for? Why don't you see if dinner is ready? And since when do ducks shoot the hunters?' he said, laughing. 'Why did you cut *my* hair?'

I hated him when he behaved as if he owned me. But I took no notice and changed my tone for one that would work better.

'Andrés, I'm asking you from the bottom of my heart.

I'll let you give Mapache to Heiss, but don't get Papa involved with Amed.'

'Give Mapache to Heiss? Your beloved horse? I'll see what I can do, I promise, crybaby. Stop it now, your mascara will run. Let's look after our guests, they haven't come to see us whispering in a corner.'

I went back to the women. I'd rather have listened to the men, but that wasn't done. Dinners always divided up like that, the men on one side and, on the other, us talking about childbirth, servants and hair-dos. The wonderful world of women, that's what Andrés called it.

I liked it when we sat down to dinner because the conversation became more interesting. I wrote out the place-cards and sat each person where it suited me. I put myself next to Sergio Cuenca, who was handsome and a good talker. I invited him even when I didn't need to because he was one of the few of Andrés's friends I liked. He manoeuvred the conversation and if I sat next to him I could say things under my breath that I wanted said out loud without saying them myself.

'Did you know that some Indians in Alchichica chased Heiss and his administrator Pérez off their land?' he asked. 'They didn't like the tone he used to convince them to plant sugar cane.'

'That's right,' said Don Juan Machuca, a Spaniard who never left his factory in Atlixco, but was none the less always the first to hear any news. 'They say they killed two lads. Heiss is in too much of a hurry. I think he passed a bit of money to one of the leaders so he'd talk to the peasants about renting their communal land. The peasants didn't want to but Heiss arrived and said the deal was already done. Naturally, the leader was furious and to show he hadn't agreed to anything he gave chase as Heiss was leaving. Don Miguel still has a lot to learn.'

'How is he?' I asked.

'Nothing happened,' said Andrés. 'Don Mike knows how to handle things; the problem was that the leader did the dirty on him. And there's a woman going round saying the land De Velasco sold to Heiss belonged to her father. Can you believe it?'

'But, General, that land did belong to Don Gabriel de Velasco before the Revolution,' said Doña Julia Conde, fanning herself with a fan of green feathers.

'Doña Julia always knows so much about what happened before the Revolution. Is it nostalgia?' Andrés asked her.

'As a matter of fact, General, yes. Things were different then.'

'She was twenty and now she's fifty,' I said to Sergio Cuenca, who burst out laughing. 'Besides, the land is Lola's.'

'What are you laughing about?' asked Andrés.

'The things which occur to your lady wife, General. She says the land belonged to Lola Campos's father.'

'No wonder you laughed at her.'

'*With* her, General,' said Sergio.

Then he raised his glass and told joke after joke until dinner was over.

About two o'clock in the morning Marilú entered her fox and said goodbye with her husband and the other guests. We accompanied them to the door. Doña Julia Conde fanned herself insatiably.

'I don't know, dear,' she said to Marilú, 'how you can wear that animal. It's hot all year in Mexico. We don't have a real winter. I'm always boiling.'

'Because she never left the menopause,' I whispered to Andrés, who put his arm round my shoulder and said, 'You're right, Doña Julia, our ladies aren't as tough as they used to be, we have to wrap them in furs so that they last until they've brought our children up. Don't you think so, Julián?'

'Of course he does,' said Marilú as a parting shot.

'Who told you the Alchichica land belonged to that woman?' asked Andrés when we closed the door.

'She did,' I replied. 'She came to see me about a month ago. She wanted me to talk to you, to convince you that her father inherited it from his father and that they worked it for many years until De Velasco stole it from them. Now he's gone bankrupt it's easy for him to sell something that isn't his. And Heiss is buying it cheaply on the pretext that there is a risk of land invasion. What scoundrels, Andrés!'

'What did you tell her?' he asked.

'What could I say? I told her to find another way, that I couldn't talk to you about it because you wouldn't listen. What does it matter what I said? I didn't help her. I felt ashamed when she got up and turned to go without offering me her hand.'

'If you kept it to yourself for a month, why did you have to play the know-all tonight?'

'Because I'm like that. Until it touches me I don't feel it.'

'Catalina, you still don't seem to understand. That land isn't Lola's. You can't believe everything an Indian tells you. And the textile deal I put your father on to is the most inoffensive thing that ever came his way.'

'I don't believe you,' I said for the first time in my life. 'I don't believe either of those things.'

'Do you believe I find you very attractive with short hair?'

He began kissing me in the middle of the patio and hugged me to him as we walked towards the stairs and our bedroom. He had big hands. I liked them as much as others feared them. Or perhaps that's why I liked them. I don't know.

He talked as he undressed. 'Foolish girl, poking her nose into things that don't concern her.'

He took his jacket off, then his pistol. I thought how nice it would be to wear a pistol under my dress. It took me some time to get my dress off. It was a long dress with a low back but high at the neck in front, and hard to get in and out of because there were so many buttons.

'You're so slow, Catín,' he said. I sat with my back to him as he lay on the bed.

'Come here,' he ordered. I wanted to see the sea and closed my eyes.

'Why don't you give Lola her land back?' I said.

'What an ignorant woman! Because I can't,' he answered, rocking to and fro over my body.

'But you can get my father out of Amed's textiles deal.'

'Perhaps.'

The next morning I hummed to myself as I ran downstairs towards the rear patio. He was already mounted on Listón and the lad who usually helped me mount was holding the reins of a roan mare.

'And Mapache?' I asked.

'He's got the owner you wanted him to have,' said Andrés. I clenched my fists until my nails dug into the palm of my hand.

'Deal completed then,' I said as I mounted the roan mare.

I set off after him with the mare going like the wind, and I soon left him behind. I went through Manzanillo till I got to the Costes's wood and then continued on to La Malinche, forgetting Checo's flu, breakfast and Lilia, who always wanted to hear about the dresses the ladies wore the night before. I used to sit in the garden with her and criticize them to my heart's content, delighted that she laughed so heartily at my gossip.

At the mere thought of Heiss on Mapache I sobbed out loud as the wind whipped my face and dried the tears that poured down my face.

I got back at about eleven. Andrés had already left, the girls were at school, so there was only Checo mulling over his flu.

'Serves you right for not going to school,' I said, stretching out on the bed beside him. Then I called our butler Ausencio and asked him to find the maid whom Señora Amed had just kicked out of her house.

'Tell her we want her to come and work here. Say we know all about everything, so not to worry.'

Lucina arrived the next day with her clothes in a cardboard box. She had dark eyes and a spotty face. She didn't talk much, but from that day on she told Checo all the stories I didn't know, made dolls for Verania and massaged my back when she saw I was sad. She mothered all of us.

Her baby appeared one morning without much fuss. It was a five-months foetus and dead. She mourned the loss for a day. Ausencio, the children and I went with her to bury it in her village. Between us we carried the little white wood box into the tiny wall-less graveyard, an open field sown with simple tombstones. At the end under a tree was the hole for her child. Ausencio put the box inside and Lucina hurriedly threw in a handful of earth.

'It was better this way,' she said.

Verania wanted to sing *O Mary, Mother of God* and we joined her.

On the way back to the car we were all silent until

Lucina said, 'Don't be sad. My baby is in the sky. He is a star. Isn't that true, Señora?'

'Yes, Lucina,' I said.

After that Marilú Amed spread the story that I'd spirited Lucina away, made her have an abortion and kept her as a slave to look after my children. Marilú never got over her pique.

A few days later I went out for a walk after dinner with Checo. I took him to the top of Guadalupe Hill to see the first stars come out.

'Mama,' he said suddenly, 'do you think Lucina's baby really is a star in the sky?'

'Why d'you ask?'

'Because Verania thinks so, but I know it isn't true. Lucina's baby is in a hole.'

'In a hole?'

'Yes, in a hole. Like Celestino. Yesterday Papa said they should find a hole for him.'

'Who did he say that to?'

'Someone who came to see him from Matamoros.'

'You didn't hear properly. Your father wouldn't say a thing like that.'

'He did say it, Mama. He always says that. Go and find this one or that one a hole. And that means they have to kill him.'

'Darling, what an imagination you've got,' I said. 'D'you think killing is a game?'

'No, killing is work. Papa says so.'

A noise rumbled deep down in my stomach and rice, meat, tortillas, cheese, jelly, pancakes, came gushing back out while Checo watched me, not knowing what to do but asking from time to time, 'All right now, Mama?' Then came something yellow and bitter, then nothing.

'Race you home?' I said. And I began running down the hillside as fast as I could.

'You're crazy, Mami. Papa's right. You're crazy as a coot,' the child yelled behind me.

We reached home exhausted. Verania was in the doorway holding Lucina's hand. She was a beautiful little girl, with enormous eyes, thin lips, pale like me, naïve like my sisters.

'Why are you so late?' she asked.

'Because Mama was ill,' said Checo.

'What with?' asked Lucina.

'Her tummy. She sicked up all her food,' said the five-year-old. Five crazy years.

Our children couldn't live in the clouds. They were too close. When I'd decided to stay with Andrés, I'd decided for them too, and there was no way I could keep them in an ivory tower.

They lived on one floor of our huge house and we lived on another. We didn't even have to see them if we didn't want to. The afternoon I was sick I decided to close the maternal-love chapter of my life. I handed the children over to Lucina. From now on she would bathe them, dress them, listen to their questions, teach them to pray and believe in something even if it were only the Virgin of Guadalupe. From one day to the next I stopped spending the afternoons with them or thinking about what to give them for lunch or how to amuse them. I missed them at first. For years my life had revolved round them, they had been my passion, my entertainment. They used my bedroom like a playroom. They'd wake me up early even if I'd had a late night, play with my necklaces, try on my shoes and dresses; our lives were inseparable. That night I locked my door. When they came next morning I let them knock, I didn't answer. In the afternoon I explained that their father

75

wanted peace and quiet on the ground floor and asked them not to come in again.

They got used to it, and so did I.

CHAPTER SEVEN

I also decided to find out what Andrés was up to in Atencingo. The first thing I learned was that the Celestino Checo had heard about was Lola's husband and that his death was just one of a long line. Then I made friends with Heiss's daughters. Especially Helen. She had two children and was divorced from a *gringo* who had mistreated her cruelly till the day she'd plucked up the courage to leave.

Helen had returned to Puebla in the hope that her father would help her, but not unexpectedly he gave her nothing for free. He sent her to work in Atencingo. Her job was to spy on a certain Señor Gómez, the administrator, and assess how loyal he was. To do this she'd gone to live in a half-empty, inhospitable house which had a swimming pool with freezing cold water and hundreds of flies in the afternoon.

I used to go and visit her. The children would swim in her dreadful pool while I sat and chatted to her.

'There aren't many men around here,' she'd say. And she'd tell me her latest experience with some Puebla gentleman. She was determined to marry one of them, and I was just as certain that none of them would get into a mess like that. *Gringas* were all right for a while, but no one wanted one day in, day out. She wanted to get married, have a Talavera dinner-set and a house with a sloping roof.

I don't know why she needed the sloping roof. But when she talked about her future, she included it as if it were indispensable.

One day as we were watching the children swim and sipping the daquiris she prepared and drank non-stop, we heard shots nearby. I ran out in my swimsuit, cutting my feet on the spines and stones round the house. Checo followed me with my sandals.

'Go back to the house,' I said. I put the sandals on and ran to the mill. A man lay dead. 'A drunken brawl,' said Gómez, the manager.

A woman sat on the ground weeping softly, as though she had her whole life ahead of her to do just that.

When I went up to her to ask who the dead man was, she lifted her face.

'My husband,' she said. 'Help me. If I stay here they'll kill me too, and who will care for the children?'

Juan, my chauffeur, had followed me and I asked him to lift up the body. I gave Gómez a governor's-wife glare as I informed him, 'I'm taking the body.'

'As you wish. But the woman stays, doesn't she?' he asked, seeing me with my arm round her.

'She's coming with me too,' I replied.

We walked back to Helen's house. There, she began talking to me as though I weren't the wife of the governor. I listened in silence, my head in my hands. Her story was terrible. No one could have invented anything like that.

When she finished, Helen stopped drinking for a minute to say in her silly *gringo* accent, 'I believe it, Cathy. These men are monsters. What dreadful relatives we have.'

'I want Mapache back,' I told Andrés when he came to bed.

'A deal's a deal, Catín. Your Papa is no longer with Amed.'

'But you killed those peasants in Atencingo.'

'What?' said Andrés.

'The only survivor, a woman, told me so. They killed her husband at the mill this afternoon. I saw him. They killed him because he came to tell the peasants there how two days ago Heiss's men, and yours, killed the people defending the land that *gringo* crook bought from De Velasco for a song. She said there were more than fifty in all, including children. She said you'd sent the army in to disarm them and then turned machine-guns on them. Give me back my horse. No one can resurrect the dead, but if everybody is getting something out of this, I want my horse back or I'll tell Don Juan from *Forward* the truth.'

'You keep your mouth shut. That's all I need, the enemy in my own bed. The governor's wife spilling the beans to the honest journalist! Just who d'you think you are?'

'I want my horse,' I said, and went to sleep in our little day room.

I sat in the blue armchair I used to while away the afternoons in. They were so far away now. Every time I found out about one of Andrés's barbarities, my whole past seemed so very far away. For days I would be in a trance, churning things over in my head, wanting to leave, ashamed and terrified, certain I'd never have another peaceful afternoon, that the disgust and fear would never leave my body.

That night I felt more horror than usual. I lay down to sleep trembling. I didn't want to close my eyes in case I saw the face of the man spread out on the ground at the mill and his wife crying into her shawl.

I finally did sleep. I dreamed of my children with blood on their faces. I wanted to wipe it away, but my handkerchief merely oozed more blood. When I woke, Lucina was knocking at my door. I opened and she came in with my tea, milk, sugar and toast.

'The general says be down in an hour.'

'Is it a nice day?'

'Yes, Señora.'

'Have the children gone to school?'

'They're having breakfast.'

'Poor little things. They are, aren't they, Lucina?'

'Why, Señora? They're perfectly happy. What clothes shall I put out for you?'

I ran downstairs. I went into the stables calling his name. There he was, the white flash between his eyes, his elegant form.

'Mapache, Mapachito, what did that stupid fucking *gringo* do to you? Do you forgive me?'

I caressed him, kissed his face, his neck, his back. Then I mounted him and we galloped off to the mill at Huexotitla. I sang to frighten away the spirits of the dead. On the way there I could still see them, but by the time I got back I'd forgotten them.

At midday I went with Andrés to a lunch. There were some journalists there. One who wrote for *Forward* asked him about the deaths at Atencingo.

'A very unfortunate thing to have happened,' he said. 'I have asked the public prosecutor to investigate the matter thoroughly and I can assure you justice will be done. At the same time, we can't allow groups of bandits masquerading as peasants claiming rights to land to take by force what others have earned through their own honest toil and austere dedication. The Revolution is never mistaken, nor is a government that derives its authority from the Revolution.'

The journalist wanted to reply, but the master of ceremonies grabbed the microphone in time.

'Ladies and gentlemen, the governor is leaving now. Please vacate the room.'

People got up and started moving towards the door. I saw four of Andrés's men pick him up and carry him bodily from the room. A couple of others hustled me out into the street. They put us in different cars and drove off in a hurry.

'What's going on?' I asked the driver of the car I was in.

'Nothing, Señora, we're just trying out new exit techniques.'

Andrés went to City Hall and I went home.

His older children were in the games room with some friends. Marta had told me she was inviting Cristina, a schoolfriend, the daughter of Patricia Ibarra, elder sister of José Ibarra who was once my sweetheart.

We said we were sweethearts because we used to buy ice-creams at La Rosa, walk hand in hand to Concordia Park and kiss on the cheek before we said goodbye. One day we had the bad luck to be kissing just as his sister came out of twelve o'clock Mass and saw us. His family told José that as well as being poor, I was wilful and didn't know my place. His father offered him a trip to Europe.

He told me all this as though I were his mother and should rid him of this terrible punishment.

'So they won't let you be my sweetheart?'

'You don't know what my family's like.'

'I don't want to, either,' I said and ran, livid, all the way from the park to my house on 2nd West.

'What's the matter, pet?' asked Mama.

'She's quarrelled with the rich kid. You can tell from her face,' said Papa.

'What did he do to you?' said my mother, who took any offence personally.

'Nothing that's worth more than a rude noise,' answered Papa. 'Stick your tongue out at him.'

'I already did.'

The niece of that idiot, who was later married off to Maru Ponce to form the most boring family ever to stroll through the colonnades of a Sunday, was Marta's friend, and very pretty.

Andrés just happened to arrive as her mother was picking her up from our house that night and invited them to stay for dinner. Throughout the meal he flattered them, asked after the menfolk in their family and told them tales of bullfighters and politicians.

As she was leaving, José's sister said, 'Cati, it was a pleasure seeing you; you're always so elegant.'

'You didn't think so ten years ago,' I replied.

'I don't know what you mean,' she said with a twisted smile, and left hurriedly because Andrés was whispering God knows what to her daughter, who put her hat on backwards in confusion.

Within three days he'd taken her off to the ranch near Jalapa. And there she stayed right till the end, when she appeared with a little girl to claim her part of the inheritance. She didn't do too badly; she still lives with her horses, dogs and antiques, and does nothing at all useful. Even the son-in-law lives off what Cristina got.

I wasn't angry. How could I be angry when the whole Ibarra family still hasn't got over the shame of it? I actually enjoyed it. I found it amusing. The general stole Marta's friend and the mother is going slowly mad. It's even funnier imagining that prayer-monger going in and out of church in vain. 'She didn't even have time to earn herself a little respect,' I said, thinking back on José, Concordia

Park, and the kiss that dishonoured me.

Indeed, in Puebla everything happened in the colonnades. Espinosa was standing there when he received the stab wound that finished him in the cinema business, and Magdalena Maynez used to parade there in her new clothes before misfortune overtook her. Her life changed totally when they killed her father. I can see her now, never a rumpled ribbon or a hair out of place, her clothes hung on her like a model. They weren't rich, but they spent money as though they were. We used to see them often because her father did business with Andrés. Everyone seemed to do business with Andrés.

Magdalena was her father's favourite. At weekends he used to take her to the Casino de la Selva in Cuernavaca. We met them there once. Magdalena was wearing a white silk print dress, and her hair was held back by two combs. She was sipping her lemonade with an almost seductive detachment.

She and her father were sitting in the garden at a table by the pool when we arrived. We had all the children with us. When he saw us he got up and talked to Andrés while she chatted with us about how hot it was, without missing a single detail of her father's movements. Very soon he came back and left immediately; his daughter followed him asking him who knows what, transformed from a frivolous adolescent into a fierce litigant. I found the transformation a bit odd, but then so many things were odd and we didn't notice them specially. On the way back to Puebla in the car, I asked Andrés what had upset them and he told me to mind my own business. So I forgot about the Maynezes.

Months later the father disappeared. He was kidnapped one night as he walked through the colonnades.

Magda came to see me at home. She wore a tailored alpaca suit and a grey silk blouse.

'My father went to his cinema and hasn't been home for three days,' she said.

He must have a lover, I wanted to say, but I said nothing and stared at my hands as though it were my fault.

'Will you do me a favour and ask your husband about him?' she said.

'I'd be delighted, but I doubt if it will do any good. If he has him, he won't tell me.'

'People say you can handle him.'

'They also say you sleep with your father. They can be wrong.'

'I hope they're not wrong, Señora,' she said. She got up and left.

Three days later her father reappeared, chopped in little pieces, in a basket that someone left outside her door.

I heard about it during the morning, when I went to Blondie's to have my hair done and three old ladies were talking about it very excitedly. Blondie was sticking a false plait on and asking me how it felt when I saw my tears in the mirror. I stayed very still while she put the last grips in. The salon was silent, the old ladies began looking at me as though I held the knife in my hands. I stared at the nails Maura was painting and bit my lip hard to hold back my tears as I thought of her father, as handsome and intelligent as everyone said.

I went to the Maynezes' house. There were a lot of people. The widow was sitting with her younger children, staring at the floor, as still as if she had been killed as well.

Magdalena was the only one by the coffin; she saw me come in. I didn't go up to her, I had nothing to say, I just wanted to see her and find out if the wreath Andrés sent would fit through the door. Because that's the way he did things; if the corpse was his, or at least if he benefited from the death, he would send enormous wreaths, so enormous they wouldn't fit through the door of the house where the wake was being held.

As I repeated the Ave Marias I read the ribbons on the bouquets and wreaths. None said General Andrés Ascencio and family. When the litany began I went to see if it was outside, but before I reached the door two men came in carrying one of the wreaths which Andrés usually had made up at the main stand in La Victoria market. They came through the door.

I left. I thought Blondie would know what people were saying, one of the women whose hair she'd done that morning was bound to have told her something. I went back to see her.

She knew no more than what I already imagined. They said Andrés had killed him because no one could think of anything else, but there was no proof. All the same, I remembered the argument in Cuernavaca and Magdalena's eyes begging me for her father.

I went home. I locked myself in my room and started eating first my nail varnish and then my nails. I hated my general. I didn't know if I wanted him to come home so I could ask him about it or if I wanted to stay in my room and never see him again.

He came in laughing. He'd been riding and was dragging his spurs. I heard him climb the stairs and walk to the end of the corridor. He stopped in front of the sitting-room door and pushed it. When it didn't open he began shouting: 'No one locks me out, Catalina. This is my house and I'll go where I want. Open up, I'm in no mood for silly games.'

Naturally I opened the door. He didn't want to hear about the scandal.

'I know you were there,' he said. 'So you'll have noticed

it was nothing to do with me. Get that dress off, it makes you look like a crow. Let me see your tits, I hate it when you button up like a nun. Come on, don't be prudish, it doesn't suit you.' He climbed on my dress and I pressed my legs together. My suspender belt dug into me under his heavy body.

'Who killed him?' I asked.

'I don't know. Pure souls have many enemies,' he said. 'Take that shit off. It's getting harder to fuck you than a Puebla virgin. Take it off,' he said, as he rubbed his body against my dress. But I kept my legs closed, tightly closed, for the first time.

CHAPTER EIGHT

The moment I first saw Fernando Arizmendi, I wanted to go to bed with him. I was listening to him talk and thinking how much I'd like to nibble his ear, touch his tongue with mine and see the back of his knee.

My yearning was noticed. I began to talk more than usual, incredibly fast, and ended up being the centre of attention. Andrés realized and broke up the party.

'My wife isn't feeling well,' he said.

'But she looks wonderful,' someone replied.

'It's her make-up, but she's had this terrible headache for ages. I'll take her home and come back.'

'I feel fine,' I said.

'You don't have to pretend with these nice people; they're friends, they understand.'

He took my arm and led me to the car. He put me in, sent the chauffeur over to the other car and went round and got in the driver's seat. He sat at the wheel, started the engine, waved goodbye to those who'd come to see us off at the door and drove slowly off. He retained his frozen goodbye smile until we were a couple of streets away.

'You're so obvious, Catalina, you should be spanked.'

'And you're so discreet, I suppose?'

'I don't have to be discreet, I'm a man. You're a woman, and women who go round like bitches on heat wanting to fuck anyone who makes their belly-button tremble are called whores.'

When we arrived home, he got out deliberately, took me to the door, waited for a servant to open it and, when he was sure that not even our eternal companions in the car behind would see, smacked me on the bum and pushed me inside.

I ran up the stairs, past the children's room. I didn't pop in to see them as I did most nights, but went straight to bed. Under the sheets I thought of Fernando and touched myself as the gypsy had taught me. Then I fell asleep. I slept for three days, waking only to eat a lettuce leaf, a piece of cheese and two boiled eggs.

'What's the matter, Señora?' asked Lucina.

'An ailment the general discovered which can't be got rid of, not even with cold showers. But I'll feel better after a week's sleep.'

I had to get up after that because a week was long enough for a fever. And what was the first thing Andrés said to me when I went down to breakfast? That on Tuesday the president's private secretary was coming to dinner. And who was the private secretary? Fernando. The well-groomed and smiling Arizmendi.

Out of shock I began eating bread with butter and jam and swallowing large gulps of tea with sugar and milk. Andrés was ecstatic about Arizmendi's visit because he would be followed by the President of the Republic and Andrés planned to give him a spectacular reception with schoolchildren waving flags down Reforma, banners hanging from buildings and state employees hanging out of office windows applauding and throwing confetti. I had to find a little girl with a bunch of flowers to assail him in the middle of the street, and a little old lady with a letter asking for something simple so that the photographers could snap her five minutes later with her request granted. Espinosa and Alarcón had already lent their cinemas to hang the biggest banners from. Puebla was going to give the president the warmest and most colourful reception he had ever had. All those things which eventually became the norm and were given to the stupidest local mayor were invented by us for General Aguirre's visit.

I had to do something to abate my fever and I threw myself into the work as though I were being paid. Not just one little girl with flowers, but three on each block, and in the main square fifty of them on horseback in local Indian costumes.

I went to the old folks home to choose the little old lady and found one who looked like a picture postcard, hair in a bun, a beatific smile and a tale that, naturally, we put in the letter. She was the widow of an old soldier who had been shot for refusing to take part in the murder of Aquiles Serdán. She was proud of her husband and of herself and thought it fitting to ask the president for a sewing-machine in return for such sacrifice for the motherland.

I organized the local primary-school teachers. I got all their pupils to make paper pompons like the cheerleaders in the United States. I knew the president's favourite tune was *The Boat of Guaymas*, and it was such a silly little ditty that it wasn't too hard for the children to move their pompons and feet in time to the music. The flower-sellers from the market promised to fill Reforma with flowers, as though the avenue were a huge church, and on the cobbles of the main square they would make a floral carpet with the image of an Indian woman holding out her hand to the president. When Aguirre had passed down Reforma the people there would run with their banners and flowers to the square so that it would be full when he and Andrés arrived in their open car. After his speech from the balcony the crowd would sing *Puebla the Beautiful* and the national anthem.

I sent for every town band in the state and formed an orchestra of 300 musicians who would play in exchange for a uniform of Santa Ana cotton.

When the president's private secretary arrived to consult with Andrés, he was astonished at our plans.

I decided we would eat in the garden. The menu would be the one to be offered to the president two weeks later. But that particular lunchtime, there was only Andrés, Fernando and I.

We were so formal that Andrés sat on Fernando's left and put me on his right at a round table.

After the consommé, Fernando began praising my talents: my intelligence, my charm, my discretion, my interest in the country and politics and, to cap it all, I could cook like a nun in Puebla convent.

'Also, if the general will allow me to say so, your wife has a beautiful laugh. Adults don't usually laugh like that,' said Fernando.

'I'm glad you like it, Señor. Treat this house as your own, we want you to be comfortable,' replied Andrés.

'Yes, we do,' I said, and put my hand on his leg.

He didn't move it or change his expression.

Andrés began talking about the disturbances in Jalisco. He regretted the death of a sergeant and a private, and praised the governor who gave the order to put down the rioting peasants.

'Some things just cannot be tolerated,' replied Fernando.

I, who in those days still said what I thought, butted in: 'But isn't there some way of stopping them other than sending the army in and killing twelve peasants? They took their revenge six to one. And we don't even know what those Indians were protesting about.'

'That's just like a woman. You were talking about her intelligence and then she goes all sentimental,' said Andrés.

'Perhaps she's right, General. We should find other ways,' replied Fernando and put his hand on my leg. I felt it on the silk of my dress and forgot the twelve peasants. Then he took it away and began eating as though it were his last meal.

We became friends. Whenever I went to Mexico City I'd phone him with a message from Andrés or some other excuse. I just wanted to hear his voice or see him for a moment if I could. Afterwards I spent the three hours' drive home repeating his name.

My chauffeur had a nice voice and I'd ask him to sing *With You In the Distance* while I lay on the back seat of the black Packard, listening and missing Fernando. I searched for significance in his simplest phrases and almost came to believe that he had made an oblique declaration out of respect for my general. I remembered exactly every single thing he said to me and from a 'I hope to see you soon' I was absolutely certain he was tormented by my absence just as I was by his, and that he spent his time counting the days until he bumped into me by chance. I liked thinking about his mouth, and the sensation that ran through my body when he kissed my hand. One day I could stand it no longer. We had walked to his office door after a strange conversation in which we'd discussed neither politics, Andrés, Puebla nor Mexico. We'd talked about the pain of unrequited love and I thought I saw it in his eyes. When he said goodbye, kissing my hand, I offered him my mouth. He didn't kiss me, but gave me a long embrace.

That night my poor chauffeur sang *With You In the Distance* so often that he went on to win the International

Amateur Song Contest. I was pleased something good came out of my romance, because the very day it reached its pinnacle it was dashed to pieces. Andrés was waiting for me at City Hall. I'd been to the tailor to pick up the suit he was going to wear for the president's visit. It was already very late when I arrived back but Andrés was still settling the problem of some workers who wanted to strike in Atlixco.

I looked radiant as I entered his office. Instead of carrying his suit I held it to me and danced with it.

'You're lovely, Catalina. What have you done to yourself?' he said when he saw me.

'I bought three dresses, went to the Palacio de Hierro for a facial and came back in the car, singing.'

'I hope you took my message to Fernando, and didn't just mess around, did you?'

'Of course; I did all that after I saw Fernando.'

'There's no denying it, queers are a source of inspiration,' said Andrés to his secretary. 'Women love talking to them. Heaven knows what they find so attractive. It's amazing, when we met Fernando I was even jealous and locked Catalina up. Now he's the only boyfriend I allow her and I'm delighted with the affair.'

Next day I went to see Pepa to tell her my misfortune. I expected to find her at home, because she never went out. I was surprised that she wasn't in. Her husband's jealousy, worse now because they hadn't had children, kept her a prisoner. One afternoon when she went out for a couple of hours he had met her at the door with a crucifix and forced her to beg forgiveness on her knees and swear there and then that she hadn't deceived him.

She had preferred to find things to do at home. She'd turned it into a golden cage, filling each corner with some tiny detail. The patio was full of birds and she knitted interminable covers for chairs, tables, windows and side-boards. All their food was fried in olive oil, even the beans, and she always cooked it herself. You'd think she was in love. She spent her days polishing antiques and watering plants. She behaved as though it were the only world that existed, she didn't want us saying it wasn't, and once when Mónica tried to be frank and told her we were living in the 1930s and her husband was insufferable and she should leave him and at least be free to go out whenever she wanted, she gently put her hand to her mouth and asked her if she'd like some tea and walnut biscuits.

'You're going crazy,' said Mónica. 'Isn't she, Catalina?'

'No more than I am,' I replied.

Mónica had had to work since her husband became ill. She had opened a children's clothes shop and ended up with a factory.

'Honestly, the only one here with a normal husband is me,' she said, laughing.

I sat on a wrought-iron bench in the garden under a purple jacaranda. The maid in white cap and pinny brought me some lemonade and said that the Señora always came back at 12.30 on the dot. I was mystified, but there were only fifteen minutes to go so I decided to wait.

At the precise minute the antique family clock chimed half-past twelve, Pepa came in through the door, crossed the patio and came up to me on my bench.

'You've got a lover, I see,' I said, laughing at my own silly joke.

'Yes, I have,' she said, sitting beside me with a calmness I haven't seen since.

They met in the mornings, every day from half-past ten to half-past twelve in a room rented as a storeroom over La Victoria market. Who was he? The only man her husband had allowed her to exchange more than two words with. The doctor who had attended her when she miscarried. It had happened three times. He was very handsome, the best-known baby doctor in Puebla. Half his patients would have liked to have an affair with him; some of them got more dressed up for an appointment with him than for the Red Cross ball, and he ended up with Pepa, the most difficult.

'We fuck like gods,' she said in the same sweet voice she used to say her prayers in, and she laughed a clear, happy laugh. She was radiant. My imagination would never have stretched to dreaming of her like this.

'And your husband?' I asked.

'He doesn't realize. He's incapable of rhyming dust with lust. And how are things with you?'

'The same.'

What could I say? My stupid affair with Arizmendi was fine for amusing a poor woman locked in the house all day, but I couldn't disturb this new goddess's paradise with something so prosaic. I kissed her and left, envying her her state of grace.

CHAPTER NINE

I never understood how Fito got to be Minister of Defence, but then I hadn't understood how he'd got to be an under-secretary, or that when Andrés brought him along to act as a witness at our wedding he was already director of heaven knows what.

But Andrés was surprised too when posters signed by General Juan de la Torre appeared on walls in Mexico City putting Rodolfo Campos forward as a candidate for the presidency. I think even Rodolfo himself was surprised, because he quickly put out a statement saying that it was a crude manoeuvre and that he was only interested in collaborating with General Aguirre and had no further aspirations.

I believed him. What aspirations could the poor bloke have if not even his wife respected him? Short and squat as she was, after eight days of marriage she ran away with the doctor in the regiment where Fito was paymaster. She just ran off one morning and didn't even leave a note. If someone hadn't slipped him a hint, who knows when her husband would have found out. Recently an old soldier from that regiment told me that when Rodolfo did find out he went to his general and burst into tears as he recounted his tale of woe.

'Very well, sergeant,' said the general, 'you have my

permission to go after them with a firing squad and deal with them as they deserve.'

'No, General,' said Fito, 'I want you to send a justice of the peace to order them to come back, nothing more.'

The general sent the justice of the peace and they came back. When Chofi got off her horse, Rodolfo threw himself at her feet, crying and asking what he'd done to deserve being abandoned like that. He begged her to forgive him, kissed her ankles in front of everyone while she, hands on hips, didn't even deign to lower her head.

Sofía was always haughty and they say she used to be pretty. But I doubt it. What she did do though, as her husband rose through the ranks, was to exchange her philandering for piety. If she fucked some priest or other no one ever knew, and it certainly never showed on her face.

I'll never forget the day Fito was nominated for president because it was the day Tyrone Power came to Mexico.

I went to the airport with Mónica, since it so happened that Andrés wanted me to pay Chofi a courtesy call. Mónica had imagined herself waiting for Tyrone Power on the aircraft steps, but when we got to the airport it seemed that thousands of women had exactly the same thing in mind.

Her husband had been ill for so long that Mónica had spent years keeping thoughts of fucking to herself while she made clothes and money. When she saw Tyrone Power all her latent desire came rushing to the fore and she turned into a wild animal. She left me standing by the ticket counter and threw herself, pushing and kicking, into the fray.

In two minutes, she was on top of the poor man.

'Tyrone, I've seen all your films,' she shouted. She got to him before the multitude, so she managed to give him a kiss which he returned with his studied, puppet-like smile. That was the last smile he managed, the police and fire brigade had to spirit him away from the airport. The women left him without a jacket and not a single button on his shirt. I saw him being carried aloft by firemen; his hair was standing on end and he was missing a shoe.

Mónica looked like a cat who'd got the cream. It was a pleasure to see. Not many people are happy with so little.

From the airport we went to Chofi's house. She was looking very smart when we arrived, which I found strange, because she was almost always still in her dressing-gown and slippers at one o'clock. That day her hair was done in tight little pin curls and she had a dark dress on. One couldn't expect total elegance, so I thought it a bit much of Mónica to observe that it wasn't done to wear diamanté brooches like the one she had between her tits during the day.

She was sitting in an armchair in her Louis XV drawing room, having her picture taken by several photographers.

When they'd gone, I assumed we had to congratulate her but I didn't know why. I asked the last photographer and he said that Martín Cienfuegos, Governor of Tabasco, had signed a pact with politicians from various parts of the country to support Rodolfo Campos for president.

Chofi was all in a tizz; she showed us the badges with her husband's photo which had just arrived from some factory in the USA, and talked about the pro-General Campos committees that were springing up all over Mexico.

I assumed that Andrés knew all about this, but had sent me there without explaining so that I wouldn't refuse to visit Chofi as though I were her lady-in-waiting. I was furious with him, but listened to Chofi's stories with a beatific smile. When she'd finished I allowed myself the luxury of expressing my congratulations and asked her to accept Andrés's too, explaining that local matters made it impossible for him to rush to his *compadre*'s side. Then I said goodbye with the excuse that I wanted to get back to Puebla before dark.

'Imagine! Six years of those bores ahead of us,' said Mónica at the door. 'How awful! I prefer indigenism.'

We went to the Tampico for dinner. Mónica flirted with the men at adjacent tables until the waiter arrived with a bottle of champagne we hadn't ordered, a note saying our bill had been paid and two roses with a card saying, 'With our sincere admiration – Mateo Podán and Francisco Balderas.'

I looked around for Balderas, who was the Minister of Agriculture and had dined at my house several times. He was sitting not very far from us, at a table for two, with a man with a pointed nose and deep-set eyes whom I assumed was Mateo Podán, a journalist Andrés hated.

'You say the one on the right wants to be president too?' asked Mónica. 'Well, my dear, I hope he makes it.'

They came over to our table and chatted. Mateo Podán had a quick, cruel tongue which he used to describe our friend Campos as if I were Dolores del Rio or any woman except the wife of his *compadre* Andrés Ascencio. Balderas was smitten with Mónica and asked for her address among other things.

We left the restaurant at about seven. We got back to Puebla so late that Mónica's husband nearly recovered enough from his paralysis to get up and hit her, and mine already knew all about everything, even that I had liked Podán's long hands.

'Who gave you permission to go out whoring?' he asked when I waltzed into our bedroom at about midnight.

'I did,' I told him so calmly that he had to stop himself laughing before he began his tirade. I halted him in his

tracks when I put on my nightie and said, 'Don't get so
worked up. Are you so sure that Fattie will be president?
It's best to light several candles. And take those bodyguards
away. They're not worth their wages. Besides, I'm in your
team and you know it.'

Early in the New Year Rodolfo's candidacy became
inevitable, especially after General Narváez was killed.
He'd had it coming to him, according to Andrés, because
he was stupid and stubborn. Who'd be foolish enough to
take up arms against the government?

As Defence Secretary, Rodolfo ordered the army to be
magnanimous to prisoners and allow the few who were still
armed to surrender. Then he resigned so that people
couldn't say he had taken advantage of his position to
curry support.

'He's crazy, that bastard,' said Andrés. 'He's going to fall
between two stools.'

By now he'd already decided that it wouldn't suit him if
his *compadre* was president. He even thanked me for the
attention I had paid Balderas and wanted us to invite him
to dinner with Mónica. We also invited Flores Pliego and
then, one by one, the whole cabinet. But Rodolfo was
already well on his way. In Veracruz a meeting was held
for the twenty-four governors supporting him and Andrés
had to go. Biting his balls, as they say in polite company,
but he went. He came back cursing his *compadre* behind our
bedroom door and applauding his success outside it. The
one he had absolutely no love left for at all was Martín
Cienfuegos. He couldn't bear being pipped at the post and
not even having been told of Rodolfo's candidacy before it
was a *fait accompli*. Worse still, Rodolfo had found a pal in
Cienfuegos and even stopped consulting Andrés about a
load of things he usually did ask him about.

Only when a Revolutionary Committee of National Reconstruction was formed to support the candidacy of General Bravo did Fito remember he had an intelligent *compadre* and even came to Puebla to talk to him. It was the day Colonel Fulgencio Batista, who had just come to power in Cuba, came through our city. Rodolfo and he lunched at our house.

'Know when the hero of Cuban democracy is going to hand over power?' Andrés asked me when they'd gone. 'Never! If that bastard's not thrown out, he'll be there for forty years.'

I asked jokingly if that was what he'd like to see happen in Mexico.

'Of course I would,' he said, 'and if it were like that, neither that idiot of a *compadre* Fito nor his pal Cienfuegos would get to the eagle throne before me. But all that palaver just for a puny six years? No, I'm better off building a lasting little power base, and even the most macho president will end up running my errands.'

He talked like that because he was appalled at the avalanche of support for his *compadre*. One day playing dominoes he called him a fool and swore he would never be president. Three days later a meeting of governors was organized and all of them backed Campos for president. Instead of going to the function in the Regis cinema, Andrés went to a lunch Balderas gave for the press where he said democratic elections weren't possible because he was sure the governors would rig the polls.

A few days later the CTM decided to support Fito, and the CNC convention in the Mexico City Arena ended with the peasants waving their machetes and sombreros, and shouting, '*Viva* Campos!'

We returned to Puebla. Andrés was as grumpy as a wet

hen. I didn't even talk to him. I just listened to him growling and cursing. Then one morning something he read in *Forward* changed his mood. After he'd left the house whistling, I picked up the paper with more than my usual curiosity. I couldn't see why he was so pleased, because it was full of accusations against him and his *compadre*. Their names were linked, the much praised presidential candidate was the governor's accomplice in the crimes of Atencingo and Atlixco; he had a house near Heiss's mill built on what had been communal land, he and Andrés were in cahoots with Heiss to spirit money out of the country and everyone knew that between them they had more than 6 million pesos deposited in dollars in *gringo* banks. It ended by saying that the Office-holders' Responsibility Law should be applied before nominating as candidate a pillager and plunderer and accomplice of a governor who was guilty of many deaths, no matter how much silence and fear covered them up.

Not long afterwards *Forward* reported the disappearance of its editor, Don Juan Soriano, and begged the public to unite in urging the government to bring about his prompt reappearance. A few days later his body was found dumped on a hacienda in Poloxtla near San Martín. Newspapers all over Mexico published protests and articles accusing Governor Ascencio of the crime. I was present at the interview with the correspondent from *Excelsior*. Andrés used him to state that he had asked the Senate to intervene in the matter. It was in their hands and justice would be done.

The following weekend Rodolfo appeared at our house in Puebla. I was sitting in the patio facing the door and saw him walk slowly in.

'How are you, *comadre*?' he said affectionately and kissed me. 'Your husband?'

I accompanied him to the bottom of the garden. Andrés was in the games room beating Octavio at billiards. Marcela was keeping score with discs hanging on a wire, in league with her brother whom we all knew let Andrés beat him.

'*Compadre*,' said Rodolfo from the doorway with a firmness in his voice that was new to me.

'*Compadre*,' replied Andrés, walking towards him.

They embraced.

'And now what?' I asked after saying goodbye to Rodolfo that afternoon.

'Now we'll both be president,' he replied.

I still remember the rest of that year and the whole of the next as though I had fallen into a whirlpool. Andrés named me his representative. I was forever at meetings, gatherings, civic functions and a host of other things that bored me to tears.

I bought a house in the Las Lomas area of Mexico City. Sometimes I had it all to myself. The children and Andrés spent Monday to Friday in Puebla. At weekends Octavio and Marcela arrived, soi-disant to help me.

'Catín, can we change the two beds in my room for one big one?' asked Marcela one day.

I agreed, of course. From then on they slept in the same bed. They still do.

At first her father tried everything to get Marcela married. Octavio begged me to reject the suitors. I did such a good job that one day Andrés said, 'So you think they make a lovely couple too.' And burst out laughing.

The Party's convention came. Fito was officially named candidate and began a country-wide tour. The first place we visited was Guadalajara. Fito gave a speech in a park.

He defended the family and spoke of the respect children
owed their parents. He seemed more like a priest than a
presidential candidate. Marcela, Octavio and I nudged
each other and winked when he got too bombastic. I was
grateful to them for coming with me. Apart from the nice
company, they gave me an excuse to get away from Fattie's
unwelcome attentions.

Suddenly, in the middle of the night, he'd send for me
via one of those soldiers lent to him by the presidential staff
who treated him like a president already. I didn't know
what to do. I didn't fancy Fito one little bit. I wouldn't
have wanted to touch him even if he'd been president of
the whole world.

Once he sent for me in the afternoon to show me the
biographies of him and Andrés which the hitmen had
published in almost every newspaper. They began by
reminding readers that Fito had been a postman, then
went back to the business of them having been with Huerta
in La Ciudadela, and followed that with a letter from Heiss
to his government saying that they could depend on the
'Ascencio and Campos boys' to defend US interests in
Puebla, and ended with a list of all the familiar crimes.

'Don't be upset,' I told him. 'Andrés never paid any
attention to what they wrote about him during his cam-
paigns. You're going to win anyway, aren't you?'

'I want you to come with me to the parade,' he
answered, nodding his head. The next day he sent for me
at my house. The chauffeur delivered a bunch of flowers
with a note saying, 'For bringing me luck on May Day.'

We watched the Labour Day Parade from the balcony of
the CTM offices in Madero Street with Álvaro Cordera,
thin and refined, standing next to Fito with his usual
podgy, half-smiling face, totally miserable. Everything went
well until the railway workers marched by shouting for

Bravo and throwing rotten oranges at the balcony where we were. I thought Rodolfo would have a fit, but instead his boring features set into a solemn stare and he stood firm, without losing his half-smile, next to Cordera.

I was wearing a pale chiffon dress. Suddenly an orange burst against my skirt. Given Rodolfo's detachment, I thought the right thing to do would be to smile also and keep still. So I did. When the parade was over, Fito asked Cordera if he didn't think I had behaved like a wise queen. Cordera said calmly, yes I had.

'Sofía couldn't have faced it. What a good choice Andrés made!' said Fito. 'You're a perfect and brave woman,' he kept repeating in the car on the way home. When we arrived, he walked me to the door and said goodbye, kissing my hands and my stained skirt.

'Does he write his own speeches?' I wondered as I climbed the stairs to my bedroom. 'He's so banal he'd do well writing speeches.'

Andrés rang in the afternoon to thank me. He completed the other half of the eulogy as to my qualities: 'You're a fucking trooper. You learned your lesson well. Now you can go into politics. Keep Fattie sweet for me,' he said.

I imagined him sitting at his desk, piled high with papers he never read. I could almost see his mouth spouting guffaws of appreciation. There was something about him I still liked.

'When are you coming?' I said.

'You come here tomorrow. President Aguirre is arriving on the fifth.'

I went. The parade went off perfectly. Thousands of children dressed in regional costumes marched before us in a mass of brilliant, disciplined colour. Aguirre thanked Andrés, Doña Lupe went with me to the hospice and donated breakfasts for the next six months. Then a car took us up to the mountains. Andrés had organized a line of Indians willing to ask the President for things. We spent the afternoon listening to them. At about eight o'clock I took Doña Lupe for coffee and cake. At eleven we went back to where her husband was still listening to Indians. Beside him Andrés was sucking on his cigar, immutable and satisfied. Doña Lupe and I went off to bed. It was four in the morning when my general came into the bedroom we shared.

'The bastard never gets tired,' he complained as he got into bed. He put his arms round me. 'I was forgetting how fanciable you are.'

'That's because you've got so many,' I replied.

'No slander, Catín. If you're clever, you'll keep quiet.'

'What do presidents feel when their turn is up?' I said. 'Poor General Aguirre.'

'Aren't I right about you being fanciable?' he replied.

CHAPTER TEN

Bibi was a bit younger than me. I met her when she was married to a doctor who was embarrassed about charging. When asked what his fee was he'd say what the Indians say – whatever you wish. He was a good doctor, he cured children's indigestion and flu and mothers' anxiety. Once, when Verania swallowed a sweet and turned purple, I ran to him in a panic. I thought she was going to die and I was terrified at the thought of hearing the general yelling 'careless murderer' at me.

No sooner had I stepped into his surgery at 3rd North than I felt relieved. The child was still purple, but the doctor greeted me calmly and made her drink some hot herbal tea which dissolved the sweet and let her breathe again. When she coughed and turned from purple to white I started crying, I hugged the doctor and began kissing him. We were in the middle of it when Bibi came in.

'He saved my daughter's life,' I said, apologizing, although I didn't know who she was.

'He's like that,' she replied, quite unperturbed.

'This lady is General Ascencio's wife,' the doctor explained to Bibi.

'And what does that feel like?' was all the greeting I got.

I shrugged my shoulders and we burst out laughing, much to the doctor's surprise.

I didn't see much of her after that. We'd sometimes meet in the street, ask after each other's husbands. She'd praise mine and I hers, we'd ask after the children, she'd complain that hers was delicate and I that mine were savages. Then we'd say goodbye with one of those kisses that fall on the air while we touch cheeks.

Years later she told me that those meetings made her feel important.

One day her husband died. Without any fuss, he was like that, and without leaving her a penny, he was like that. I went to the funeral to thank him for curing my children's bruises and because in Puebla people went to funerals for the same reason they went to weddings, christenings and first communions – to pass the time of day.

Bibi was holding her son's hand. I put some money in an envelope and gave it to her after I hugged her.

'This is what I owed your husband,' I said, with that do-gooder air I so enjoyed.

'Always so discreet, Catalina,' she replied.

She didn't cry. I remember her looking lovely in widow's weeds. She looked younger than ever and her dark eyes shone. She was very pretty, so pretty that she couldn't bear the idea of wasting her beauty in Puebla with a son who would grow up while she grew wrinkled from worrying about what to sell to pay his school fees. She went to Mexico City to be with her brothers who worked on a newspaper owned by General Gómez Soto.

And I saw her next at Gómez Soto's house. It was a huge, ridiculous house like ours. Bibi was in the garden. She was wearing a dress cut very low at the front and back, and a perfect smile.

'You look lovely,' I said.

'I'm not as poor,' she replied.

'Congratulations,' I said, thinking of my mother, who said that when she was pleased at someone else's good fortune but preferred not to examine too closely where it had come from.

We sat beside a pool full of gardenias and floating candles.

'It's divine, isn't it?' she asked.

'Divine,' I said, and we began talking about divine things: the nylons she'd got from the States, how much she liked the Angel of Independence, if I thought it correct to accept flowers from a married man. I laughed. What a crazy question. She should go and ask one of the women who accepted car keys wrapped up as a present from Andrés – with the car standing outside the front door of course.

'As Aunt Nico used to say, "Before marriage, from a man nary a flower." You're not thinking of taking that saying to heart, are you?' I asked.

This led on to her confessing that General Gómez Soto had asked her to be the lady of that house.

'Just this house, nothing else?' I said.

'His wife and children live in the others. They haven't got this one yet.'

The general's wife looked like the back of a bus. She was the same age as Bibi, but hers were the forty-five years of a woman who'd been a camp follower and had had nine children. The children were grown up now, some of them married even, and she was a grandmother who had never expected much from life but whose husband had become rich. From what I knew of these generals, he would never leave her publicly and marry Bibi.

'Say yes, but have him put the house in your name,' I advised.

'I can't do that, Catalina. I daren't. He's so good to me, he already gives me such a lot,' she said, and she blushed.

'He gives you crumbs,' I said. 'They all do. Nothing they really miss. He decorates your pool, but he doesn't put it in your name. What a joke! D'you want to be a kept woman?'

'To start with. But I'll keep working on it,' she said in the voice of a fifteen-year-old.

A month after that conversation she came to see me in Puebla. She got happily out of a car as big as mine. She didn't have her son with her, and she was wearing a fur coat in March. I said rude things about General Gómez Soto again and even linked him to Soriano's murder. It had suited him just as much as Andrés because he ended up adding *Forward* to his chain of newspapers. She didn't want to hear.

We were standing on the terrace looking out over the city and the dozens of churches with their shining domes. I liked the view from there. You could see the streets of Puebla perfectly and almost reach out and touch the house you liked best.

'I'm tired of feeling unprotected, Catalina. It's horrible being a poor widow. Everyone wants to put their paws on you, but nobody gives you anything, hardly. At least the general is generous. Look at the car he gave me, look at the servants he pays for. He's promised to take me to Europe, he'll buy me anything I want. We'll go to the theatre, I'll see things I'd never see stuck in this hole or bent over a typewriter in America Studios watching María Félix until I'm old and grey and she's as beautiful as ever.'

'You're right about that,' I said. 'I'm the worst example and I'm not grumbling. Why should you? Of course I didn't have anyone to compare him with, and I don't really think I had any choice. I've never known a normal everyday husband who hasn't enough to buy vermicelli soup. I sometimes think I'd have liked to be married to a doctor who knows where children's tonsils are. Although it might well be the same old boring life without the fur coats. Why don't you marry your brother-in-law's brother? He's nice, and handsome,' I said.

'Because he's already married. He's one of the many gropers.'

We became friends. She ended up going and living with Gómez Soto, who was true to his word as far as cars with frosted windows and the house with the pool were concerned, but didn't come up with the trips to Europe. He didn't let her leave the house, not even to buy clothes. Everything was delivered to the house: clothes, shoes, Paris hats. As if the poor soul needed hats with veils to walk up and down the corridors in her house. He even built a theatre at the bottom of the garden. He brought actors. They had private shows. They invited everybody. Even Chofi, who was so puritanical, came with her husband one day. Fito needed Gómez Soto's newspapers for his campaign and was ready to pay the necessary courtesies.

'Don't worry,' Andrés told him as we were driving to Bibi's house. 'Gómez Soto knows which side to be on, and he's grateful. I lent him money to buy his new machines.'

'The state government's money?' asked Rodolfo, as if he were completely dumb.

'Of course, my friend, but the state is me, and a debt is a debt. He knows he owes us. Besides, it'll be fun, his parties are always amusing. Aren't they, Catín?'

'Yes,' I said, looking at Chofi who was so furious her snout stuck further in the air.

'Well, I don't like having to put up with his mistress,' she said.

'What d'you mean, put up with? She's charming,' said Fito. Chofi's snout grew longer.

Bibi came to the front gate. We hadn't seen each other for about three months. She had stopped coming to Puebla and when I saw her I knew why. Inevitably, the general had given her a bun in the oven.

Pregnancy suited her rather well. In her long full dress she looked like a Greek goddess. Her arms were a bit fatter but her face was even younger.

'I warned you. First the fun, then the bun.'

'Don't remind me. I'm afraid the poor kid will be born with his nose.'

'Don't worry about the nose, what about his bad habits? I don't know how we dare reproduce them.'

'They don't have to turn out the same,' said Bibi, patting her belly. 'Beethoven was the son of an alcoholic and a lunatic.'

'Who told you that?'

'I don't remember, but there's hope for us yet, eh?'

'And your other son, how is he?'

'Fine. Odi wanted us to send him to school abroad for a while; he's in a lovely boarding school in Philadelphia.'

'At nine?'

'He's very happy. It's run on military lines, very expensive. They have three different uniforms and beautiful playing fields. He needed to be with other boys, he was too close to me.'

'Is that what you think, or Gómez Soto?'

'Both of us.'

'What a perfect couple! In agreement on everything,' I said, giving her a hug.

'Well, what d'you want me to say?' she asked.

'Don't treat me like an idiot. You can tell that tale about your son being happy to Chofi. I'll even help you with the details. But with me, you can cry. Is that what you want to do?'

'No, I don't. Not because of that. I do cry sometimes, but because I've a great big belly and I'm shut away here.'

'Having a big belly is horrible, isn't it?'

'Horrible. I don't know who invented the idea that women are happy and beautiful when they're pregnant.'

'Men, probably. But even some women put on contented faces now.'

'What else can they do?'

'They can be angry at least. I was furious during my two pregnancies. Miracle of life, huh, the nightmare, you mean. You should have seen how I cried and hated my six-month pot with Verania when the garden was full of fruit and I couldn't pick it. I was always the champion climber, I used to beat my brothers and sisters by at least three baskets, and, suddenly there I am at my parents' house watching them climb the trees with no competition at all.

'"You see, pet, what you get for being a busy-body," said Papa. I started crying and I haven't stopped yet.'

'Liar. I've never seen you cry.'

'Because you're not there at midnight, and during the day it's not done, I'm the First Lady of the State of Puebla.'

We walked from the front gate round the whole garden. Fito, Andrés and Chofi in front, us behind. When we reached the front door the general welcomed us and they all embraced and patted each other on the back. Men are funny, they can't kiss each other or say something tender, or pat a pregnant belly, so they guffaw and give each other big noisy hugs. I don't know what fun there is in that.

'You look very pretty pregnant,' said Chofi. 'It makes your face look softer.'

'It makes it fatter,' said Bibi.

'Well, yes, nothing you can do about that. You can't be expecting and thin. But motherhood is noble. I don't know a single woman who is ugly when she's pregnant.'

'I do, lots,' I said, remembering Chofi, who looked dreadful from day one. You couldn't tell if she was coming or going, she had a belly as big as her bum, and tits like an elephant. Poor thing, you couldn't help feeling sorry for her. She was going to be the president's lady and even so she couldn't stop eating.

'You know lots? Who do you know who looks ugly when she's pregnant?'

'Lots, Chofi. You don't want me to name them, do you?'

'You just say it to be different.'

'OK, I'll say all pregnant women are beautiful if you like, but I don't think it's true. I never felt so ugly.'

'Well, you didn't look it. You're too thin now. And how do you feel, Señora?' she asked Bibi.

'Very well,' said Bibi. 'I'm doing exercises, they say it's good for you.'

'But that's terrible, it can't be good. You'll harm the baby. You should rest during pregnancy. You don't want it to be premature like Catalina's was last time.'

'That was nothing to do with exercise, my womb rejected it,' I said.

'Don't be silly! Since when have wombs rejected babies? You went riding.'

'The doctor said I could.'

'Of course, Dosal is crazy, he lets you do anything. When I heard him saying after you'd had Checo that you didn't have to drink atole and chicken soup for the first forty days, I thought he was crazy. Crazy and irresponsible. You shouldn't play with children's lives like that. Perhaps he's a queer. Queers hate children and women. Yes, he's a queer for sure.'

'How do you like the flowers in my pool, Doña Chofi?' asked Bibi, opportunely.

'Ah, they're lovely. I hadn't seen them. Do they grow near here?'

'Odilón has them sent from Fortín every week.'

'What an attentive man,' said Chofi. 'There aren't many left like him. How long does it take from Fortín to here?'

'Seven hours,' I said. 'We're all mad.'

'Why d'you say that, Catalina? Don't be jealous.'

'Who wouldn't be? But it's mad to bring flowers from Fortín. Obviously the general is deeply in love.'

'Ah, yes,' replied Chofi. Her breasts swelled when she went all romantic, and she sighed as if she'd like someone, please, to fuck her.

We went to sit in the living room, which was like the lobby of a *gringo* hotel. Carpeted and huge. That's why we all invited so many people to our parties: we had to fill the rooms or we'd rattle round like peas in a pot.

There were masses of people at Bibi and her general's party. They were celebrating the newspaper's anniversary, so anyone who wanted to be on the front page next day was there. Bibi wasn't much good at organizing the food; she handed it all over to some very expensive girls, French apparently, and there was never enough. On the other hand, they had imported wine and waiters who filled your glass as soon as it was half empty. Not much food and a lot of wine: the party ended in a spectacular binge. The men started off by going red in the face and smiling a lot, then they became talkative, then stupid and angry. General Gómez Soto was the worst. He always drank quite a lot. To start with he was almost charming, a bit disconnected but intelligent. Unfortunately, it didn't last long. He soon began insulting people.

'Why've you got such bandy legs?' he asked the wife of Colonel López Miranda. 'The things you must've been made to do for them to get so bandy. This Colonel Miranda must be a randy bastard, look what he's done to his wife.'

Nobody laughed louder than he did, and nobody left the party quicker than López Miranda and his wife with the bandy legs. After that, the general began talking about his father, saying that no one had done so much for Mexico and received so little recognition.

'Yes, my father supported Porfirio Díaz, what do you expect, you bastards? You couldn't do anything else in those days. But we've got my father to thank for the railways and thanks to the railways we had the Revolution. Isn't that right, you bastards?' he shouted from a table top.

'How many times a week does he get like this?' I asked Bibi, who was sitting beside me, looking at him with contempt rather than horror, as though he were a stranger.

'Once or twice,' she said, unperturbed. 'I'll get him off the table so he doesn't fall – he's worse injured than drunk.'

'He can't be.'

'You have no idea. He gets a cold and thinks he's dying, he won't let me leave his bedside, he complains like a wounded lizard. I can't bear to think of him with a broken leg.'

She went up to the table Gómez was standing on. I'll never forget her white figure holding up her hand.

'Come down from there, darling,' she said. 'It's dangerous. You'll hurt yourself if you fall. Come on, get down.'

'Don't talk to me like that!' Gómez shouted at her. 'Think I'm an idiot? Think I'm your idiot of a son? You treat me like you do him. D'you treat him as though he were me? Sure you do, I've seen you putting him to bed, kissing him, whispering to him, you'd rather fuck him than me. Dirty whore!' he cried as he jumped off the table onto Bibi. He put his hands round her neck and began to strangle her.

'Do something,' I said to Andrés.

'What d'you want me to do? She's his wife, isn't she?'

Chofi started shrieking hysterically and Fito put his arms round her to calm her down. No one intervened.

Bibi struggled with the general's hands without losing her elegance.

'Help her,' I said, taking Andrés by the hand to where the general was puffing and blowing.

'Don't go overboard with your love, Gómez,' said Andrés, forcing his hands between Gómez's hands and Bibi's neck. Gómez let her go and I hugged her.

'It's nothing,' she told me. 'He's just playing, aren't you, my love?' she asked Odilón, and in seconds his wild, lunatic expression changed to that of a playful puppy.

'Of course, Catita. Think I'd want to hurt this beautiful girl? I adore her. We play a bit rough at times, but it's only a game. Forgive me if I alarmed you. Music, please, maestro.'

The band began to play *The Little Star*. Bibi smoothed her dress, put one hand on the general's left shoulder and gave him the other, as she leaned her head graciously against his chest, ready to dance.

Soon everyone had forgotten the incident and Bibi and Odi were once again the perfect couple.

'You're a genius,' I told her as I said goodbye.

'Did you like the party, angel?' she asked, as if nothing had happened.

CHAPTER ELEVEN

Hardly any of the other states gave women the right to vote, but Carmen Serdán had won this for women in Puebla. We were in the forefront for once, so on 7 July I did myself up more elegantly than usual and paraded around with Andrés, playing my official lady role. The polling-booths weren't very crowded, but we found some journalists and I put on my best smile, went hand in hand with my general to the ballot box as though I didn't know what to do, pretending I was as stupid as I looked.

I voted for Bravo, the opposition candidate, not because I thought much of him, but because he was bound to lose and it was nice not to feel in the least bit responsible for Fito's government.

It all passed off quite quietly in Puebla. As First Lady I probably wouldn't have known if it hadn't, but we heard that in Mexico City the people had forced President Aguirre to shout 'Viva Bravo' when he went to vote, and that PRM militants had had to safeguard the Revolution by stealing the ballot boxes where Fito was losing. They arrived by car waving pistols and invented complaints which forced the booths to close early.

Bravo had the foresight to be called away suddenly to Venezuela. The Armed Uprising Plan was replaced by the Surrender Plan. His followers rose up anyway and were killed like flies. So my candidate didn't come back. Since I'd proved a disaster as a voter, I thought it only right to recognize my error and applaud Congress when in September it declared Fito the winner by 3,400,000 votes to Bravo's 151,000.

Like me, the United States government chose to recognize Fattie's victory, and promised to send Secretary Bryan as special envoy to his inauguration ceremony.

Bravo came back not long afterwards. I've never seen Andrés laugh as much as the day he read the speech my ex-candidate gave to the press the afternoon he arrived.

'This bastard is really funny. Listen to this,' he said. '"Since my resoluteness was due neither to vanity nor ambition, I have returned to abdicate, before the sovereign people of Mexico, the office of President of the Republic which they honoured me by electing me to last 7 July." What a hoot,' stamping as he roared with laughter. 'He has shining intentions, profound piety, unflagging gratitude, confidence in a free and happy Mexico. He's got everything except balls.'

'What did you expect?' I asked. 'That he let them kill him?'

'Yes. That was the least he could do. All that farting and no shitting, just a load of hot air,' he said, and didn't stop laughing all morning.

He had the brilliant idea of sending me to help Chofi look after Secretary Bryan's wife at the reception at the *gringo* embassy. We got there just as a huge crowd was throwing stones at Washington's statue. We went in through the back door and from inside could hear shouts and shots as several very serious waiters plied us with caviar titbits and champagne. Señora Bryan was pale but put on a 'nothing's happening' face worthy of the best actress. She must have been ruing the day they'd sent her husband to a country of savages, but she smiled from time to time and even asked me what the weather was like in Puebla.

'Chilly,' I said.

'How nice,' she replied.

As we came away from the dinner we heard that a Major Luna had died trying to arrest a group of terrorists who were planning to assassinate Generals Aguirre and Campos.

'Poor Major Luna, he died serving his motherland,' said Chofi to the lieutenant who acted as her bodyguard and had told us the awful news.

'It hasn't taken her long to confuse herself with the motherland,' I thought. 'It happens to all of them, but I thought it happened more slowly,' I murmured as she went on about the vocation of service and Major Luna's deep sense of loyalty.

Back in Puebla I was reminded of it when Mónica, Pepa and I were discussing Fito's ridiculous stunt of declaring his total worth; two ranches, Las Espuelas and La Mandarina, a country house in Matamoros, their residence in Lomas de Chapultepec worth 20,500 pesos. No numbered account in any credit institution whatsoever.

'They're so vulgar,' said Mónica. 'Forgive me, Cati, but who are they trying to fool with this honesty bit? Don't tell me they haven't even got a chequebook. Does Chofi keep her pennies under the mattress?'

'No bank account in Mexico,' said Pepa. 'Your *compadre* is insufferable; six tedious years ahead of us. Pious and anti-communist. I thought my husband was the only one of those left,' she said, laughing with the cheek she'd got from her rendezvous in La Victoria market.

'Know why they call Rodolfo the inland revenue?' asked Mónica. ''Cos he's so bloody taxing.'

We laughed. Like all good Puebla girls, my friends hadn't got a kind word for anyone. They said all the things I wanted to hear but never did. I loved seeing them. I was so happy I almost forgot it was Rodolfo's inauguration next day and I didn't know what to wear.

Papa did me the favour of taking the decision out of my hands. I went to see him when I left Pepa's house. He was having his coffee with cheese and some hard bread he was slicing very thin.

'What d'you think about the war? Will anything worse than not having nylons happen to us?' I asked him.

'I don't intend living long enough to find out,' he answered.

I joked about his eternal pessimism and began complaining about my lot; the wife of Andrés Ascencio, the *comadre* of Rodolfo Campos, a poor soul who couldn't bear the idea of a long speech read in that mental-defective tone which pervaded Fito's oratory at his supreme moments.

'My poor little girl,' he said, stroking my hair. 'Things will get better. You need a nice boyfriend.'

'I've got you,' I replied, wrinkling my nose and getting up to kiss him.

We started fooling around as we always did. I went up with him to put his pyjamas on and was lying on the bed next to him when my mother arrived with a face which said it's very late for you be out alone. She was never out of the house after five in the afternoon, especially not without her husband. She thought I was scandalous. I got up.

'I don't know what to wear tomorrow,' I said.

'Wear something black, that's always smart,' replied Bárbara, coming into the bedroom.

'I'll see what I can find. Look after my boyfriend for me.'

I had to find something black. By dawn, Papa was dead.

I don't like talking about it. I think we all saw it as a betrayal. Even my mother, who was sure they'd meet again in heaven. Bárbara took charge of the funeral and things like that. I don't remember anything except that I cried in public, something a governor's wife should never do. Nor do I remember anything about Andrés's last months as governor. When I came to my senses we were already living in Mexico City.

CHAPTER TWELVE

I wandered round the house in a dream, conjuring up people I needed near me. I was so desperate for company that in the end I even needed Andrés. When he was gone for a few days, as he so often was, I began complaining about him being away with none of the pretence I used in the early days.

'What's wrong with you?' he asked. 'Why are you pouting? Aren't you happy I'm home?'

I couldn't think of any reproach that would convey my boredom, my fear when I woke up in bed without him, my anger at having cried buckets in front of the children, with only their grumbles for company.

I became useless, strange. I began hating the days he didn't come home, I worried about the dinner menu, was furious when he was late and he didn't phone, didn't turn up – the same old story, I don't know why it began upsetting me so much.

Worse still, my friends were no longer just round the corner, and Bárbara had gone back to being my sister in Puebla, not my private secretary or any of that rubbish. Pablo was in Italy, Arizmendi was an invention, the only possibility was Andrés and he left me in our house in Las Lomas for days on end, pacing from the living room to the front gates to see if he was coming, reading the papers to see if he was with Fito and where.

I established a rule of iron in the house, as though I were expecting the curtain to rise at any moment. There wasn't a speck of dust, a lopsided picture, an ashtray out of place or even a shoe in the dressing room without a tree and a box. Day in, day out I curled my eyelashes, renewed my mascara, tried on dresses, did exercises, hoping that suddenly he'd arrive and give me a reason for existing. But he was always so late I felt like putting my pyjamas on at five o'clock, eating biscuits and ice-cream or peanuts with lemon and chilli, or all of it at once, until I had a bloated stomach and some kind of calm between my legs.

After one of those afternoons, when I was four kilos heavier, crying a bit less and was even beginning to get interested in a novel, Andrés came in with his lets-sleep-together face. I wanted to insult him, throw him out of what my home had become, run on *my* time and *my* whims. He arrived in a very chatty mood, making fun of my fat legs and going on about some quarrel he had had with someone he didn't know how to get the better of.

'Suggest something,' he said. 'You're not interested in my affairs any more. You're always in a dream.'

'You've abandoned me,' I replied.

'You're starting to get on my nerves, always bitching about being abandoned. I'll abandon you for good if you're not careful. I'll pack up and go where I'm better looked after, where someone's pleased to see me. You're unbearable. What you need is something to do. Your principal ally is dead, your lording it as governor's lady is over and you can't find your niche. Get it into your head. Things change. You can't queen it here, nobody recognizes you in the street; you can't give parties or come with me to the mountains, and you don't have charity concerts to organize

any more. Women here don't tremble at your every word –
many of them probably think your views are old-fashioned
anyway. You poor thing. Why don't you talk to Gómez
Soto's Bibi? Or get involved in the National Association of
Parents? There's lots to be done there. They're organizing
a campaign against communism and need people. I'll
introduce you to someone tomorrow.'

I knew he was doing the anti-communist bit to screw
Cordera, head of the CTM. I'd heard him say on the
phone to the Governor of San Luis Potosí, an ex-president
turned industrialist, that only opportunists and spongers
were into communism. 'You did well. That was a good
hiding you gave Cordera,' he went on. 'He deserves every
bit of it. Count on me if you want to do it again. What
about coming to dinner at the house the next time you're
in Mexico City? My wife would be delighted to see you.'

'Who will I be delighted to see?' I asked when he hung
up, so I'd know what type of dinner to plan and when.

'General Basilio Suárez,' he said, and laughed.

'I'll be delighted to see that ass? Liar! And since when
have you been so delighted? Didn't you say he was a
fucking counter-revolutionary?'

'Until yesterday, pet. And until yesterday you thought
he was an ass. But from now on, for our whole family, he is
a prudent and almost wise man. Imagine it, he called
Cordera's fuck-ups "social experiments based on exotic
doctrines". You can't deny he's a find.'

'I like Cordera,' I said.

'You don't know what you're talking about. Cordera is
ambitious and a stirrer – all that talk about class struggle
and workers' power. The general is right, he's a demagogue.
He was always rich. His father rented me and my brothers
mules to cart maize in. They had a huge hacienda before
the Revolution. What does he know about hunger – don't

make me laugh – what does he know about poverty or any of the things he goes on about? He knows nothing, and cares even less. But he shouts a lot. He's not going to fuck us up now. He fucked us up when we were poor, let's see him try to fuck us up now we're rich.'

'I like him,' I said.

'You're going to say you like his grey suit next. Think he's only got one? Bloody idiots. The bastard's got 300 others. He's got them all fooled. The workers' leader! The bastard's got it coming to him. I won't rest till we strip him of his sinecure – defender of the poor! Wait and see what happens at the Convention. I'll get my own back for everything, even your stupid "I like him" bit.'

'Well, I do like him,' I said, happy to have found something that annoyed him. In actual fact I'd seen Cordera that time at the march and I liked his protruding cheekbones and wide forehead, but I hadn't really spoken to him.

'Why do you like him, you nitwit? When have you talked to him? You don't know what you're talking about,' replied Andrés, livid.

'I know what I see,' I said.

'Shut up. What have you seen? Tell me that. What?'

'Just that.'

'Don't make things up, Catalina. Are you trying to provoke me? You haven't seen any more than I've seen.'

'Did you notice what a nice laugh he has?' I asked.

'Go to hell,' he said. 'Just wait and see what a nice laugh he has a month from now.'

The following day he took me to the Parents' Association. We arrived at a big house in Santa María, and went to the office of a certain Señor Virreal. He was sitting behind a dark wood desk, he was thin as a rake and was going bald.

I learned later that he was married to a fat woman called Mari Paz with whom he'd had eleven children, one after another.

'This is my wife,' said Andrés. 'She's very interested in working with you.' He turned to me, 'I'll send Juan back for you in an hour.'

Andrés left through one door and a lady with a pearl necklace and a medallion with the Virgin of Carmen came in through another. She was thin, well dressed, with a sanctimonious smile of satisfaction that annoyed me from the word go.

'Come with me,' she said. 'I'll show you round our premises and introduce you to some of our colleagues. My name is Alejandra and I'll be delighted to be your guide and friend from now on.'

I thought she was vulgar, but followed her.

The dark old house had lots of adjoining rooms with doors that served as windows. They were all set out like classrooms with tables, chairs and blackboards. We went into one with several women in it.

'We're making bags of goodies for the prisoners' party,' said my guide and friend, so that I'd understand why fifteen women were sitting round a table without talking to each other. You could only hear the murmur of their voices counting to three, marshmallow and coconut biscuits, to seven, animal-shaped biscuits, to five, a handful of green sweets, to two, packets of cigarettes.

'Good afternoon,' they chorused when they saw us.

We were doing the introductions when Mari Paz came in, three children hanging onto her skirt, clutching a box.

'I've brought the *pambazos*,' she said. 'I don't know if they'll be enough to put one or two. I made 200. How many prisoners are there?'

'A hundred and fifty,' said a fat lady with a moustache,

continuing to fill her bags with marshmallow biscuits. They were piling up beside the next lady with the animal biscuits, who had been chatting to the one with six aniseed sweets without a thought for the moustachiocd lady's production-line of bags.

'So, a hundred too few or fifty too many,' replied Mari Paz, making a huge mathematical effort.

'If we have fifty over we can share them out among the guards and visitors,' said Alejandra.

'There aren't enough. There are always more guards and visitors than prisoners,' said the moustache again. She had no more room for her bags, so she said, 'I'm sorry to trouble you, Amalita, but if you don't hurry up with your animal biscuits and Ceci with her aniseed sweets, I can't carry on.'

'Ay, forgive us, Irenita, we've got behind, but we'll hurry up now, don't worry, we have to be first to finish anyway, we left our houses in a mess. We came so early we didn't have time for the housework.'

'We're all in the same boat,' said Alejandra, who was clearly not in the same boat at all, you could tell by her face and hands she had four maids per floor. I learned later that her husband had shares in Palacio de Hierro and Coca-Cola, owned a paper factory in Sonora and a textile factory in Tlaxcala. No one believed her house was in a mess while she devoted herself to good works, but everyone listened to her as though her words were gold.

Almost all the other women looked poor, perhaps wives of Alejandra's husband's employees, or discontented bureaucrats, or even workers. They started talking about the parish and Father Falito. They all knew each other from there apparently, and this particular Father heard all their confessions.

Alejandra and Mari Paz were the leaders. They put the

box of *pambazos* on the table, and I sat in front of it with instructions to put one in each bag that came my way. They went off to whisper in a corner. Pricking up my ears, I could hear them.

'She's General Ascencio's wife,' Alejandra was saying.

'We have to be careful. Father Falito says you can't trust people like that,' replied Mari Paz.

'Falito's exaggerating,' said Alejandra. 'She looks a nice person to me, I think she should be given a chance to do some good. Besides, we need people with class, Mari Paz, people who can socialize. This lot is all right for the prisoners, but we can't take them to talk to high-society ladies.'

'You may be right, but I doubt it,' said Mari Paz.

I pretended to count. One, one, one, I said, putting the cakes in like a diligent schoolgirl.

Mari Paz rustled luxuriantly up to me with her three kids.

'What do they smell like to you? Did they come out all right?' she asked coquettishly.

'Good,' I said. 'They'll go down well with the prisoners.'

'Yes, I think so too. They're getting sausage stew and fried beans. I was told not to give them meat, but poor things once a year at least they should be saved from that mush the government feeds them. Ay, forgive me! Your husband is . . .'

'In the government, yes,' I said.

'Oh dear, I'm so sorry. Yes, I can imagine how difficult it must be to feed so many every day. And to make it for them. They get plenty considering they're there as a punishment, don't you think?'

'I don't know,' I said. 'I also don't know why you should be so concerned about them.'

'Don't think it's the only thing we do. This was Father

Falito's idea. He's a very good man, and very impression-able. One day he went to prison to confess a dying man and came back very sad. He told us how dirty the building was, and that dozens of men are crammed together in tiny cells. Remembering it made him cry. So he decided to ask for permission for us to visit them, pray with them and take them some titbit or other. We thought it a good idea, permission was granted, you see this government isn't against Catholics like the others were. So we're going this afternoon. We've got the *piñatas*, the rosaries, the bags of goodies and ten scapulars that Father Falito wants to raffle.'

'You mean you raffle scapulars?'

'No. Usually they're for sale, people buy them and ask Father Falito to put them on. But the Father wants to raffle these ten and put them on those who win.'

'And if they don't want them?' I said, watching the door in the hope Juan might appear.

'What do you mean?' she asked. 'Of course they want them; how could they not? It's an honour. Winning one in a raffle is as if God sent it. They're not going to say no to God.'

'You're right,' I said. 'They can't possibly say no to God.'

Juan appeared. God certainly sent him. He stood in the doorway smiling his accomplice smile.

'What is it, Juan, are they waiting for us?' I asked. He knew the answer to that question was, 'Yes, Señora, it's urgent.'

I feigned surprise and said goodbye hurriedly, promising to be at Lecumberri Prison at five o'clock sharp.

Out in the street I shook my arms and stretched my legs. There was a warm February sun. I took off my jacket. It was colder inside than out. Outside everything suddenly seemed pleasanter. The morning gale had left the sky bright blue and I loved the trees.

'Take me to the Alameda, Juan,' I said.

Usually when I wanted my spirits revived I bought an ice-cream. Juan parked the car and I walked along the Alameda de Santa María. The ice-cream stand shone in the sun and the benches were filled with mothers, old folk, nannies, children and lovers.

I bought a newspaper. I sat down on a bench to read it. It was very amusing. Delegates to the preliminary session of the Mexican Federation of Labour Congress were accusing Don Basilio of harvesting the seeds sown by Sinarchism and National Action and raising the flag of opposition to Rodolfo. They said General Suárez's speech was an attack on ex-President Aguirre and demanded that Fito keep his promise to further the aims of the Revolution.

'The trouble has started,' I said. 'And Andrés is in there. I know where he is.'

I regretted having stopped reading the papers, and once again I wanted to know things and be involved in what Andrés said didn't concern me; since we'd been in Mexico City and my governor's-wife duties were over, he'd treated me like all his other women. I'd cut myself off without realizing it, but from now on I was going out and about again. I even blessed the stupid Parents' Association which would be my excuse for a while.

'Juan, teach me to drive,' I said to the chauffeur.

'The general will kill me, Señora,' he replied.

'I swear he'll never find out how I learned. Teach me.'

'All right.'

Juan was about twenty-seven, a simple and good man. I got into the front seat beside him. He began to tremble.

'If the general finds out, he'll kill me.'

'Stop saying that, and explain what I have to do,' I said.

The theoretical lesson took all morning. We went round the Alameda about fifty times. Then he took me home and went to pick up Andrés from the Government Palace.

'Lend me Juan again,' I said to Andrés at lunch. 'I'm going to need him at the Parents' Association.'

'What for?' he asked. 'He can take you there and pick you up. I need him.'

'And when you're not here?'

'I'm here now.'

'I read the manifesto of the delegates to the CTM meeting.'

'Where did you read it?'

'In the *Universal*. I bought it while I was out. I don't know why I cut myself off so, but now I've been out and about again I feel different. If you can't lend me Juan, give me another chauffeur or let me learn to drive.'

'What a nuisance of a woman you are. I was sure you wouldn't keep quiet for more than six months. How did it go at the Association? Will you be any use?'

I said nothing for a moment. It was no good lying to him, he was like an invisible spy, always lurking in the background, knowing everything.

'Of course I won't be any use. If I'd wanted to do that I'd have become a sister of mercy and at least I'd have known my place in the world. But get mixed up with those confused old bags? No fear! I don't need Father Falito to show me the light; I've too many things to see to waste my time in a freezing cold house filling sweetie bags for prisoners who get scapulars raffled for them. Besides, communists have never done anything to me and I don't like gratuitous enemies. I think that if you go in for good works, you should do it in a big way, be Saint Francis at least, with the poor kissing the ground behind you. I'd rather die than be some idiot in Father's Falito's flock, blowing kids' noses and praying for prisoners.'

Andrés burst out laughing and I breathed a sigh of relief. 'What did you say the priest's name was? Falito? You mean, like "phallus"? Incredible! You're right, it's one thing to get those idiots to help me fuck Cordera up, but my being mean enough to put you in there is quite another. I could have taken one of the girls. Marta's that way inclined and she'd be a good informant. But what ever possessed me to take you there? Did I think you were crazy? It's your fault for not treating me nicely.' He laughed again. 'Hey, did you meet Falito? How many of the ladies have seen his "name" at close quarters, d'you think? How could I take you to such a place? I'll have to make amends. From now on you're coming with me everywhere. Your confinement is over.'

No sooner said than done, because he wished it so, because he was like that. He ebbed and flowed like the bloody sea. And that day he decided to flow.

'I have to go back to the palace. Fattie can't do anything by himself,' he said. 'Come with me. You can go to the centre and see what you can buy in three hours. When the shops shut at eight you can pick me up and I'll invite you for dinner at Prendes. How d'you like that idea?'

I got my coat and was in the car in three minutes; he wasn't taking this invitation back. It was cold, one of those rare mid-February days when you can wear a fur coat without feeling hot crossing the street. I had on a fox fur. The most beautiful coat I ever had. Furs can be vulgar, but I wore this fox with boots and felt like a Hollywood star.

We arrived at the main square and drove round to the Government Palace. Ever since some gallant hero had tried to assassinate Fito, the procedures and searches you had to go through to get in were excessive. They searched every car, including Fattie's, in case someone had climbed into the boot at some corner or other. That afternoon the guards even searched my coat pockets. Andrés was furious at all these precautions.

'Rodolfo's such a baby,' he said in front of the guards and whoever else wanted to hear.

When we eventually managed to get in, Andrés got out of the car quickly, gave me a lot of money and told me to buy whatever I wanted. But all I wanted that afternoon was an ice-cream and to be able to walk along, licking it without anybody bothering me.

CHAPTER THIRTEEN

Juan bought the vanilla ice-cream and left me at Sanborn's in Madero Street. I felt protected there because it has walls of Talavera tiles. One's own little quirks. With Talavera I always felt safe, that's why the first thing I bring into all my houses is my Talavera dinner service. One of the yellow-and-blue ones, for fifty people. It costs a fortune nowadays apparently, but in those days it was thought a bit vulgar. Everyone had Bavarian china, not rough, breakable pottery from Puebla.

I stood in the doorway of Sanborn's for a while, leaning against the wall like a tart, feeling like Andrea Palma in *Woman of the Port*. Then I crossed the road and passed the Bank of Mexico, whose director in those days was an idiot with thick glasses whose name I always forget. He was stupid and ugly. Besides, he had pinched the job from a nice intelligent man whom I liked very much because he was the only one who hadn't laughed at me when Andrés commented at dinner one night that I'd cried during the national anthem after the results.

I crossed the street again to the Bellas Artes. I liked the building, it reminded me of a First Communion cake. I went in. The theatre doors were closed, but I could hear some music, like a long repetitive whine, coming from upstairs.

I went up, pushed the door and it opened. The theatre seats were empty but there was an orchestra on stage. A man facing it ordered the music to stop and began to talk rapidly and passionately, explaining something feverishly, as though it meant his very life to him that the musician he was pointing to with his baton should understand. He wasn't very tall, had a broad back and long arms.

I walked to the front and heard him say, 'Right, once again, from the twenty-fourth, everyone. Ready,' and he hummed the melody.

The music sounded sad and strange again, even more drawn out. I'd never heard anything like it. I sat down without a sound. I studied the ceiling and empty boxes, and let myself be carried away by the sounds, which seemed to come from the conductor's arms.

What an amazing job these men had, so different from any men I'd been around. The conductor stopped them, talked to them, waved his arms once again, and the music returned. Suddenly he broke off, violently. He looked at a young violinist sitting in the third row and said, 'Where are you, Martínez? You're not following me. Where's your tempo? What can you be thinking about that's more important?'

Martínez kept watching me, but didn't answer. The conductor turned round and saw me sitting in one of the front rows, pressing my hands against my coat, speechless.

'Who gave you permission to come in here?' he said, furious. I had no choice but to be a journalist.

'All this disruption,' he said. He had enormous dark eyes, and white skin. 'Wait for me at the back and don't move, it puts us off.'

I got up and walked slowly down the aisle.

'Ready?' he asked.

'Ready,' I replied and lowered my eyes. When the music returned, I got up slowly and walked to the door on tiptoes. I pushed it and went running down the stairs. In a second I was out in the street. I sat on a bench in the Alameda and tried to hum what I had heard, but couldn't. Instead I started to cry, without knowing why. I thought I was getting old and had inherited my mother's gift for premonitions.

'He is enchanted,' I said.

When Juan found me it was very late.

'The general's been waiting at the Palace for ages,' he said and took me to pick him up.

'Where've you been, dimwit?' asked Andrés, calmly.

'Just walking around.'

'You must have been in every single shop. What did you buy?'

'Nothing.'

'Nothing? What did you do then?'

'I listened to music.'

'I bet you found a *mariachi* band in the Alameda. Why are you so vulgar, Catalina?'

'I went to the Bellas Artes. The symphony orchestra was rehearsing.'

'You must have seen Carlos Vives then. He's the conductor.'

'Do you know him?' I said.

'Of course I know him. He's the most stubborn man I know. His father was a general, but he turned out a bit odd, he fancied music. He's just come back from London with the idea that this ranch here needs a National Symphony Orchestra, and he convinced Fito. Who doesn't?'

'Let's go for dinner,' I said, hearing my voice as if it no

longer belonged to me, as if someone else was making me
talk and move.

We got to Prendes. I left my coat in the cloakroom.
Andrés left his hat and went in as though it were his dining
room at home.

'Usual table, General?' asked the maître d'hotel.

'Same one, chief,' he said.

I never understood why Andrés liked this place. It was
horrible, it was like a convent refectory. The food was
good, but not good enough to merit eating in a place with
no windows. Especially not day in, day out, like he did.

My oysters arrived at the same time as his *tortilla* soup
and I began eating them quickly, as he talked.

'It was fucking good, the speech I wrote for Rodolfo.
Cordera won't know how to reply. He's always pegging his
stupid nonsense on democracy, so I've got Fito saying that
democracy should be understood as incorporating the class
struggle into the bosom of our liberties and the law. And
since the law is us, he's fucked. Look who's here.'

I swallowed my last oyster and looked up to see who it
was. The conductor was walking towards us with his
dazzling smile and a navy blue coat. I wanted to
disappear.

'I was waiting for our interview, Señora,' he said as an
introduction. Then he shook Andrés's hand and sat down.

'How are things?' asked Andrés. 'Catalina told me she'd
been to hear you this afternoon. How come you let her in?'

'She just came in.'

'What did she say?'

'That she was a journalist and wanted to interview me.'

'The girl's a liar. Why didn't you say, "I came in
because I felt like it"?' he asked me, like an amused father.

'I was frightened of him,' I confessed.

'Frightened of him? He's just a kid, he's only a couple of

years older than you. He was twelve during the war. His mother and he lived in Morelia and his father, who was my commanding officer, used to take me to their house sometimes when there was a truce. This kid would always be playing a reed pipe.'

'What a good memory you've got, General.'

'You weren't so formal then.'

'You weren't who you are now.'

'I was just beginning, like you are now. But I didn't get ahead so quickly. Of course, in war and politics you make more enemies than in music. Why did you plump for music?' asked Andrés. 'You could have been a good politician. Your father was.'

'Sometimes one isn't like one's father.'

'You say it with pride.'

'On the contrary, General. But each person has his own battle.'

'And yours is a battle? What a strange young man. Your father was right.'

They began talking about the past, about how as a boy the conductor used to steal Andrés's uniform buttons and shake them inside a pot to hear what sound they made, about the day Andrés and his father took him to see a hanging; they stood him under the gallows and made him look at the purple faces and tongues hanging out.

'Weren't you scared?' I asked.

'Very, but I wasn't going to show those two bastards, my father and your husband.'

I couldn't eat my fish or my dessert. I ordered a cognac and drank it down.

'What's the matter with you?' said Andrés. 'Since when do you drink things neat?'

'I think I'm getting the flu,' I replied.

'My wife's a bit mad, don't you think?'

'I think she's lovely,' replied Vives.

They went on talking about themselves. Of the difference between music and bulls. Of how Carlos's father loved my general, and how he fought with his son, who disappointed him by his determination to be a musician instead of a soldier.

'Your father was always right,' concluded Andrés.

'To your health, General,' said Carlos. 'To your health, noseyparker,' and he winked at me and patted the hand that was on the table.

'Your health,' I said, and downed another cognac in one gulp, and did nothing but smile the rest of the evening.

When we went out into the street, the moon was shining yellow and round over our heads. In a doorway, sitting there as though it were five in the afternoon, not three in the morning, a blind man was playing a trumpet.

CHAPTER FOURTEEN

I always thought that the only thing I needed to be truly happy was to have Andrés with me every day. But when, instead of rushing out the next morning, he announced he was moving his office into our library, I could have easily murdered him. It was like having an old wardrobe in the middle of the house. Everywhere you turned it was there. His noise was all pervasive. And to cap it all, he started being affectionate. He wanted to fuck every morning and take me with him wherever he went. He made me his private secretary and took me to the sessions he'd organized to plan the ousting of Cordera from the CTM, and to all his meetings with politicians; he even wanted me with him when he went for a pee.

Two days earlier I would have been happy. Not only having his explosive presence around again, but also being invited to places that had been out of bounds, to the meetings I'd always had to reconstruct by harassing Andrés with exhaustive questions as I tried to glean some idea of what was going on. Now I went to all of them. I could even have expressed an opinion had I wanted to, except that I had just climbed the steps of the Bellas Artes and fallen in love with another man.

I was unfaithful long before I touched Carlos Vives. There was room for nothing but him. I had never loved

Andrés like this, never spent hours trying to remember the exact size of his hands or wishing with my whole body that he were there. I was ashamed of behaving like this just because of a man, of being so unhappy yet so happy over something beyond my control. I was unbearable, and the more unbearable I became the better Andrés liked me. I had never had so much freedom to do as I pleased, but I had never felt that everything I did was so utterly pointless, stupid and unwelcome. For, of all the things I had and wanted, the only thing I really desired was to see Carlos Vives in the afternoon.

One day at breakfast Andrés discovered that my hair had grown and was shinier than it had been in years; he found my legs lovelier than a geisha's, my teeth like a child's, my lips like a film star's. I, on the other hand, had never so loathed my hips, my mouth, my eyelashes. I had never felt so stupid, so deceitful, so ugly.

He was going to the Government Palace. I went with him.

'So you're going shopping after all?' he said as he got out of the car.

'Maybe,' I replied.

Juan pulled away from the curb and I asked him to take me to the Bellas Artes. When we arrived, I leaped out of the car.

'What time shall I come back, Señora?'

'Don't come back.'

'Is eight o'clock all right?' he said, as if he hadn't heard me.

I ran up the steps. I couldn't hear any music. I was sure he wasn't there.

I pushed the door.

'Right everybody, let's start at the seventh again,' said his voice.

The music began. I slid in like a cat. I sat down right at the back. I put my hands on my thighs and without thinking rubbed my skirt up and down. I watched him from a distance. Again the arms and the voice giving instructions.

'That sharp means sharp, Martínez. Stress it, don't be afraid. That's how it sounds. Good afternoon, Señora, how nice to have an audience,' he shouted. 'It would be helpful if you didn't make that noise with your hands on your skirt.'

I'm going from one madman to another, I thought, but I didn't run away. I liked seeing him from a distance. I couldn't do an imitation of him, but I remember him as well as the sea and the night at Punta Allen.

I went up to the boxes on the second floor. I liked the way his hands moved, the way others obeyed without stopping to think whether his commands were right or not. It did not matter. He had power and you could feel it. It filled the hall, it entered the others, it invaded my body leaning over the balustrade, my head on my arms, my eyes following his hands.

Eight o'clock came and went, the music still flowed back and forth. Juan would be at the door and Andrés would be furious, but I did not move from my red-velvet seat until Carlos suddenly dropped his arms.

'Better. Much better, gentlemen. See you tomorrow. Thank you for this afternoon.'

He got down from the podium and disappeared through one of the side doors. I was just wondering where he had gone when he appeared at my side.

'Who's taking whom for an ice-cream?'

'I'm taking you,' I said.

'You're the one who likes ice-cream. I'd prefer a whisky.'

'How do you know I like ice-cream?'

'Don't you eat ice-cream when you're nervous?'

'Yes, but I'm not nervous now, and anyway who told you that?'

'My spies. They also told me that yesterday you wanted to get out of the car and come to my hotel.'

'They told you wrong. What do you take me for?'

'A woman married to a lunatic twenty years her senior who treats her like a teenager.'

We went down the stairs. Juan was waiting at the door, pale as death.

'Señora, the general will kill us,' he said, opening the car door.

'Tell him we're walking, we won't be long,' ordered Carlos.

'No,' said Juan. 'I'm not going back without the Señora.'

'Wait here then; we're walking.'

He took my arm and we crossed the street to Madero.

'I like this building,' I said as we passed Sanborn's with the tiles.

'I can't buy it for you. Why don't you ask your general?'

'Go to hell,' I replied.

'Your wish is my command,' he said, pushing the door of Sanborn's and going in just as Juan caught up with us and held a gun at my side.

'Forgive me, Señora, but I have a family to support. Just come with me and pick up the general.'

'All right, Juan,' I said and we ran to the car. We arrived just as Andrés was saying goodbye to some people at the entrance to the Palace.

'Hi, princess, had a good time?' he asked.

I couldn't get used to his new tone, it made me feel silly.

'I went to see Vives,' I said, as if I were undressing completely.

'Good idea,' he replied. 'Where is he now? Why didn't he come for dinner with us?'

'I told him to go to hell.'

'What did he do to you?'

'He treated me like a fool. He said if I liked the Sanborn's building so much why didn't I ask you to buy it for me.'

'Do you like the Sanborn's building?'

'I like the tiles,' I replied, and we went off to dinner arm in arm.

The next day General Basilio Suárez came to lunch at the house. I had told the cook to make *mole* the Puebla way especially for him because I knew he loathed it.

General Suárez was as simple as chilli and *tortillas*. What mattered to him was making money and that's why he'd joined forces with Andrés. They were trying to get some road construction contracts but it wasn't working because the Minister of Public Works was a certain Jesús Garza whom they hated because he was an Aguirre man and who doubtless hated them as well. They wanted to find some way of discrediting him, and Suárez, who hadn't much imagination, said, 'We could accuse him of being a communist. It would be true, too, because the fellow is a communist. And we didn't make the Revolution so that the Russians could come and take it away from us.'

'You're right, General. I'll talk to the Parents' Association today and ask them to extend their campaign against Cordera to certain other people who've got it coming to them. It's time we named names. So, in one fell swoop we oust Cordera from the CTM, install Alfonso Maldonado, who's no bright spark, and prepare the ground for screwing those two big-shots Aguirre bequeathed us.'

I was going to say something to contradict them when Vives came in.

'You're late,' said Andrés. 'We're talking politics, do you mind?'

'I do mind, but I'll put up with it. I realize everything is politics in this house, but I accepted the invitation to lunch anyway.'

'We said two o'clock, and it's half-past three,' said Andrés.

'You invited him?' I asked.

'I didn't tell you, so it would be a surprise,' said Andrés.

'It is,' I replied. 'Lucina, bring another place setting, please,' I said, adopting the lady-of-the-house role, pointing to a chair for Vives besides General Suárez. Andrés was at the head of the table, I was on his left and the General on his right.

'I prefer the other side if the general won't take offence,' he said, looking at Suárez.

'No son of General Vives can offend me,' said Suárez. 'Especially not if he chooses to sit next to a beautiful lady rather than an ageing ex-president.'

'Just sit down and stop interrupting,' said Andrés.

'Forgive me, Chinti, I'll behave myself now.'

'What did you call him?' I asked with a laugh.

'Don't tell her, she'll be unbearable afterwards.'

'Of course not, General. Besides, your wife and I are not speaking. Yesterday she left me in the street in mid-sentence.'

'You upset her,' said Andrés, 'and she's very sensitive.'

'Let's get on with lunch,' I said, and turned to Suárez. 'Would you like more beans, or shall we move on to dessert? If we wait for Vives it'll be quite a while.'

'As far as I'm concerned we can go straight to dessert,' said Vives. 'I can give the *mole* a miss.'

'Strange friends you have, Andrés. Not only does this musician muscle his way in, he's fussy, too.'

'What can I do? He's the son of the only bastard I ever respected. I can't have him killed just because he doesn't fancy your food.'

'He can die of starvation for all I care,' I said. 'What would you like, General?'

'I want apple-bread and goat cheese,' said Carlos. 'I haven't had goat cheese for years.'

'Poor you,' said Andrés. 'We forget you've come back from self-imposed exile.'

'There are worse cases, there are exiles who can't come back,' said Suárez.

'You mean President Jiménez.'

'Who else?' asked Suárez.

'I don't think it'll be long before Jiménez comes back,' said Andrés. 'I even think we need a bastard with his balls.'

'It's because he wants to keep his balls that he'll lay low at home and keep quiet when he does come back,' said Carlos, spreading cheese on his bread.

'Think so?' said Andrés, with a respect unusual when he talked politics, at least with novices.

'I can assure you, Chinti,' said Carlos. 'Trust my instinct.' And he began humming the *Barcarole* between bites of bread and cheese. Andrés roared with laughter.

'Cheers, Vives, good to see you again,' he said. 'Cheers, General Suárez, treat this house as your own.'

A diminutive hunchback appeared in the doorway with a huge file and a mountain of papers in his arms.

'With your permission, General,' said Andrés, beckoning him in. 'We were expecting you. Come in. Stand here. No, better between the Señora and this gentleman,' he said pointing to me and Vives. 'Read it, please.'

The man stood between us, opened the file and began: 'On this day, 1 March 1941, the said property . . .' To cut a long story short, Andrés had bought me Sanborn's, with the tiles.

'Just sign here, Señora,' said the tiny man, handing me a pen. Andrés watched us, amused.

'How did you get them to sell it?' asked Carlos.

'They sold it to my wife. She's the buyer.'

'Your wife can't even buy a piece of chewing-gum for herself,' he said.

'What's mine is hers,' replied Andrés.

'She must be a millionaire then.'

'Nothing she doesn't deserve. Sign it Catín, and do what you want with your Sanborn's.'

'I'll never have another coffee there,' said Carlos.

'Don't be bitter, Vives. What do you care who the owner is? It's a nice place.'

'It was. Now it's been bought with heaven knows whose money.'

'Don't you come here and talk to me about my money. Where do you think the British got the money for your grant? Are you going to tell me that was clean money? All money is the same. I get it where I find it because if I don't some other guy will. If I don't give Catalina that building, Espinosa will give it to Olguita, or Peñafiel to Lourdes. It was mortgaged to the hilt, the owner was done for anyway, either I got it or the bank did. Better I get it and make my wife happy; I haven't seen her look so radiant for ten years, until you poked your nose in, that is. You're a wet blanket.'

I was amazed to hear Andrés justifying himself, tolerating any smear on his honesty, even accepting that his money wasn't clean. Why didn't he yell at Carlos? Who knows. I never really understood what went on between them.

'Go on then, Señora, sign,' said Vives.

I took the pen and wrote my name the way I'd done since I married Andrés.

'Your whim has been satisfied,' said Carlos. 'Now what? Are you going to sleep beneath the tiles? Do you feel like the owner? I'm warning you that there aren't many people in this city who don't feel they own that building. You may hold the title deeds, but as long as anyone can go in, sit down and have a coffee, Sanborn's with the tiles belongs to everyone.'

'That's the way I want it,' I said.

'Of course, the great benefactress, to be admired and loved. How this woman wants to be loved!' he said.

CHAPTER FIFTEEN

Of course I wanted to be loved. I spent my whole life wanting people to love me. The night of the concert more than ever.

The Bellas Artes was full when Rodolfo and Chofi arrived, so the papers said, accompanied by Andrés and myself. We went up to the presidential box. Right in the centre of the theatre. Everybody turned to look.

In the adjoining boxes were the ministers and their families. Down below were special guests and the kind of people you look at from afar and think are happy, I can't think why.

Beneath me was the seat I sat in when I saw Carlos for the first time. He would be down there near me, he could look up at me.

The orchestra was tuning its instruments. The musicians were wearing black suits, their shoes were shined and hair slicked back, they were not as I'd seen them at rehearsal with their different-coloured shirts, tousled hair, old shoes and worn trousers. Neat and spruce, they seemed unreal, they all looked the same when really they were as different from each other as their instruments. Finally Carlos appeared, in his bow-tie and tails, his baton in hand and hair freshly combed. The audience applauded as he walked to the podium. Standing on it, he turned round and bowed low to us.

'What a clown Vives is,' said Andrés.

I was moved. We sat down and Carlos conjured up the music with his arms.

At the end of the first part the theatre erupted in applause, as though he were God. I stayed silent, looking downwards.

'What's the matter, Catín? Didn't you like it?' asked Andrés. 'You look as if you were about to have a baby.'

'Yes, I liked it,' I said, getting to my feet. 'He's good, this Vives.'

'How do *you* know he's good? *I* haven't the slightest idea. This is the first time we've ever been. It's too theatrical for my liking. Town bands are more lively, they don't send you to sleep.'

We left the box for a drink and a chat. Chofi was proud of her husband's discovery.

'He's a genius,' she said to the ministers' wives surrounding her like chickens round their hen. She was wearing one of those horrible fur stoles with foxes' heads at the ends. As if her broad shoulders, huge arms, and protruding breasts weren't enough. The foxes' heads waved like tassels on her nipples as she sang Vives's praises.

Such was her euphoria that she got all hot. So she took out a fan and fanned herself over her furs. Anything but take them off. The other ladies joined in the eulogy.

'He's very handsome,' said the wife of the Secretary of State.

'I think we're all in agreement on that fundamental point,' replied the Finance Minister's wife with a guffaw. 'He doesn't even need to be a good musician.'

They all laughed with her.

'But he's a great musician as well,' said the Foreign Secretary's wife, rolling her eyes in ecstasy. She was the daughter of Porfiristas who hadn't come down in the world and treated us all like parvenus in matters of international culture. Her father had been an ambassador and she'd spent her childhood in France.

'Yes, he's a great musician,' said Chofi, clutching her foxes.

Intervals end, thank goodness. I don't know how Rodolfo's ministers all came to marry such stupid women.

The second part of the concert was a very long, sad bit, which always seemed as though it were about to end and just when you thought it had, it started up again like a curse. This was the music I had climbed the staircase to find, which had stuck in my head, but which I was afraid to hum.

For the first twenty minutes Andrés made an effort to stay awake, then he began to talk to Fito.

I watched Carlos. I watched his back and his arms twisting to and fro. I watched his legs. I watched him as though he were the music, not the man who could talk, make fun of me and joke with Andrés over a meal. He was someone else, his whole being in something which had nothing to do with us, which came from somewhere else and carried him who knew where.

'This Señor Mahler could have done with a bit of fucking,' said Andrés near my neck.

Several times people began clapping, thinking that a thunderous bang of the drum was the last, but the music began again, almost inaudible, the barest whistle, joined by a violin, then a cello, rising to a deafening cacophony. So when the end actually came, only I who had heard it many times knew it actually was the end and began to clap alone.

I interrupted Fito and Andrés chatting and Chofi

nodding off. They stood to applaud him, so did the whole theatre. Carlos, who had dropped his arms and was standing quietly in front of his orchestra, finally turned round and I could see his face with his quiff of hair tumbling over his eyes. He did another low bow, got down from the podium and disappeared.

'Who's taking whom for an ice-cream?' I wanted him to come and say as the applause continued. When he reappeared he didn't stand on the podium but signalled to the orchestra and again bent his head to touch his knees.

They are right, those silly fools, I thought, he is very handsome. And they haven't heard him speak, walked with him down Madero, wanted to insult him in the middle of the street.

I went on clapping, everyone was, and Andrés was yelling as though it were the Fifteenth of September.

'Something good had to come out of General Vives. This boy has political talent, no one without political talent can milk so much applause out of a theatre. Just look at him, he looks as though he's made the speech of his life. You weren't even like that when you took office,' he said to Fito, roaring with laughter.

'Vives, Vives, Vives,' shouted the audience, while the orchestra applauded or tapped their music-stands with their bows.

Vives appeared through the side door with his hair in place.

The applause grew louder as he came in. He got on the podium, invited the orchestra to stand, turned to face us and bowed to the ground again.

'He'd make a good politician,' said Andrés. 'He's an excellent actor, very dramatic. It's a pity we don't bow, it would be very effective. Why don't you introduce it, Fito?' he asked Fattie. 'Just look at our wives, they've gone wild.

I'll practise bowing if you promise to give women the vote. The Chamber has a bill before it that was never approved under Aguirre. I assure you that with them voting and me bowing I'll get to be President and no one will say it's bad taste because I'm your *compadre*. I'll make Vives president of the Party the day after I'm nominated and he can tour the country, orchestra and all. What do you think, Catín?'

Vives disappeared and came back for the fifth time, and the orchestra sat down and stood up, but no one had stopped clapping. Least of all the ladies. All Chofi's flock in the adjoining boxes applauded as though he had fucked them.

'Let's go,' I said to Andrés. 'We'll congratulate him at the dinner. This is too much, whoever it is.'

'I think so too, even for a bullfighter. You'd think he'd risked his life,' said Andrés.

'Don't go,' asked Rodolfo, who was incapable of ordering. 'I can't be so impolite.'

'But we're not you,' I said.

'But you're his people,' said Chofi, who took the *compadre* business very seriously.

Meanwhile, Vives came running back on stage, got on the podium and with his head and arms at the same time made the orchestra play over the applause. As though he had said, 'Everyone, again, from the twenty-fourth.' Except that the music was something you could hum, something my father might have requested. I can't remember the number of mornings I heard him humming this, he sometimes stood at the door to our room and whistled for a while until we stirred under the sheets and cursed the sun and our early-bird father.

Why wasn't my father here for me to talk to, moan to about life's mistakes, ask what to do with the uncontrollable desire welling inside me?

The whole orchestra was my father whistling in the mornings, and I – as I usually did when I felt his presence, when something reminded me that his words and embrace would only ever be a memory, only my stubborn nostalgia – I began to cry, hiccupping and snivelling, almost as loudly as the orchestra.

I left my seat and sat on the floor, so no one could see the scandal. Andrés, who never knew what to do at times like these, put his hand on my head and stroked me like a cat. Anyway, by the time the orchestra finished playing I had a dirty face, swollen eyes and tousled hair.

'There, there, my love,' said Andrés. 'Unfortunately I told Vives that the only music you knew was the song your father sang all the time.'

The audience had suddenly risen and was clapping, shouting, clapping, shouting, this time as though it really was at a bullfight. I stayed on the floor. Through the brass balustrade of the box I saw Carlos laugh as he lifted his head after his last bow. My father used to laugh like that sometimes. I stopped crying.

People kept on applauding, but Vives didn't come back. Before the national anthem and the saluting the flag that was always done when Rodolfo arrived and left, I ran to the ladies' room to try and do something with my face.

The party was in Los Pinos. In the wood-panelled room with enormous chandeliers. Carlos was already there when we arrived with Rodolfo, Chofi and the national anthem again.

'Excellent, Vives,' said Fito, shaking his hand.

'Maestro, I don't know what to say,' sighed Chofi, patting her foxes.

'Vives, you are a natural political talent. Don't waste it,' said Andrés.

'Thank you,' said I.

'Thank you all,' said he, smiling even more broadly.

I began to tremble, it was horrible what was happening to me. I thought everyone realized.

I took Andrés's arm and said let's go.

'But we've only just arrived. We haven't had dinner. I'm dying of hunger, aren't you? Besides, Poncho Peña is here; I need to talk to him,' he said, and left me in the middle of the room half a yard from Vives and his admirers. They stole him away. Even Cordera had come to say hallo. Vives embraced him and over his shoulder saw me standing quietly, watching him. He took Cordera's arm and brought him over to me.

'Do you know each other?' he asked, but didn't give us time to reply.

'How do you do,' we both said, preferring to forget where we knew each other from.

'Why don't we go into the garden?' said Carlos. 'There are too many people here.'

He took my hand and walked quickly towards the door. Cordera came with us. As we passed Andrés, Carlos said, 'I'm taking your wife for some fresh air. It's too stuffy in here.'

'See if it wakes her up a bit, she was wanting to leave,' replied Andrés. 'Good evening, Álvaro,' he said when he saw who was with us, and pulled me towards him. 'Pay attention to what they say,' he whispered in my ear before kissing me. 'See you soon,' he said out loud, winking at Carlos.

'How are things going at the Congress?' Carlos asked Cordera when we were alone in the garden, walking through the trees.

'Very well,' said Cordera, looking at me.

'Will you be re-elected?' asked Vives.

'That doesn't depend on me, the Assembly will decide,' he replied.

'But who controls the Assembly? Don't tell me you're letting it choose for itself?'

'Why not? That's how it should be.'

'Don't play games, my friend.'

'What d'you want me to say?' asked Cordera, holding up his hands.

We were walking towards the middle of the garden. Carlos had put his arm round my waist and, before answering, he pulled me to him.

'The Señora knows her husband is a national disgrace. Don't let him put his oar in. He wants to screw you for good, that's obvious, you're a hindrance. If you're re-elected and can mobilize the workers like six years ago, you might even make it to president.'

'Ascencio is in it already. Our deputies in the Chamber have declared war, and who do you think wrote the speech the President gave this morning? Who else would have thought of that bit about a road which is moving forward is not identical in every section? That meant that his policies are not straying from Aguirre's, but he wants the proletariat to revise its methods, and be more self-critical. Revise methods is a way of saying revise people and positions. They want to screw us, my friend, they want to silence us. They want us to sell out in the most pathetic way. They're with Suárez, who is in politics for business reasons.'

'But you're going to fight them, or aren't you? You're not tired already?'

'No, it's not that; it's more complicated. Let's talk about it tomorrow, shall we?' he said, looking at me suspiciously again.

'Are you afraid to die? You used not to be.'

'Afraid no, but I don't want to, either. Besides, it's not

up to me. I'll see you tomorrow. Goodbye, Señora, thank you for your discretion.'

'How do you know I will be?' I said.

'I know,' he replied and walked off in the opposite direction.

'What a country!' said Carlos. 'You're either afraid or bored. Are you afraid?'

'I was bored.'

'Now you're not?'

'Not now.'

'What do you want to do?' he asked.

'When?'

'Now.'

'Whatever you want. What d'you want to do?'

'Me? Fuck.'

'With me?' I asked.

'No, with Chofi,' he replied.

When I woke up, Carlos was sleeping by my side, his mouth in a pout.

The flat had a living room with a piano that took up half of it, a kitchen the size of a cupboard and a bedroom with photos on the walls and a large window looking out over the Bellas Artes. I wanted to stay. Carlos opened his eyes and smiled.

'Where shall we go?' I whispered in his ear, as if someone might hear us.

'To the sea,' he said, still half asleep.

'Let's go then.'

'What time is it?' he asked, yawning and stretching.

'I don't know. Why don't we die now?' I said.

'Because I've still got lots of things to do. I've never conducted in Vienna.'

'Will you take me to Vienna?'

'When I'm invited.'

'Haven't you been invited?'

'The war has to be over first and I have to conduct better.'

'You won't love me by then.'

'I love you now,' he said, and began kissing me. Afterwards, he stretched an arm over me and tried to reach the watch that was on the bedside table on my side.

'It's four o'clock. I think we are going to die today. Juan must have forgotten.'

'Forgotten what?'

'He was supposed to call us when Andrés was ready to leave Los Pinos.'

'What for?'

'So you'll get home before him.'

'But I don't want to go home.'

'You have to. You can't stay here.'

'What a fool I am,' I said, picking up the clothes I'd left sprayed around the floor. I was so furious I jammed the zip on my dress and pulled at it till it broke. I looked for my shoes anyway. With my coat on no one would see the back open.

'You and Álvaro are just kids.'

'You've got lovely hair for a Puebla girl,' he replied.

'What do you know about Puebla girls?' I yelled.

The bell rang. It was Juan.

'Señora, the general doesn't want to leave Los Pinos. He says you told him you'd be in the garden, so you must be there and he can't leave you.'

'Who is he with? Isn't the party over?'

'He's with Don Alfonso Peña,' replied Juan.

'Still? You have to be drunk to put up with Peña for so long.'

'Come on, darling,' said Carlos, already dressed and standing in the doorway.

We got to Los Pinos. Juan went to park the car and we got out near the place where we had been with Cordera.

We walked. Carlos had his arm round my waist and held me to him. We went into the lounge. It was practically empty. Andrés and Peña were sitting at the far end, a waiter on each side and a bottle of cognac in front of them. We went up to them.

'Had your fresh air?' asked Andrés, slurring his words.

'We weren't long. How did you find time to drink so much? I've never seen you so drunk, Andrés. Why?' I said, in surprise. I was used to seeing him drink for hours on end without getting drunk.

'Because to live in this country you have to be crazy or drunk. I'm nearly always crazy but this time I wanted to gain some wisdom and I didn't stop. Isn't it true, my friend?' he asked Peña, who was even drunker. His eyes were crossed and he was staring at the ground.

'I'm warning you, they're bloody dangerous communists,' he said. 'You shouldn't let your wife go with them.'

'He has started hallucinating,' said Andrés. 'He thinks Vives is a communist, now he'll see a purple elephant and Greta Garbo in her knickers. Take him home, Juan; we'll stay here talking.'

'Let's go to our house,' I said. 'It's not proper to stay here any longer.'

'Ah yes, hark at her, very concerned about the proper thing,' said Andrés, getting up. 'A good idea. We'll go home, but Juan must go and get some singers from Ciro's.'

'Ciro's will be shut by now,' I said.

'He'd get them even if it were three in the morning. Juan, bring a trio that can sing *Fear*.'

'Let him take us home first,' I said.

'Haven't we got another car? What about yours, Vives?'
asked Andrés.

My stomach turned over. We'd left Vives's car at his
house.

'I lent it to Cordera. He didn't have one,' replied Vives,
very calmly.

'That bastard Cordera, he even pinches his friends' cars.
You're going to fall for that poor little Álvaro story too.
You lend him your car; if he hasn't got one that works why
should he take yours? We're wasting time. If we miss out on
the singers, I'll kill him, I will, nothing to do with politics,
he'll die because he ruined our evening and I'll be doing
the country a favour to boot.'

We arrived home.

'Leave us at the gate, Juan, we'll walk in,' said Andrés.
'By the time I'm sitting down in the lounge I want you
back here with the singers, Juan. Ones that can sing *Fear*.'

I got out quickly and went round to Juan's window.

'His watch has stopped,' I said. 'You won't find anyone
at Ciro's. Better go to Maestro Lara's house, there'll still be
a party going on there. Tell Toña to come urgently.'

CHAPTER SIXTEEN

I had met Toña Peregrino when Andrés was governor. She and Lara had come to Puebla. I invited them to sing in the Guerrero cinema at one of those charity concerts I loved organizing. They came for two days, but stayed for five. I installed them in our guest rooms, took them to the ranch at Atlixco, drove them round all the tourist sights. They were delighted, but no more than I was. In the evenings Agustín would play the piano and Toña would sing, just for fun.

We became friends. I took her to Lupe, my dressmaker, who was a genius. In a couple of days she'd made her three dresses with trains and capes to disguise her weight. She was beautiful when she opened her mouth, but these dresses helped her reach centre stage without looking like Ninón Sevilla. I envied both of them. Since Lupe made her those first dresses, Toña only ever appeared on stage in clothes made by her. So, since she didn't manage to persuade Lupe to move to Mexico City, she often came to Puebla. She always stayed at our house. Everything happened to her, even a man entering her room shouting, 'Death to Andrés Ascencio'. In those days Andrés never slept in the same room two nights running. Sometimes he stayed in mine, sometimes in Checo's or in one of the others. The night before Toña arrived he'd slept in the guest room. The man jumped on Toña with the knife and the only thing she could think of was to sing at the top of her voice, *In Your Eyes is Emerald Green.*

The man fled and she let him go. She only told me about it years later.

'Why on earth did you sing?' I asked her.

'What else could I do? I had been rehearsing those lines about the green springing from the sea, and the coral's mouth of faded blood all day. I dropped off to sleep repeating it, and I'd said it so often I didn't know my arse from my elbow.'

We were such friends that I was sure if Juan told her it was urgent, she would come, even in her nightie.

I'd just put the ice in the whisky glasses when I heard the car pull up at the door. I opened it. Toña came in dressed as though she'd stepped out of a bandbox, in brilliant blue, her arms bare. She kissed me.

'Good evening, good evening,' she said with the voice of a goddess. 'Someone here want something sugary?'

'Toña!' shouted Andrés. 'Sing *Fear.*'

'Of course, General, but introduce me to these gentlemen first,' she said, looking at Vives as though she wanted to engrave him. 'I know, you're the conductor of the symphony. I saw your photo. I don't forget a face, do I, dear?' she asked me.

'And this is Deputy Alfonso Peña. As you can see, he found us very boring,' I said, pointing to Poncho, who had fallen asleep on the arm of a velvet chair.

'Delighted to meet you,' said Toña, taking his hand and letting it fall. '*Fear*, General? The problem is, I didn't bring a pianist, so I don't know what it'll be like.'

'Could it be anything but wonderful with your voice, Toña?' said Andrés.

'Want a pianist?' asked Carlos, sitting at the piano.

'Don't tell me you know that sort of song?' said Toña.

Carlos replied by playing the first few bars of *Fear*.

'Hark at him,' said Toña.

'That all right?' asked Carlos.

Toña joined in with the piano.

'From the beginning, Toña,' said Andrés. '"Fear of being happy at your side . . ."' he sang.

'Don't ruin it,' I said, seated in a round armchair, listening, fascinated.

'O K, General,' said Vives, and they began again. Carlos accompanied Toña as though they'd been rehearsing together for months.

Not only did he accompany her but he ran the end of one song into the beginning of the next and Toña kept to his tempo quite naturally. They were enjoying themselves, understanding each other with their eyes.

> 'There's a reason the world has a sky
> That the sea is so dark and deep.
> There's no barrier in this world
> My love would not break for you.'

'You are my obsession and the world is witness to my passion,' I sang with my little tinny voice, which could not resist joining in.

Toña nodded her head in approval and gestured to me to come close.

I sat on the piano stool with Carlos and he jumped from that song, which I imagined written for me, to *The Night of Last Night*.

'"Ah, what a night last night,"' joined in Toña. '"So many things happened to confuse me."'

'"I am bewildered, I, I who was so calm, enjoying the calm of love long past,"' sang I with what voice I had and

I leaned against Carlos, who took his hand off the piano for a moment and caressed my leg.

'You're the one ruining it now, Catalina,' said Andrés. 'Shut up and let the artists perform.'

I took no notice. I went on. '"What are you doing to me? I'm feeling as I've never felt before."' My voice was like a whistle next to Toña's but I followed her. '"I swear to you, all this is new for me."'

I even imagined it belonged to me, her voice over mine.

'"It made me understand my life was just waiting for you,"' we sang, and I let my head fall onto the piano. Pum, it banged like the end of *The Night of Last Night*.

'Catalina, stop fucking around,' said Andrés. 'I'm the one who's drunk. *Ashes*, Vives,' he requested.

'Yes, *Ashes*,' I said.

'You shut up, Catín,' he said.

'Yes, my love,' I said.

'"After suffering the pain of your abandon,"' sang Toña.

'"After all my poor wounded heart gave you,"' I joined in with her as she stood behind me with her hands on my shoulders.

'Catalina, stop fucking about,' repeated Andrés.

'*Your* interruptions fuck it about,' I said and caught Toña up at 'for the bitterness of a love like you gave me'.

'Pa pa pa,' I said, standing up to drum the piano top.

'"I can't forgive or give you what you gave me,"' we sang on.

'"In affection that dies there is no bitterness,"' pronounced Andrés from his armchair, pointing at who knows who.

'"And if you remove the ruins you caused, you will find what was once my love is no more than ashes,"' we concluded.

'Load of rubbish,' said Andrés.

'"Sing if you want to forget your heart," ' sang Toña, accompanying Carlos.

'"Sing if you want to forget your pain," ' sang Carlos, playing short sharp notes.

'"Sing, if you lose one love today. Another will take its place." '

'"Tralala, tralala, tralala," ' I sang and left the stool to dance, round and round.

Vives laughed and Andrés fell asleep.

'*Take This Life of Mine*,' I asked as I danced round the room.

'"Take it, take my heart," ' sang Toña.

'"Take this life of mine, and perhaps the pain will wound you," ' my voice joined theirs as I sat by Carlos again. Andrés was right, I ruined their voices but I couldn't have cared less just then.

'"You'll not see me, because your eyes will accompany me," ' I said, leaning on Carlos's shoulder. He ended with three chords as Toña held the final 'me'.

'Fantastic, Toña,' I said. 'My compliments!'

'What about you two?' she asked 'Are you in love or falling in love?'

We left Andrés sleeping and went into the garden to watch the sun come up.

'Señora, shall I take the deputy home?' asked Juan, who was standing in the reception room.

'Yes please, Juan. And put the general to bed. You're a saint.'

'Then come back for me,' said Toña. 'I don't want to stay for breakfast.'

The orange sun had been up for almost an hour when Checo came down to the bottom of the garden, barefoot, in his pyjamas.

'Why have you got the same clothes on as yesterday, Mama?' he asked. 'Put your trousers on. Aren't you going riding?'

'Let's go, Maestro,' said Toña, patting Carlos's shoulder. He had big rings under his eyes and was very handsome. 'Goodbye, my dear, have a nice ride. The air will do you good.'

Carlos put his hands on my shoulders and kissed me on the cheek.

'Tomorrow?' he asked.

'Tomorrow,' I answered as we parted.

He and Toña walked towards the car, Checo and I towards the house.

'Hey,' shouted Carlos from the gate, 'it's tomorrow already.'

When we came back from our ride, I was half dizzy. I got down, and wanted an orange juice. Lucina brought me one to the garden gate where I had sat to rub my legs and listen to something Checo was telling me.

'The general says you're to go up and see him as soon as you get back,' Lucina told me.

I ran up the stairs three at a time, dirtying them with my muddy boots. Only when I got to Andrés's bedroom did I pull them off, sitting on the unmade bed.

'Can I open the curtains? I can't see anything.'

'Have pity on an awful hangover,' replied Andrés, rolling around on his bed till he got hold of my waist. 'Tell me what Cordera and Vives talked about yesterday,' he said, rubbing my back.

'The concert.'

'What else?'

'Vives asked Cordera about the Congress but Cordera didn't say anything important.'

'How long did they talk? What did he tell him?'

'He just said it was going well, that the grass-roots would decide the leadership.'

'Don't give me that. What important things did he say?'

'Nothing, sweetie. He left after five minutes.'

'So what did you and Vives do all that time? You can't fool me. Vives and Cordera talked more than that. You didn't come back until two in the morning.'

'We just walked,' I told him. 'They've got such wonderful gardens at Los Pinos!'

'You talk as though you only realized it yesterday. D'you want to live there? Tell me what Vives and Cordera talked about.'

'General, if I ever hear them talking I promise I'll reproduce the whole conversation, but yesterday they only said a couple of things.'

'Tell me what they were. Remember exactly what they said; they use a kind of code.'

'Are you still drunk? What d'you mean, they talk in code?'

'Did they arrange to meet?'

'One of these days.'

'That means Thursday,' he said.

'You're crazy,' I replied, tugging at the boot that always got stuck.

'Did you sleep?' he asked.

'A bit.'

'Why all the euphoria? You usually sleep for three days when you've stayed up late, and even then barely recover. How come you went riding?'

'Checo asked me to.'

'He asks you every day.'

'I wanted to today,' I said, getting the boot off and wriggling my toes.

'You're very odd.'

'I enjoyed myself yesterday, didn't you?'
'I don't remember. Were you singing or did I dream it?'
'I sang *Take This Life of Mine*.'
I sang it again.
'Shut up. I can hear five of you.'
'Go back to sleep. Why wake up? It's Sunday.'
'That's why I woke up. Garza is fighting.'
'It's a long time till five. Go to sleep. I'll wake you at two.'
'There's no time. I invited people to lunch at one. Want to come to the bullfight this afternoon?'
'You never invite me.'
'I'm inviting you now.'
'I don't like bullfights.'
'That's sacrilege! Come.'
'If you like,' I said, kissing his head and covering him up as though making a shroud. I tiptoed out and left him sleeping.

My bathroom in Las Lomas was three times as big as my bedroom, with walls lined with mirrors and a skylight through which the midday sun shone as brightly as in the garden. Round the bathtub, big enough for five people, were lots of plants. The bathroom was my favourite spot, my escape hole for being alone.

That morning I ran in, turned on the taps and cast my clothes to the four winds. I remember my body as it used to be, immersed in the hot water, among the plants, head wet and face upwards, watching the clouds cross the piece of blue which fitted in the panes of the skylight.

'And now what do I do?' I asked, as though I had a confidante in the bath with me. I can run away. Leave the general and my children, the bathtub, the violets, the never-empty bank account. 'I want to go away with Carlos,'

I said, shampooing my hair. 'Right now. Lorenzo Garza or no Lorenzo Garza, I won't watch crimes or listen to curses one more day. Today I'll move house, sleep in another bed, even change my name. But if he doesn't want me? Yes, he wants me. He asked, "Tomorrow?" He said, "It's already tomorrow." But he didn't want us to go to the sea, he brought me home, it never entered his head to stay with me. He doesn't love me. He likes me, I amuse him, but he doesn't love me. What if I ring his bell and he doesn't open? What if he's got a girlfriend arriving from England? To hell with her.'

I got out of the tub, wrapped my hair in a towel, walked to the mirror and smiled at it.

CHAPTER SEVENTEEN

I never saw Andrés kill. Often I'd hear his voice through the door talking about death. I knew he had no scruples about killing, but not with his own hands, his own gun. For that he had men who were prepared to earn a niche for themselves by starting at the bottom.

Until I was with Vives, it had never occurred to me to be afraid of him. The ways in which I defied him before were games I could stop playing if they became dangerous. But the thing with Carlos was different. And I was frightened.

Sometimes at night I'd wake up trembling, in a cold sweat. If we slept in the same bed I could never sleep. I'd watch Andrés, his mouth half open, snoring, sure that next to him was the same silly girl he'd married, the same exuberant child, a little older and less docile, but still the same. His own Catalina, his accomplice, whom he could laugh at, who guessed what he was thinking and didn't meddle in his affairs. Everything that had been building up since our marriage invaded my body and one afternoon I got a knot in my throat. A lump formed between my neck and the top of my back. It was hard, like a single, enormous nerve and very painful.

When I told Bibi, she prescribed exercise and massages, which just happened to reduce one's hips at the same time.

Her masseuse went to her house because Gómez Soto wouldn't dream of letting her take her clothes off elsewhere, even for another woman to rub her. But I preferred going to the studio in Cuauhtémoc – presided over by a smiling woman with beautiful legs on enormous heels – where they did massage and gymnastics.

There I made friends with Andrea Palma. She was very funny; the poor thing was always complaining because she had no bum. As they massaged us on adjoining beds, we talked about the size of our stomachs and decided that a combination of our backsides would have made a perfect woman.

'If you weren't so envious and God wanted to do us the favour,' she said to me one day.

'You want God to do you the favour too, Andrea? Haven't you got enough with all the kids he puts at your disposal?'

'You're just jealous. That's because you're oppressed. What does it feel like being faithful?'

'Awful.'

'Being unfaithful feels awful too.'

'Less so.'

'You're blushing,' she cried. 'You've blushed right down to your belly button. What are you up to? No, don't tell me, your husband might threaten to cut my tongue out if I don't confess.'

'I envy you your breasts,' I said, as though I hadn't heard.

'Don't think I'm a fool, Catalina, tell me.'

'What about? I'm not doing anything. Would you dare deceive General Andrés Ascencio?'

'I wouldn't, but you would. You dare sleep with him. So why not some other outrage?'

'Because for that outrage he'd kill me.'

'Like the poor girl he killed in Morelos,' Raquel the masseuse pointed out.

'Who did he kill in Morelos?' asked Andrea.

'A girl who was his mistress and who received him one day with a "no more of that thank you",' said Raquel.

'That's a lie. My husband doesn't kill ladies who refuse him,' I said.

'That's what I was told,' said Raquel.

'Well, don't believe everything people tell you,' I said, jumping off the couch to get away from her hands.

'Catalina, don't be silly,' said Andrea. 'I thought you were more worldly.'

'More worldly, more worldly. What d'you want me to be? You're telling me that for twelve years I've lived with Jack the Ripper and you want me to lie there calmly. D'you want me to smile sweetly like the Mona Lisa? What do you want?'

'I want you to think.'

'Think what, think what?' I shouted.

Our private chat had become public. The women on the other couches and their masseuses had stopped to look at me standing there in the nude, with tearful eyes and livid face, shouting at Andrea.

'Stop shouting, first of all,' she whispered. 'Get on the bed, lie down, smile at me, finish your massage and when you get out of here find out exactly who Andrés Ascencio is.'

I obeyed her. Her insistent voice and dark eyes calmed me. I was quiet for a while, face downwards, feeling more acutely than ever the pummelling Raquel was giving my buttocks.

'Find out what, for instance?' I said.

'If it's true what Raquel says or not?'

'But how can it be true, Andrea? That's just stupid. My

husband kills for his business interests, he doesn't go around killing women who won't fuck him.'

'You see, that's much more intelligent. But why wouldn't he do both?'

'Because he wouldn't.'

'Very reasonable. Because he wouldn't. Because you don't want it. He wouldn't, and that's it.'

'Yes. He wouldn't, and that's it,' I said.

'As you wish,' she replied with her mischievous half smile. 'How's your diet going?'

'Don't change the subject. D'you think I'm stupid?'

'You're the one who ended the conversation, not me. Don't blame me if you're scared,' she said, getting up and following Marta to the steam bath.

'Are you having a steam bath?' asked Raquel.

'Where did you hear about the murder in Morelos?' I answered.

'Somewhere around, Señora, but you're right, it can't be true.'

Raquel dyed her hair reddish-blonde, she had lively eyes and thin lips. She massaged with small but strong hands. She didn't talk much. She seemed to be there to listen and keep mum. That's why I was so surprised that she had butted into my conversation with Andrea.

What if he really had killed her I kept asking myself as I sweated in the steam bath.

'I don't want to die,' I said to Andrea, who was in front of me, sticking her head out of the little brick hut they sat us in with a canvas cloth over our shoulders. We looked like monsters with huge square bodies and tiny sweaty heads.

'Especially now you're looking so pretty,' she replied.

'Andrea, it's not a game. I don't want to die.'

'You won't die, dear, don't be silly. You know your husband better than any of us, despite all the gossip we've heard about him. You say he's not a monster, so what are you worried about? Even if you were unfaithful to him, he wouldn't shoot you. And what other reason would he have?'

'None. He's not some second-rate killer.'

'You've convinced me, darling. Now do you want me to convince you of what you've just convinced me? Or are you going to come whining to me with all this about not wanting to die?'

We were talking increasingly intimately. We'd come out of the steam baths and were drying ourselves so close together that our faces and lips almost touched. Andrea was beautiful. Like that, without make-up, sweating, avid for gossip and sharing the fear that I conveyed to her as I told her the whole story, from the steps of the Bellas Artes and the dinner at Prendes, to the day I saw his house and began to make it mine. Everything. Walks round the city, tea in the main square, afternoons at the cinema, nights at a concert, early mornings rushing home to bed, exalted but terrified.

'What should I do, Andrea?' I asked.

'Gym, for the time being,' she said, and kissed me.

CHAPTER EIGHTEEN

That year 2 November fell on a Wednesday, and Andrés decided we would spend the long All Souls' weekend in our house in Puebla. He told me he was inviting some friends and would I organize everything. I was furious at the idea of waiting on Andrés's guests, away from Carlos. It would be different if he'd invite amusing people, but he invited people like the Under-Secretary for Finance and his silly wife, always dressed as though she were having her photo taken for *Maruca* magazine, the Minister for Agriculture, who couldn't even talk he was so stupid, and the latest political whizz-kid. Politicians were always in and out of fashion and Andrés often invited the flavour of the month to spend the weekend with us. He'd treat him like a king, make him the centre of attention, let him win at *frontón* and I'd have to indulge the wife's every whim.

I'd had holidays with fifteen guests, three meals a day, plus cocktails, snacks and coffee on demand. I'd spend the whole time between the kitchen and Matilde's bad moods.

All day Tuesday I cursed. Andrés told me we'd be leaving on Friday the 28th at midday and coming back on Wednesday the 2nd in the afternoon.

'Won't the country collapse around Fito's ears if you're away so long? What'll he do without his *compadre*'s advice?'

I asked, thinking how totally unbearable and boring life would be without Carlos.

I spent Wednesday afternoon with him, walking round the main square and Juárez Avenue. We dined at El Palace, overlooking the square. I had eel and he had oysters, me pastries with ice-cream and he an espresso coffee.

'I've got a room here,' he said.

'I can stay until one,' I replied, and we hurried out of the restaurant to a room with a balcony. I opened the door onto it to feel the cold air and look out over the Government Palace and the cathedral.

'We always have to fuck in secret,' I complained.

'Why did you get married at fourteen to a general who is the President's *compadre*?'

'How do I know why I did what I did at fourteen? I'm nearly thirty now. I want to decide things for myself, I want to live with you, I want that bunch of old bags who come while they watch you conduct to know that the only one who really comes is me. I want you to take me to New York and introduce me to your friends. I want you to bring me out of the closet and tell General Ascencio everything.'

'But will a little fuck do for now, eh?'

'Yes,' I said, and forgot my complaint.

As we were saying goodbye I remembered it again. I almost enjoyed having to tell him I was shutting myself away in Puebla for four days, without him, with my husband, my children, my servants, in my house, half refuge, half convent, full of corridors and flower-pots, alcoves and fountains.

'What a pity,' he said calmly.

'You don't care, of course, you don't even care,' I screeched. 'You have a good fuck and pack me off to the

other one. You pansy!' I banged the car door and told
Juan to drive off.

The whole of Friday morning I was furious. Lilia noticed
it early on.

'Don't you want to go? You used to like going back,' she
said. 'It's lovely in Puebla.'

'Would you mind telling me what you think of the fiancé
your father has picked for you?' I asked.

'He's a nice person,' she replied.

She was sixteen. She had perfect breasts, long firm legs,
sparkling eyes and a confident laugh.

'He's really a bastard. He has messed Georgina Letou
around for seven years and now he's leaving her for you,
very pretty, very young and just happens to be the
daughter of Andrés Ascencio. Don't you realize you are mer-
chandise?'

'Don't complicate things, Mama. You're in a bad
mood because you don't want to leave Carlos for four
days.'

'I couldn't care less about Carlos,' I said.

'It looks like it. Coming riding?'

'I can't. I haven't organized the meals yet. I don't even
know how many we'll be.'

'So complicated!' she said and went off, banging her
boots.

Fifteen years ago I was like Lilia. At what point had food
for other people become more important than the desire to
go riding?

I phoned Puebla and spoke to Matilde. I asked her to
make pork in chilli sauce.

'Isn't that rather heavy for the evening, Señora?' she
replied in the tone she liked to use when correcting me. I
almost always admitted she was right and so unloaded the
problem, but that morning I insisted on the pork.

'Wouldn't the chicken in herbs be better? The general loves that.'

'Make the pork, Matilde.'

'Whatever you say, Señora,' she replied.

She was a little in love with Andrés. She was my age, with a son who lived with her mother in San Pedro. She looked old. She had teeth missing, never dieted, nor did exercises, nor bought face creams. She seemed twenty years older than me. She didn't like me and she was right. I was left with the prospect of having to do battle with her the whole weekend.

I was still sitting by the little telephone table, staring at the tips of my slippers, when Carlos came into the hall carrying a suitcase.

'Are we leaving at twelve?'

I didn't answer. I scurried off to take the rollers out of my hair. I put on trousers, perfume and lipstick and went back downstairs, but he was no longer there.

'They went to the games room,' explained Lucina.

'Are you ready?' I asked. 'And the children?'

'All of them.'

The games room was at the bottom of the garden. All our houses were so huge, we almost needed cars to get around. I crossed the garden. Andrés and Carlos were playing billiards.

'Are you watching the time, Señora?' said Andrés. 'You've got until one.'

'I'm ready. Lili isn't back from her ride yet. Who else have you invited?'

'Only Deputy Puente and his wife. I just want to see some Puebla people and relax,' said Andrés, eyeing up the ball. He aimed and missed. 'I'm playing so badly. What are you standing there for? Hurry your kids along. We'll need three cars, get Juan and Benito. Who else is there?'

'I can drive my own car,' said Carlos.

'Perfect,' replied Andrés. 'Catalina, you go with him, take Lilia, the little ones and the nanny. I don't want to have to listen to domestic chit-chat. Carlos likes it because he's a bachelor. But no one is to leave after two. We'll go in a convoy. See that Lilia doesn't only take trousers and swimsuits, she'll need something dressy, because the Alatristes are inviting her one evening.'

'You've already arranged it?' I asked.

'Yes, I already arranged it. Don't ask in that tone of voice. She's my daughter and I'm looking after her future. Don't interfere!'

'When it suits you she's your daughter, when it doesn't she's our daughter. You handed her to me when she was ten with a speech about her needing a mother. Now all of a sudden she's your daughter again.'

'Because now she needs someone to assure her future, not someone to wipe her nose and help her with her homework.'

'I won't allow you to force her into a marriage,' I said.

'Don't worry, she'll get married of her own free will.'

'Why don't you marry off one of the two older ones?'

'Because it so happens she's the prettiest.'

'Emilito's no beauty. He can perfectly well marry Marta.'

'Because you love her less.'

'That's right. I love her less and she's older. Lili is just a poor, silly little girl.'

'She's about the age you were when we got married.'

'But Alatriste's son is a dumb-bell. You're what you are, but not because your father organized your life for you.'

'How could my father organize my life if I didn't even

know him? My poor mother had a terrible time. Don't make me go over that old story again. I'm delighted Milito has his future assured, all the better for my Lili. Are you having your turn or not, Vives?'

'I'm waiting till you've finished arguing.'

'Don't wait, you bastard, play. I'm arguing because I'm waiting for you, otherwise I wouldn't waste my time on this eternally stubborn lady. She should have been a lawyer. "Little drop of honey" her father used to call her. Can you credit it? He didn't know his daughter at all, poor Don Marcos.'

'And his son-in-law even less,' I said.

'I've played,' Carlos informed him.

I winked at him while Andrés concentrated on chalking his cue. Then I went out.

We left at five. Andrés was red-faced, with rage he said, but really with brandy. He still had to pick up Deputy Puente. The cars drove off, one behind the other. In the first, Carlos with us, then Benito driving Lucina, the older girls and two friends, and last Andrés, driven by Juan.

It was a fun journey. Verania and Checo sang some songs from school, then had a fight over a book and finally went to sleep. Lilia was in the back with them. She chatted to us for a while.

'I wrote to Loli,' she said.

'Who's she?'

'Don't you know? The one who writes the agony column in *Maruca*.'

'What did you ask her?'

'Oh, you know.'

'And what did she say?'

'Shall I read it? I signed it "Carmina from Puebla". This is what she wrote: "Fondness can lead to love, it depends on whether you find in him the qualities your Prince Charming has in your dreams. But if reality doesn't live up to your dreams, love will not follow. You can be sure."''

'Are you fond of Milito?' asked Carlos.

'A bit.'

'But he has nothing in common with the Prince Charming of your dreams.'

'Not much.'

'So love will not follow,' I declared. 'What you should do tomorrow is tell him to go to hell. Nicely, without being rude, but send him straight to hell. You say that you're not sure, that your mother says you're too young, that you want to meet other boys, so it's best just to be friends.'

'And what do I tell Papa?' she asked.

'Leave your father to me.'

'Promise? He says it's what's best for me. You won't change his mind.'

'How does your father know what's best for you? This is what's best for him. This is how he links his business with Don Emilio.'

'You cope with him then, Mama,' she said finally, and soon dropped off to sleep too.

It was a bright afternoon and the volcanoes seemed near and enormous. In Río Frío, Andrés overtook us and waved us down. We parked in front of the village store-cantina. It was getting dark and the trees looked like ghosts behind us. The children got out noisily.

'If you want a drink ask for one, if you want a pee have one. Don't pass up this chance because we're not stopping again until Puebla,' said Andrés.

We arrived at about nine. Carlos pointed out that you couldn't see the house from below, it was hidden, and yet from our terrace you could see the whole of Puebla getting ready for bed. Puebla people didn't stay out in the streets after eight o'clock, but turned in early behind their huge doors.

Andrés took our guests to their rooms while I went to see how the dinner was coming along.

'Only lay ten places,' I said to Lucina. I put my finger in the pork casserole. 'We'll eat in twenty minutes. Send out hot *tortillas* as soon as they're ready.'

I went to see which room Carlos had been given. I asked Juan to bring up a huge fern and put it in the room. Then I went to get changed. I had new clothes in my Puebla wardrobe. I never packed a case to go from one home to the other.

I put on one of my governor's-lady dresses. A heavy red material, clinging over the bust and draped to the floor.

'Are you going to let me take it off you?' said Carlos, approaching me as I came into the drawing room.

I began thinking about how I would escape up to the third floor at midnight. Andrés made it easy by going up to bed as soon as dinner was over. Deputy Puente and his wife weren't tired, nor were my girls and their friends, so we stayed chatting in front of the fire.

Four nights I spent in Carlos's room, creeping up when Andrés went to bed, using Checo's cold or talking till late with Lili as an excuse.

Andrés played *frontón* every morning. Carlos lost the first game to him, then came swimming with the children and me.

On Sunday we went to the square in Atlixco for an ice-cream. There he introduced me to Medina, the local head of the CTM, a good friend of Cordera's.

'Excuse me saying so, Señora, although Carlos says you're to be trusted, but Andrés Ascencio is a bastard. He wants to screw us just to show Álvaro that he still gives the

orders around here. The C R O M people are in the pay of
the presidency, they're just stooges. They have been for
ages, not just now. They're the people he put in at La
Guadalupe after that strike which ended in shooting.'

'What was that?' asked Carlos.

'I wouldn't like to say in front of the Señora, although
everyone round here knows.'

'I don't,' I said. 'What happened?'

Slowly, Medina told me bit by bit. La Guadalupe had
been on strike for a month. The workers wanted a pay rise
and proper jobs for casual labourers. They were confident;
it was General Aguirre's sixth year and there were strikes
all over the country. They forgot that in Puebla Andrés
Ascencio was the boss. They'd had their banners out for a
month when the governor arrived.

'Start the machines,' he said to one worker, who refused.
'Start walking then,' he ordered. He took out his pistol and
shot him. 'You start the machines,' he told another. He
refused too. 'Start walking,' he said, and shot him too. 'Are
you all so stubborn?' he asked the hundred workers who
were watching in silence. 'What about you?' he said to a
youth. 'Do you all want to die? We'll have no problem
replacing you tomorrow.'

The youth started his machine, and the rest followed
suit, until the factory groaned to life again, shift after shift
without a penny rise in pay.

He had done the same thing with the strike at La
Candelaria: twenty dead. The papers said someone had
been accidentally injured.

Medina had plenty of stories to tell. At first I wanted to
hear them, but in the end I went off to chase the children
round the square while he talked to Carlos. When we got
back to the stand all hot and sweaty for another ice-cream,
Medina stood up, gave me his hand and his thanks in

advance for my silence. I didn't tell him that although I believed half his stories, the bit about Andrés personally killing one worker after another was an exaggeration. I didn't tell Carlos either. Instead I talked about the countryside and sang with the children the *corrido* of Rosita Alvírez. We got back to Puebla very late. Andrés had already asked for dinner to be served and was seated at the head of the table.

'Where have you been to get so filthy?' he asked.

'We went to Atlixco for an ice-cream,' said Verania, who adored him.

Monday I stayed at home. For years I hadn't played with my children. I found them so clever I couldn't want for better company than their games and inventions while Carlos went over to see Medina again.

We spent the morning playing Snakes and Ladders. At two o'clock I was still laughing and squabbling like a little girl.

Tuesday I got everything organized early and by ten I had no other duties than to go with Carlos wherever I wished. No one saw me crouching on the floor of the huge Chrysler as we left those city streets full of peeping Toms. After that came the countryside, and no one bothered anyone there.

I persuaded him to take the Cholula road till Tonanzintla, which was covered in *cempazúchil*, the flowers of the dead. The fields were orange and green; *cempazúchil* and alfalfa grew together in November. We went into a church full of round-eyed, frightened little angels.

'Pretend I'm the bride,' I said. 'Pretend I'm walking down to the wedding march, to marry you. The wedding march played by your orchestra.'

'I can't conduct and get married.'

'Pretend you can.' I ran to the door to make my entrance slowly, one step, another step. 'Ta-ta-tatan, ta-ta-tatan,' I walked singing up to where he stood before the altar by the ancient velvet hassocks.

'You're crazy, Catalina,' he said, but raised his arms to the choir-stalls as though he were conducting.

'You have to receive the bride. Come on, we kneel here. People are watching us. You promise to love me in sickness and in health, for richer, for poorer, as long as I may live. I accept you as my husband and promise to be faithful, for richer, for poorer, in sickness and in health, and love and respect you as long as I may live.'

'You know it by heart. You've been rehearsing. But why are you crying? Don't cry, Catalina, I promise to be faithful, with husband, without husband, in laughter and in fear, and to love and respect your lovely bum as long as I may live.'

We kissed kneeling on the hassocks, beneath the gilded ceiling and walls, in front of the Virgin in her niche. We went on kissing till an old lady wrapped in a shawl stood in front of us, her face covered in wrinkles and warts, and so tiny that our eyes met.

'Have you no respect for God?' she said. 'If you must do disgusting things, go and do them in a stable, don't desecrate the house of the Virgin.'

'We just got married,' I said. 'God favours lovers.'

'Love, what love? What you've got is pure lust. Away with you,' she said, lifting her scapulary to her face, and, covered from chin to eyes, began to pray. Then suddenly, while we stared at her as though we'd seen a ghost, she took out a bottle of holy water and, sprinkling it on us, said more prayers in her shrill voice.

'Where's the stable?' asked Carlos as he got up, pulling me with him.

'Souls in purgatory! God have mercy on your souls, because your bodies will surely burn.'

We found a place among the fields. We lay on the orange flowers, crushing them as we undressed. Sometimes I saw the sky, sometimes the flowers. I made even more noise than usual; I wanted to be a goat. I was a goat. I was me. I didn't think of my father, I had no children or house, or husband, or desire for the sea.

We laughed a lot. We laughed like a couple of idiots who have no future, home or any bloody thing at all. I don't know why we laughed so much. I think we laughed because we wanted to.

'You're covered in orange from the *cempazúchil*,' said Carlos. 'It would be lovely to have a grave smelling like this and going all orange at All Souls'. When I die I want you to have me buried here.'

'You'll die in New York, on a trip like you did last month, or in Paris. You're too international to die here, so near. Besides, you'll be so old you won't care what your grave smells like.'

'Whenever I die, I want my grave to smell like your body does now. Let's get going, it's two already. If you're not home to preside over the lunch table, your husband'll kill us.'

'I'm tired of my husband. Every day there's something he's going to kill us for. Why not kill us and be done with it, we'll be buried here and can fuck underground where no one can bother us.'

'Good idea, but while he's killing us let's get going.'

We got up and walked towards the car. I picked some flowers and when we got home I put them in a terracotta bowl as a centrepiece for the table.

'Who put that dreadful thing there?' asked Andrés, coming in for lunch.

'I did,' I said.

'You get madder every day. This isn't a grave. Take them off – they're bad luck and they smell horrible. Excuse my wife. Sometimes her romanticism is mistaken,' he said to the guests as he seated them.

'Where do you want to sit, Carlangas?' he asked, when only the seat next to me remained. 'Next to my wife?'

'Delighted,' said Carlos.

'No need to say so,' he replied. 'What kind of soup is it, Catalina?'

'Mushrooms and courgette flowers.'

'You don't say. You're obsessed with flowers. But the soup's good, it's very filling; I recommend it,' he said to Puente, deputy for the CROM.

'Did you stay up late last night?' asked Carlos.

'No more than the others,' replied Andrés. 'We had a lot to talk about didn't we, Deputy?'

'And still have, General,' said the deputy.

'Oh no,' begged his wife. 'Then he comes to bed very late and I get very cold.'

She was a small squat woman, with big eyes and very black lashes, well rounded tits and a waist which was always squeezed with sashes or belts. She liked her husband. Heaven knows why, because he was ghastly, but she was always stroking him and whenever he expressed an opinion she listened as though he were a genius, nodding her head up and down. Perhaps this was why the deputy finished his most eloquent contributions by asking, 'Isn't that right, Susy?' to which she replied, 'Absolutely, my love,' and moved her head one last time. They were a team. I could never have formed a team like that. I didn't have the dedication.

'How did the game go?' I asked.

'Good,' said Andrés. 'I don't ask you two how it went

because I can imagine. I don't know why you like the countryside. You can tell you've never worked in it. Did you see your friend Medina?' he asked Carlos.

'There wasn't time. We stayed in Tonanzintla. The church is impressive. I want to give a concert there.'

'Give it. We'll arrange it tomorrow instead of you wasting time seeing Medina.'

'Medina is a friend of mine, and he's got problems.'

'Load of rubbish. The only problem he's got is following Cordera and wanting to be the CTM leader in Atlixco. Because as sure as my name is Andrés Ascencio, the CTM in Atlixco is going to hell and Medina with it.'

'Why interfere, Chinti? Let the workers decide who they want,' said Carlos, with that older brother air which irritated the general so much.

'It's you who shouldn't interfere. Stick to your music and your intellectual pursuits, stick to complicated women if you like, but don't interfere in politics, because it's something you have to know how to do. I wouldn't dream of conducting an orchestra and I can assure you it's much easier standing there moving your hands in front of a bunch of *mariachis* than governing cowards and bastards.'

'Cordera and Medina are friends of mine.'

'And what about me? Aren't I your friend? See, Puente, that's how I'm repaid.' He looked at me and went on, 'Don't you agree, Catalina? Has the great artist convinced you that "the Left united will never be defeated"? Women are a disaster. We spend our lives educating them, explaining things to them, then one little parrot comes along and they believe everything it says. Cati is convinced, Deputy, that that bastard Álvaro Cordera is a saint who is willing to throw in his lot with the wretched of the earth. She's only seen him three times, but she believes him. Anything to contradict her husband. Because that's her new style. You should have met her when she was seventeen – such a sweet, pretty thing, a sponge soaking up everything I said, incapable of seeing anything bad in her husband or of not being in his bed at three in the morning. Ah, women! There's no doubt they're not the same nowadays. Something's ruffled them. Let's hope yours stays as she is, Deputy, there aren't many of them left. Even the most docile ones kick their heels. You should see mine.'

Andrés knew me so well that he smiled before eating a spoonful of sauce and then, with his mouth full, said, 'When I say mine I mean you, Señora de Ascencio. The others are just anecdotes, necessary but not indispensable.'

'The general doesn't mince his words,' said Deputy Puente.

Carlos put his hand on my leg under the table.

The meal was interminable. When the Santa Clara cake and coffee arrived I sighed with relief. Everyone would soon be going off to have a siesta. Andrés never bothered me at this hour of the day. After his second or third brandy he got up, went to the kitchen, thanked the servants and, no matter who the guests were, said, 'Please excuse me. I have some private business needing urgent attention.'

Then he'd go into a little back room which was completely dark in mid-afternoon. He'd sleep for exactly an hour and a half and wake up ready for dominoes. I wasn't required for that either, all I had to do was see there was enough coffee, a lot of brandy and a dish of chocolates, then I could easily disappear until dinnertime.

'Shall we go to the square?' I asked Carlos.

'Which room is the square in?' he replied.

We were laughing when Andrés returned from his demagogic thanking of the servants and stood behind me.

He put his hands on my shoulders and pressed down on them.

'Please excuse us. We have some urgent business,' he said.

'I told the children I'd take them to the square for a balloon and then to the Forts to climb trees,' said I.

'You're an exemplary mother. Tell them you'll take them when the dominoes starts.'

'Oh, Mama,' said Verania, 'come on.'

'Andrés, I promised,' I said.

'That's fine, promises don't hurt anyone. I promise thousands of things. Promise them you'll take them at six. You can't now.'

'We'll wait for you here, Señora,' said Carlos.

'Will you tell us about your father?' asked Checo.

'Whatever you want,' said Carlos.

'Don't be long, Mama.'

'No, my love.'

Andrés went into our bedroom and closed the door. He sat on the edge of the bed and asked me to sit next to him.

'Where did you go?' he asked.

'You know. You have me followed and then you ask me.'

'I sent that fool Benito but he lost you when you came out of the church. What message did the old hag give you?'

I laughed.

'She said she'd rid us of the devil and sprinkled us with holy water.'

'And gave you a message from Medina.'

'No, what d'you mean, message from Medina?'

'Benito said she said something about a stable.'

'I didn't hear her.'

'And you didn't hear the bit about the souls in purgatory either?'

'Yes, I did. She prayed to them.'

'How did the prayer go?'

'I don't remember, Andrés. I thought she was crazy. She wanted to throw us out of the Virgin's house and all sorts of other silly things.'

'Well, remember.'

'I don't remember. Can I go now? Who's going to follow us this afternoon?'

'This afternoon you stay here in this bed with your husband. Because you're useless as a spy and you're beginning to like the role of girlfriend.'

I took off my shoes. I swung my feet onto the bed and sat with my body hunched over, head between my legs. I sighed.

'Why d'you want me to stay? Why do me the favour now? You haven't touched me for months.'

'It's done you good. You're very beautiful.'

'And Conchita?'

'Don't ask tasteless questions, Catalina.'

'It's out of politeness. I'm interested in the health of the women you sleep with.'

'You've become very vulgar.'

'And since when have you been so refined? You must have caught it from José Ibarra's niece. So well-bred, the Ibarras. D'you still keep her in the ranch at Martínez de la Torre? I know you gave her velvet curtains and Louis XV furniture so she wouldn't feel lost among all those Indians. When were you last there? Doesn't she get bored? She probably sews "petit poa". Poor thing. She's bound to wear a hat with a veil riding among peasants and bulls.'

'She had a daughter.'

'Are you bringing her here?'

'She doesn't want me to.'

'The others didn't want you to either.'

'The others weren't good mothers and she is. She loves the child and asked me to let her keep her so she wouldn't be so lonely.'

'Don't feel you have to be generous to me. I've too many children around already, not to mention teenagers.'

'Don't complain. My Lilia's going soon.'

'Your Lilia? Now you sweetly call her your Lilia. You've screeched at each other ever since I've known her. She loves me more than you and I'm only her stepmother.'

'She doesn't quarrel with you; that doesn't mean she loves you.'

'It must mean something. You brought her to me when she was ten. She'll be sixteen soon.'

'So she's your creation?'

'I don't create anyone. I feed them and listen to their problems; the rest is up to them. In our house they grow up as best they can. Your children, our children, I suppose you think I bring up Checo too?'

'You bring him up badly. Look, don't start philosophizing. Take your jumper off and come closer.' He pulled me towards him. 'Your waist's thinner. How did you do that?'

'Making love,' I replied.

'Don't think you can provoke me, you little fool. I know you're more faithful than a thoroughbred mare. Come here, I've neglected you. Since September, is it?'

'I don't remember.'

'You used to count the days.'

I yawned and stretched my legs, then snuggled beside him. I was wearing velvet trousers and let him caress them.

'It's amazing how attractive you still are. No wonder you've got Carlos following you around like an idiot.'

'Carlos is my friend.'

'Conchita, Pilar and Victorina are my friends too.'

'And the mothers of your children.'

'Because women are like that. They can't fuck without having babies. Don't you want Carlos's kids?'

'I've got enough with yours, and I don't fuck Carlos.'

'Look at me, you damn woman, and say that again,' he said, putting his face over mine and holding my chin so that my gaze met his.

'I don't fuck Carlos,' I said, looking him straight in the eye.

'That's good to know,' he replied and began kissing me. 'Take your clothes off. It's hard work getting you to take them off these days.' He pulled at my trousers. I let him do it. I thought of Pepa saying, 'In marriage there's a moment when you have to shut your eyes and say an Ave Maria.' I shut my eyes and tried to remember the fields.

'So you don't fuck Carlos, eh? And what were you doing to get your body covered in orange?' he asked.

'Rolling in the flowers.'

'Nothing else?'

'Nothing else,' I said, without opening my eyes. He put it in. I kept my eyes shut, under him I imagined the beach, thought about the next day's meals, going over what was left in the fridge.

'You're my wife. Don't you forget it,' he said afterwards, lying beside me, stroking my belly. On my back, seeing my limp body, I said, 'I'm not afraid now.'

'Of what?'

'Of you. Sometimes you frighten me. I don't know what you're thinking. You look at me and say nothing. In the mornings you go out with your whip and pistol without asking me to go anywhere. I begin to think you're going to kill me like you've killed others.'

'Kill you? How could you think that? I don't kill what I love.'

'Why do you wear your pistol every day then?'

'So that those who want to kill me see it. I don't kill. I'm too old for that.'

'But you have people killed.'

'That depends.'

'On what?'

'On lots of things. Don't ask about things you don't understand. I'm not going to kill you, no one's going to kill you.'

'And Carlos?'

'Why should anyone kill Carlos? He doesn't fuck you; he didn't visit Medina; he's my friend, almost my younger brother. If someone kills Carlos he'll have me to answer to. I swear on the head of Checo who loves him so much.'

Then he fell asleep with his hands on his stomach and mouth half open, one boot on, one boot off, no trousers and his shirt unbuttoned. I stayed with him a while, watching him sleep. I thought he looked awful. I ran through the list of his other women. How could they love him? What did they see in him? I had met him, had loved him, had even thought no one more handsome, more intelligent, more charming, more courageous than he. There used to be days I couldn't sleep without his body next to mine, months when I missed him terribly, and so many afternoons spent wondering where he was. Not any more. Today I wanted to go away with Carlos to New York or Juárez Avenue, be just a silly idiot of thirty years old with two children and a man she loves more than them, more than herself, more than anything, waiting for her to go to the square.

I sprang up. I dressed in seconds. Carlos was downstairs and up here I was stupidly contemplating that sleeping bear.

'Farewell,' I said quietly, and pretended to take a dagger from my belt and do him in for good before leaving.

I went out into the patio, shouting, 'Children, Carlos, let's go. I'm ready.'

It was getting dark. There was no one in the inside patio. I went into the back garden. I went up the steps, calling them. They weren't there. Their bedroom lights were off. I knocked at Lilia's room, the only one with the light on.

'What's the matter, Mama? You're shouting as though the sky's falling in.'

She was lovely, with her robe tied at the waist, her clean, childish face. She was taking out her rollers, her hair fell in curls about her ears.

'Where are you going?'

'To dinner with Emilio,' in the same tone of voice her father told me 'to the office'.

'What a waste, my angel. Sixteen years old, that beautiful body, that head which has so much to learn, those sparkling eyes, and all the rest of you, ending up in Milito's bed. Stupid Milito, opportunist Milito, useless Milito, just a Daddy's boy, with a gangster of a Daddy like yours, and who puts on airs to boot. It's such a shame, my love. We'll always regret it.'

'Don't exaggerate, Mama. Emilio plays tennis well; he's not very nice but he's not ugly either. He's charming, dresses beautifully and it's good for my Papa if I marry him.'

'That's true enough.'

'He likes music. He takes us to Carlos's concerts.'

'Because they're all the rage and it's a good chance to sit down for two hours without anyone noticing he has nothing between his ears.'

The bedrooms gave out onto a long open veranda with a plant-covered balustrade.

'It's cold. Let's talk inside,' said Lilia. I followed her into her room. She sat at the dressing table to brush her hair.

'Where are the others?' I asked. 'Why did they go without me?'

'Because they don't love you any more.' She still laughed like a little girl.

'No message, either?' I asked. Then I remembered the plant-pot in Carlos's room.

'You look lovely, angel. I'll be at the dressmaker's. Come and see me,' I said and ran to the plant-pot with the fern. I searched among the leaves and found a note in his handwriting:

My dearest love,
I waited for you to come back soon, dressed or not. I had to go out because a message came from Medina asking me to meet him at six in front of the San Francisco Church. I took the children and an exact image of your round backside with me. Kisses, on the mouth unfortunately.
ME.

I ran down the stairs. I was crossing the inside patio as Andrés came out, just having woken up.

'Anyone want to play dominoes?' he asked.

'I don't know. Carlos and the children went to San Francisco. I'm going to fetch them. I haven't been in the games room but I'm sure you'll find some takers there. I'll tell Lucina to bring the coffee and chocolates,' I told him hurriedly, without stopping.

'Carlos took the kids? Who gave him permission?' shouted Andrés.

'He always takes them,' I shouted back as I went down to the garage.

The car nearest the door was a convertible. I got in and drove off, skidding down to San Francisco. When I reached the park I drove more slowly. I knew Carlos wouldn't talk to Medina right in front of the church and would want the kids to go off and play somewhere. I didn't see them among the trees, or walking along the edge of the fountains, or drinking the dirty water that spouted from the mouths of clay frogs. They weren't on the swings or the slides, in none of the places they usually played. Neither did I see Carlos sitting on one of the benches or having a coffee at one of the stands. I was furious with him. Why did he have to get messed up in politics? Why didn't he stick to conducting his orchestra, composing strange music, chatting to his arty friends and fucking me? Why this stupid political fever? Why did he have to be Álvaro's friend and not someone less complicated? Where were they? It was cold.

'I'm sure they went out without sweaters,' I thought. 'The three of them will get colds and I'll get pneumonia from driving around in this daft open car. Where are they? Have they gone to the square?'

I parked the car and ran to see if they were still at the church. Perhaps they'd be waiting for me there. The church with its façade of tiles and tall, thin towers stood at the top of a long flight of steps and there in front of the closed door, sitting on the ground, were the children.

'What happened?' I said when I saw them alone, so peculiarly quiet.

'Uncle Carlos went off with some friends and told us to wait here,' replied Checo.

'How long ago? And who were these stupid friends, Verania?'

'I don't know.'

'Wasn't it Medina? Remember, the man who was with him when we went for an ice-cream in the square at Atlixco.'

'It wasn't that man, Mama,' said Verania, who was ten then.

'Sure?'

'Yes. Checo said they were friends because they took his arm and said, "Let's go, friend," but he didn't want to go. He went because they had guns. That's why he told us to stay here. He said you'd be coming to get us soon.'

'Why didn't you call the priests? Where were the priests?' I asked.

'They'd just closed the door,' said Verania.

'Useless priests. Priests! Priests! Priests!' I shouted, banging on the door of the church.

A monk opened.

'What can I do for you, sister?' he said.

'An hour ago a man who was here with my children was taken away, taken by armed men, forcibly, and your door was closed at six in the afternoon. You kicked up so much fuss about having your churches open, yet you close them. Who told you to close the door?' I said, attacking the monk.

'I don't understand what you're talking about, sister. Calm down. We closed the door because it got dark early.'

'You priests never understand when it doesn't suit you. Come on, children, into the car, quickly.'

CHAPTER NINETEEN

I ran into the house shouting, with the children hanging on to my coat in silence. I jumped the stairs to the games room five at a time and when I reached the top their hands, infected by my panic, were still stuck to my body.

'What's the matter?' asked Andrés, opening the door. He was chewing on a cigar, and had a brandy in one hand and a domino in the other.

'Someone kidnapped Carlos. The children were alone in front of the church,' I said slowly, quietly, as though I were telling him something expected.

'Who'd kidnap him? He must have gone where I warned him not to go. And he left the kids alone? How irresponsible!'

'The children say they took him away by force,' I said again, as though I were taking it calmly.

'Your children have vivid imaginations. Wrap them up and put them to bed, that's what they need.'

'And what are you going to do?'

'Open the game; I've got a double six.'

'What about your friend?'

'He'll be back. If he isn't, I'll speak to Benítez and get the police to look for him. Are you putting those kids' pyjamas on, or not?'

'Yes, I'll put their pyjamas on,' I said, as though I were

someone else, as though I'd been muzzled. My arms round
the childrens' shoulders, I went down to the second floor.

Lilia was coming out of her room. She was wearing a
black dress with red piping, very high heels and black
stockings. Her hair was scraped up in two silver combs and
her mouth painted. Dressed like that she wasn't going to
call me Mama.

'Cati, will you lend me your astrakhan coat? I spilled ice-
cream down mine yesterday. Did you find Carlos?'

'No,' I replied biting my bottom lip.

'Poor Mama,' she said and hugged me.

I wanted to scream, go and look for him, tear my hair,
go mad.

Lilia stroked my head.

'Poor you,' she said.

I slowly held her perfumed body away from me.

'You look very lovely,' I told her. 'Are you going now?
Let me look, walk away, so I can see if your seams are
straight. You always put your stockings on crooked.'

I made her walk down the veranda.

'Come here, let me straighten the left one,' I said. 'Take
whichever coat you want from my room and don't kiss
Emilio. Don't waste yourself on him.'

She kissed me again and ran downstairs.

I put the children to bed. When they were asleep I turned
off the light and lay down next to Verania, face downwards,
hands under my armpits, and began to cry slow, enormous
tears.

'As long as he's not in pain,' I told myself, 'as long as they
don't kill him slowly, don't hurt him, touch his face, or
break his hands. Please let some good person have shot him.'

'Señora,' said Lucina coming into the room, 'your
husband wants to have dinner.'

'Please serve it,' I said in a hoarse voice.

'He wants you to go down. He told me to tell you the governor is here.'

'And Señor Carlos?'

'No, Señora, he's not here.' She came up and sat on the edge of the bed. 'I'm so sorry, Señora, you know I love you very much, it was a pleasure to see you so happy, I . . .'

'Have they killed him? Did Juan tell you?'

'I don't know, Señora. Juan pretended to be ill when they sent for him. Benito drove. We wanted to tell you but we couldn't, you were in with the general.'

I hid my face in my arms again. I had no more tears.

'And Benito?'

'He hasn't come back.'

I got up.

'Tell the general I won't be long and ask Juan to come up.'

I dressed in black. I put on the earrings and medallion Carlos had given me. They were Italian, the medallion had a blue flower on it and said 'Mamma' one one side and '13 February' on the other.

I went into the dining room as Andrés was seating the guests.

'Your humble servant, Señora,' said Benítez.

'She doesn't deserve it, Governor, she's late,' said Andrés.

'Please excuse me, I fell asleep with the children,' I said. There were more people than expected.

'You know the state prosecutor?' asked Andrés.

'Yes, of course, happy to have you here,' I said, but didn't offer him my hand.

'And the chief of police?'

'How do you do?' I said, pretending not to know him just to annoy him.

'The governor was good enough to come with them when I informed him of our friend Carlos Vives's disappearance,' said Andrés.

'Wouldn't it be better to be out looking for him?' I asked.

'They wanted further details of the case,' said Deputy Puente.

'I hear your children were left alone in the street,' said Susy Díaz de Puente. 'I think Don Carlos was kidnapped by an admirer.'

'I hope so,' I replied.

'Señoras, this is a serious matter,' said Andrés. 'Carlos was a friend of Medina's and Medina died this morning. Do you know what happened there, Governor?'

'More or less. It seems he was killed by his own people. There's a big radical element in the CTM and Medina had convinced the grass-roots to throw in their lot with the CROM. They thought this prudent move was treachery and some lunatics took their revenge.

'I don't believe Medina wanted to go over to the CROM,' I said.

'Why don't you believe it?' asked Andrés.

'Because I knew Medina. Carlos liked him a lot.'

'Well let's hope he didn't like him enough to try and defend him,' said Andrés. 'He always was reckless. Only today at lunch I asked him to stick to his music and stop running risks. But he likes trouble.'

'He's a nice man,' said the prosecutor, 'and an excellent musician.'

'Let's hope nothing has happened to him,' proferred the chief of police, who was a horrendous man, deputy chief when Andrés was governor. He was known as 'Salami' because he had a blotchy skin. As for what had happened, he knew perfectly well.

*

Dinner was served. Andrés began praising my talents as a homemaker and the conversation moved on to other things. Lucina was waiting on table.

'More beans, Señora?' she said, standing beside me, and then, in a low voice, 'Juan says they've got him in Number Ninety.'

'Thank you, just a few,' I replied.

'Really, Señora, it's all very delicious,' said Benítez.

'Thank you, Governor,' I said, lifting my face to look at him. Next to him my eyes met those of Tirso Santillana, the prosecutor, a respected notary who would never work with Andrés. I was surprised he would with Benítez. He was a strange man. When I looked at him I felt he was interested in me.

'You are worried, aren't you?' he asked.

'I have a high regard for Carlos,' I replied.

'I promise I'll do everything in my power to find him,' he said.

'I thank you for that,' I said, and turned to the others. 'Shall we have coffee in the drawing room?'

'Fine,' said my husband. He got up and the others followed suit, like tame monkeys. In the drawing room I manoeuvred myself near Santillana again.

'You trust your governor, don't you?'

'Of course, Señora,' he replied. I smiled as though we were talking about the weather.

'They're holding Carlos in Number Ninety. Save him.'

'What are you talking about?'

'Number Ninety is a prison for political enemies. My husband set it up when he was governor and it still exists. Carlos is there.'

'How do you know?'

'It's not important. Will you go? Say you overheard it in the street. Go there and I'll send someone to advise your office. But please hurry.' I laughed again and he laughed too, to keep up the pretence.

'Governor, allow me to take my leave. I want to see if my office has any news,' he said.

'Ah, Santillana, so efficient. I always wanted him with me when I was in office, but there was nothing doing. How did you manage, Felipe?' said Andrés.

'I was lucky,' replied Benítez. 'Goodbye then, Santillana.'

Pellico, the police chief, was annoyed. If the prosecutor was going, he should too and it didn't look as if he wanted to. He was happy with his brandy, his coffee and his armchair.

'You'll stay won't you, Señor Pellico?' I asked.

'If you ask me to, I have no choice, Señora,' he said, settling into his armchair and eating chocolate mints.

'I'll see you out, Señor Santillana,' I said, taking the prosecutor's arm and accompanying him downstairs to the front door. All round the doorframe Andrés had placed coats of arms and war memorabilia. Juan was hiding in the shadows.

'What happened, Juan?' I asked.

'Benito left them in Number Ninety, that's all he knows.'

'Take me there,' said Tirso.

'I'll go with you,' I said.

'Do you want to ruin everything?'

I let them go and went back to the drawing room, trembling.

'Why are you talking to yourself, Catalina?' asked Andrés as I entered.

'I'm repeating my times tables so I don't look foolish when Checo asks me,' I replied.

'If she were a man, she'd be a politician. She's tougher than all of us put together.'

'Your wife has many qualities, General,' said Benítez.

'I'll ask them to bring wood for a fire. It's very cold,' I murmured.

The singer Andrés had invited to play the guitar for us that night was called Charro Blanco. He was an albino who sang in a sad voice, and it was all the same to him whether people wanted to listen or talked during his tune.

He sat by me at the side of the fireplace and began to sing: 'In the far-off mountains, a horseman is riding; he wanders alone through the world, looking for death.'

'Charro, play *Lightning* and stop singing such miserable songs – can't you see we're worried?' said Andrés. Charro Blanco merely changed the beat and began again: 'It's all because I love her so, it's because when I see her I'm afraid and want to see her no more. Lightning, fury of the sky, if you take away my hope . . .'

'What a fucking awful song. Start again,' Andrés told him.

And Charro Blanco started again and all those present joined in because when Andrés sang no one dared keep talking. Charro Blanco was now the centre of attention. Andrés started calling him brother and requesting song after song.

'Sing, Catalina,' he said. 'Don't stick so close to the fire, it's not good for you. Sing *With You in the Distance*.'

'Let's do that one, Catita,' said Charro Blanco, but he sang it alone. He was just finishing when Santillana came into the drawing room.

'I found Vives,' he said. 'He's dead.'

'Where did you find him? Governor, I demand justice!' shouted Andrés.

'What happened, Tirso?' asked Benítez.

'I'd like to speak to you in private, Señor, but right now

I hand you my resignation. I found him in a clandestine prison. The people there say they take orders from Major Pellico.'

Chaos broke out. Pellico looked at Andrés.

'Demand his resignation,' Andrés yelled at Benítez. 'What is this place? Where's Carlos? Who took him there?'

'Tirso, substantiate your accusation,' said the governor.

'I don't know what he's talking about,' shouted Pellico.

Puente's wife fainted. Puente began a speech for the Chamber. I left.

Juan was standing by Tirso's car holding Lucina.

'Where is he?' I asked.

'In here, but don't look,' begged Juan.

I opened the door and saw his head. I stroked his hair; it was caked with blood. I closed his eyes; he had blood on his neck and jacket. A hole in his neck.

'Help me take him upstairs,' I asked.

Between us, Juan, Tirso's chauffeur, Lucina and I carried him up to the room with the fern. We laid him on the bed. I asked them to leave. I don't know how long I was there, kneeling beside him, looking at him. I stopped when Andrés came in with Benítez.

'I told you. Why didn't you take any notice?' he said, going up to Carlos.

'We'll bury him in Tonanzintla,' I said, getting up off the bed and walking to the door.

I went outside. The veranda was dark. Just enough light showed from below to walk beside the flower-pots without falling. The guest rooms were on the third floor, next to the *frontón* court and the swimming pool. There should have been a light, but Carlos and I had broken it two nights previously so that I could creep up without being seen. The children all slept on the second floor. Only Andrés and I were on the first. There were five minutes of stairs and verandas from our bedroom to the fern room. I walked through the darkness with the experience of other nights; I went to the garden and then to my room. I did my hair, put on a black coat and went to look for Juan in the kitchen. He took me to see Gayosso.

'You called, Señora?' said a sleepy man trying to be polite.

'I want a plain wood coffin, wood coloured, no wrought iron, black bows, crosses or anything,' I said.

The coffin arrived at about nine. At eleven we were in Tonanzintla. It was sunny and crowded. Benítez brought along teachers, music students and Party activists. Cordera came from Mexico City and walked behind the coffin with me.

The graveyard in Tonanzintla has no walls. It lies beside the church, at the foot of a small hill. It was 2 November, many people were visiting the other graves, covering them with flowers, pots of *mole*, bread and sweets. I had the whole field we had rolled in the previous day harvested; it made fifty bouquets of flowers. I asked these to be distributed among Benítez's flock and Cordera's workers so they all had flowers to throw in Carlos's grave.

The grave-diggers placed the wooden coffin by the hole they had dug. Then Andrés stood by it and said, 'Comrade workers, friends: Carlos Vives was a victim of those who want to prevent our society from marching forward along the fruitful paths of peace and harmony. We do not know who cut short his life, the beautiful life they saw as such a danger, but rest assured that they will pay for their crime. The loss of a man like Carlos Vives not only brings grief to those like myself, my family and his friends who had the privilege of loving him, it is also an irreparable loss to society. I would like to list for you his many qualities, the endeavours in which he served his country, the ways in which he enriched our Revolution. But I cannot. My grief prevents me, etc., etc.'

After that Cordera spoke. I felt as if I was watching a film. I could not feel.

'Carlos,' he said, 'the memory of your honesty, your intelligence, your courage will be a source of inspiration to us. We will demand justice. In helping us to seek justice you lost your life. We know who killed you; those with power, those with weapons and prisons. The poor did not kill you, not the workers, students and intellectuals. You were killed by the caciques, despots, oppressors, tyrants, those who exploit, etc., etc.'

When he finished, the peons lifted the coffin to put it in the hole. It was then I threw my flowers in.

'Now you've got your flowery grave, imbecile.'

Before I had time to cry I turned and walked quickly to the car.

The following week was one of statements. I was so confused that those of the CROM, the CTM, the governor, Rodolfo, Cordera, Andrés, all seemed the same to me. They all agreed that Carlos had been a great man, his death had to be avenged, the murderers brought to justice, the country saved from traitors and the threat of violence. His friends published a letter in the paper demanding justice, and talked about Vives's virtues and the irreparable loss to the Arts. I read the names of people whom I had heard him speak to on the phone, whom he'd mentioned in his conversations with Efraín and Renato. I didn't know them, he had said it was better not to mix things, that no one would understand, they would be suspicious, Efraín and Renato were OK because they were his bosom pals and because they did such crazy things with their own lives they were bound to understand other people. I cut out everything about him in the papers and put the cuttings in a silver box identical to the one I kept locked in the back of my wardrobe with all his notes, a photo we had taken on the main avenue and the press clippings of his concerts. I even kept advertisements and bad reviews. I had a photo of him conducting his orchestra, his hair falling over his forehead and his hand uplifted. I stroked it and stroked it.

Tirso denounced the goings on at Number Ninety, the governor got rid of Pellico and declared his sorrow and surprise. Pellico came to the house to see Andrés. I was leaning over the second floor balustrade when I saw him go into the study.

Within a few days, with the newspapers up in arms, Benítez declaring war on corruption, and Andrés reiterating his confidence in the law and institutions; Pellico was jailed.

Some months later seven men escaped from San Juan de Dios. Pellico was among them. Until quite recently we still got a Christmas card from him from Los Angeles.

CHAPTER TWENTY

I stayed on in Puebla. The thought of going back to Mexico City frightened me. In the house on the hill the walls and memories were familiar, so I felt protected. I didn't want challenges or surprises. Better to grow old supervising other people's love affairs, sitting in my garden or by the fireside, or in the little brick house I bought beside the graveyard in Tonanzintla where I went when I wanted to cry or hide. It was only one room, just big enough for a hammock and a table for my box of photos and cuttings. The sun didn't penetrate because the bougain-villaea that wound around the huge tree in the patio reached over to the roof, covering the tiles and drooping down over the windows. In that tiny house I would sob my heart out till I fell asleep on the floor, then when I awoke with swollen eyes I'd go back to Puebla ready for another period of calm.

After Carlos's death, Lilia began to rebel against her father. She didn't trust him, and wouldn't leave my side. We'd go together to the La Victoria market to buy fruit, or she'd make me take her to Puerto de Veracruz to help her choose clothes and shoes. The fashion at the time was to cover your arms in gold bangles with huge coins hanging from them. When she walked along she sounded like a cow with its bell.

I didn't like shopping in Puerto de Veracruz because Andrés's mistresses shopped there. He had an account with the owners that could be signed by his daughters and by the latest cutie he was going around with. I never went. I only started going for Lilia. I liked her; she was inquisitive and poked her nose in things, like me. Andrés's other daughters weren't like that.

After a period of obeying her father and going to dinner with the Alatristes whenever they asked her, she decided to fall in love with young Javier Uriarte. He had a motorbike and she'd sneak out and tear up the road to Veracruz with him. I shielded her, and even made friends with the boy. He amused me and had saved me from the fate of being related to the Alatristes.

Emilito went back to Georgina Letona, who forgave him everything and had put up with him for the eight years they were engaged. She was very beautiful and was madly in love with him. I'd never seen anyone with eyes like hers. She had tight dark eyelashes, eyebrows as if they were pencilled in and, in the middle, two honey balls exactly the same colour as the hair that fell in ringlets over her shoulders. I never heard her laugh; she smiled. She showed her little even teeth through open lips with an enviable spontaneity.

Lilia and I bumped into them once walking down Reforma hand in hand. When he was with her, Emilito lost that idiotic manner I remember him having.

'Imagine how ridiculous I'd be, marrying him. I'd have horns on my head even before the wedding,' said Lilia after that encounter.

I put an arm round her shoulder and said she was right and blessed the day Uriarte had appeared to save her from ridicule.

Four days after we'd met them in Reforma, Emilito

gave Lilia a piano serenade that blocked the whole street. Not only was there a piano, Agustín Lara was playing it and Pedro Vargas was singing. The whole X E W radio station transferred *en bloc* to our house in Puebla.

Lilia came running down to our room, barefoot and wearing a pink robe.

'What shall I do, Mama?'

Her father had got up to spy out of the window.

'Put the light on, silly, what d'you mean, "What shall I do?"'

'If I put the light on, he'll think . . .'

'Put it on,' shouted Andrés.

'Not if she doesn't want to,' I said. 'The boy will be unbearable if he thinks he's been accepted.'

'Not to me he won't, and I'm going to be his father-in-law.'

'But Lilia doesn't want to,' I said, while outside they played *Little Lantern* and the girl peeped between the curtains.

'He's so ugly,' she said. 'He looks like he's in pain.'

'Of course he's in pain,' said Andrés. 'You've swapped him for the idiot with the bike.'

'That's not why. You know perfectly well he's in love with Georgina Letona.'

'Shut up, Catalina. Don't you go putting ideas in her head. Turn the light on, Lilia.'

'I want it quite clear I don't agree with this,' I said, getting out of bed.

'Come here, child,' said Andrés. 'Take no notice. She's just bitter.'

Lilia got into the place I'd left in bed. They stayed there, listening to the music with the light on, while I went downstairs to the servants' quarters to wake Juan. I asked him to sneak out the back way and tell Uriarte about the serenade.

As I expected, the boy appeared within fifteen minutes, with ten friends, a guitar and a rifle.

There was a terrible uproar.

'Lilia! Come out and tell this nitwit who you like best,' asked Javier Uriarte, while his friends attacked the piano, put Agustín Lara into a car and pushed Pedro Vargas in beside him. Some bodyguard protected Emilito with a bear hug, but Javier jumped on him, arms flailing. The friends fired shots into the air and shouted, 'Fair fight, fair fight! Leave the two of them to it!' Emilito disentangled himself from his bodyguard and squared up to Uriarte. In no time they were locked together, wheeling round.

Andrés forgot he was partisan and watched the proceedings as if he were at a boxing match. Emilito defended himself, but he wasn't much use. Lilia watched them, leaning out of the window with her father, biting her nails.

'What are you upset about? You should be happy,' said Andrés, but she couldn't stand it. She left the window, did her robe up, soon appeared at the front door and walked towards the young men. Without more ado she pushed in between them.

Emilito was gasping for breath with his tie around his nose. Uriarte pulled Lilia towards him and kissed her. A second later Andrés was at the door, calling her. She detached herself from Javier and went back to the house. She passed her father and went upstairs to where I was waiting on the veranda.

'He'll kill him,' she said calmly, 'just like he did your Carlos. He'll kill him.'

We went to her room, arms round each other's waist. Her sisters and the children were there looking out of the window. They applauded as she came in. We saw Andrés pat Emilito on the back. Javier and his friends went off towards the fountain and in a few minutes the street fell silent again.

The following week Uriarte phoned Lilia. She told him on the telephone in her room, 'I can't. My father's here.'

Soon afterwards we heard his bike. He rode round the house blowing his horn until she threw him a note, which fell between his shirt and his jacket. 'I love you,' it said.

Six months went by, during which time she refused to talk to Emilito. For six months she was ecstatically involved in a love affair that ended when Javier went over a cliff, bike and all. No one knew how exactly, but he didn't survive.

His parents recovered the body and buried it in the French Cemetery. There was no fuss. I accompanied Lilia to the grave and let her cry and ask forgiveness for who knows what reason.

Not long afterwards Emilito came to speak to the general.

Andrés received him in his study. It was an odd study, long like a corridor, with saddles on one side and bullfighters' costumes from Andalucía and Mexico on the other. At the end, the large desk was covered with cigars and lighters. He had about 400 different lighters, and while he listened to whoever had come to do business he lit them one by one to keep himself amused.

When they had finished their talk, Andrés called me. 'Lili is marrying Emilio Alatriste in a few months' time. Tell her and start making arrangements.'

I smiled and took Emilito's arm. We went out to Lilia in the garden.

CHAPTER TWENTY-ONE

A year later they were married at our ranch in Atlixco. Everyone who was anyone in Mexico was there, from the President and his ministers to the chiefs of the military zones, fifteen governors, all the rich people in Puebla and Lucina and Juan who ended up embracing in the middle of the dance floor without anyone bothering at all.

I'll never forget Lili dancing with her father, leaning on him as though she liked his protection, letting herself be led all round the centre of the immense garden: century-old trees and a river into which flowers had been thrown in the early morning at Matamoros so that at three in the afternoon they'd be floating past the ranch where General Ascencio's first daughter was getting married.

I had chosen Lilia's dress. She looked beautiful in a mass of organdie. She danced with her father, throwing her head back, twirling her feet rapidly to follow his steps in the *paso doble*.

Then the band played *Over the Waves* and Andrés handed her over to Emilito so he could hold her as they listened to 'their song'. I don't know when they decided it was their song; Lilia couldn't care less but she clung to the roles she was given like the best of actresses.

They whirled round the floor as the guests applauded.

'Kiss! Kiss! Kiss!' They looked at each other a moment,

looked at the floor, touched lips and went on dancing in silence.

Andrés came back to the table we were sharing with the in-laws. He asked for a cognac, took out a cigar and began blowing smoke rings.

'My dear fellow,' he said to Emilito's father, 'are we on all the radio stations?'

'How could we fail to be, my dear chap?' replied Don Emilio with a smile.

'Everything has turned out beautifully, Catalina, congratulations,' said Emilito's mother.

'Nice of you to say so, Doña Concha,' I replied, catching sight of a very handsome man at a table with Bibi and General Gómez Soto.

'Not at all,' said Doña Concha. 'Going to all this trouble for a girl who isn't even yours. Who is Lili's mother?'

'As far as I'm concerned, I'm her mother.'

Bibi noticed me looking at her table with curiosity and came over to save me from Doña Concha. I followed her back to the man, elegant as Clark Gable, who got up and held out his hand: 'Quijano, at your service,' he said.

'Thank you,' I replied.

'Don't you know Quijano, Catalina?' asked General Gómez Soto. 'He's from Puebla, he's a famous film director now.'

We began talking about films and actors. He invited me to the first night of his first film, *The Lady of the Camelias*. I accepted and told him how much my mother liked the novel and what it had meant to us at home. They all laughed.

'Really, it was our Bible. In my house no one could cough without her believing we were slipping away into the other world. My mother had a bottle of radish-and-iodine syrup in every room. Whenever any of us coughed she'd get out her spoon and save us from Marguerite Gautier's terrible fate,' I said.

We danced. I passed under Andrés's inquiring eye in the arms of that perfect man. I don't know if it bothered him. I would have liked to dance with Carlos like that.

'Shall we change?' said Lilia as we danced by her and Emilito.

I let go of Quijano and tried to follow Emilito's clumsy steps. I thought of Javier Uriarte and the fun we would have had, and I was angry. Lilia came back. 'Shall we change?' and, letting go of Quijano, she began to dance with me while the two men just stood there in the middle of the dance floor.

'He's so handsome. Where did you find him?'

'Lili, you're crazy. I love you very much,' I said.

'Tell me where.'

I kissed her and we went back to our partners. Quijano whirled me round the floor and I enjoyed the feeling of doing it well. We were never out of step; it was as if we'd rehearsed all our lives. The afternoon was turning cool and Lilia came to say she was leaving.

'Emilio doesn't want to stay till the evening for the *pozole*. Will you come with me to get changed?'

'I'll wait for you,' said Quijano, taking me to the edge of the dance floor. I thanked him and went with Lilia to the ranch house.

In her bedroom were four half-packed cases, with things all over the place in what seemed like an irreversible chaos. I unpinned her veil and crown. Free of the hairpins she shook her head violently, and flowers and tulle flew in all directions. Her black mane fell down her back and she breathed as though she'd been holding it back for hours. She stepped out of her shoes and undid her dress. I tried to help her unbutton it when she actually had it half off. She pulled it up over her head. Her long brown legs were encased in pale stockings and half way up her thigh was one of those old-fashioned garters, elastic covered in white satin and lace. I told her how in my grandmother's day the bride used to throw the garter into the air and a friend had to catch it round her foot before it touched the ground. That way she passed on her good luck and her friend would have a fiancé and a wedding.

'Come on, catch the garter,' she said, prancing around in her bra and pants.

'I've got a husband.'

'This is so you'll get another.'

She kicked the garter in the air and I caught it with my toe. For a moment our feet were entwined together in the lace, until she got hers out with a little jump. I hitched up my dress and arranged the garter round my thigh.

'I've always liked your legs,' said Lilia, putting on the skirt of her suit. It was made of tergal and fell perfectly. She put on a red silk blouse and then the navy blue jacket which matched the skirt. She had lost a shoe. We found it under a suitcase.

'Your stocking seams are crooked,' I said.

'You always say they're crooked,' she said, standing with her back to me so I could straighten them just like any other day.

'So? I put myself there and that's it?' she asked.

'Put yourself where?'

'Underneath him.'

'Yes, underneath, and let him get on with it,' I said and kissed her.

'Give me your blessing then. Like you did when I was little and you were going away,' she said, hearing Emilio calling her.

She was inquisitive and bossy like her father. And, like her father, totally arbitrary.

I put the tip of my fingers on her forehead, lowered it to her chest, then from one shoulder to the other, and watched her hold back laughter and tears, misty eyed and rosy cheeked.

'In the name of the Father, Son and Holy Ghost, may everything work out well for you, especially with the Holy Ghost.'

I sat on the floor till a servant came and asked me if he could take the suitcases down. I got up and, closing the door on Lilia's mess, left the room with the luggage.

Down in the garden there was a kerfuffle as the newlyweds were about to leave in the Ferrari, a present from Andrés to his daughter. 'Just married' had been painted in lipstick on the back and old boots tied to the bumper for sound effects as they drove along. Lilia got in and waved goodbye like a film star. The one who seemed *de trop* was Emilito, looking wistfully towards the bottom of the garden as though expecting someone.

'Goodbye,' said Lilia, puckering her lips to kiss her father, who was presiding over the riotous send-off. Emilito pointed to a black Plymouth which was parked behind: 'We're going in that one, darling. The luggage is already in it.'

The Alatristes senior came up to say goodbye. They kissed their son and Doña Concha began to cry. Lili had not moved from the Ferrari.

'Get out, Lilia,' said Emilito.

'I want to go in this,' she replied.

'We're going in the other one.'

'If that's how you want it, each in his own,' said Lilia, moving over behind the Ferrari's steering wheel and revving up. The boots made a terrible noise and the Ferrari disappeared scandalously through the front gates.

'She's all woman,' said Andrés, fuelling the rage of Milito, who set off after her in the other car. He then offered me his arm, asked me where I'd been and led me on to the dance floor. When we returned to the table of honour, Doña Concha and her husband were no longer there.

'Let's thank our guests,' said Andrés, grabbing a bottle of champagne and two glasses. We went from table to table drinking toasts. Andrés was a genius at the art of giving each guest a special word, thanking them for coming and for their presents.

As he solemnly embraced his *compadre*, Rodolfo said he had to get back to Mexico City. Martín Cienfuegos was with him, they would be leaving together. When he heard this, Andrés laid the cordiality on even thicker and drank the Secretary of the Treasury's health. They hated each other. Each was sure that the other was his deadliest rival on the road to the presidency, and lately Andrés was more sure than Cienfuegos. We accompanied them to the gates.

'That arselicker Martín is singing his own praises to Fattie. And it doesn't take much to convince him, the present of the house alone was enough to get Martín the presidency and his backside too,' said Andrés, when we went back to the table. He said it angrily, and for the first time with regret.

At Bibi's table, Gómez Soto was mumbling in his beard, totally drunk. Quijano got to his feet as we came up.

'Has your daughter gone?' he asked.

'She's gone.'

'They dance beautifully, these two,' said Gómez to my

general, pointing to us. 'You and I are too old to dance.'

'*You* may be too old,' said Andrés. '*I* still do my duty. Don't I, Catín?'

I tried to smile gracefully.

'Don't I, Catalina?' he repeated.

'Of course you do,' I replied, gulping down my champagne as though it were lemonade.

'Will you be coming to Mexico City?' asked Quijano as he kissed my hand.

'Yes, soon,' I said. Andrés was discussing with Gómez Soto who was younger and who had more children.

Bibi watched me with a 'here's your chance, take it' expression, and I remembered I had to go and see that the *pozole* was heated up before everyone got as drunk as her general.

With the food came the fireworks and another band. It was about five in the morning when Natalia Velasco and María Bautista, two of the girls who'd liked me least at cookery class, came up dragging their husbands to thank me for the invitation.

I said goodbye with a smile and all the social etiquette I now handled like a queen after so many years of having none. It was my most exquisite revenge, especially in cases like these.

Inside the house again I went to see if the cheese-and-chilli *tortillas*, dried meat, coffee and bread were being prepared for breakfast. There were about forty women in the kitchen making *tortillas* and sauces. I passed one who was in charge of a huge pan of chilli sauce.

'Don't make it too hot,' I said, without stopping to look at her.

'It is a bit hot,' she replied. 'You don't remember me do you, Señora?'

I looked at her. I said yes and tried to look as though I

knew her, but she must have noticed I couldn't remember when we'd met.

'I'm the widow of Fidel Velázquez, the one they killed in Atencingo. D'you remember the day you took me to your house? I met Doña Lucina then and she asked me to come today. I often see her and she tells me about you.'

'And your children, how are they?' I said, to show her that I did remember something.

'Growing up. Soon I'll only be working for three of them. I work in a textile factory in Atlixco. I supplement that with anything else I can. Today I came here, next week I'm going to cook figs to sell in Puebla.'

'I'll buy them. Come to the house, bring me all you have,' I said, tasting the tomato sauce and asking Lucina for a cup of tea and an aspirin. I had a headache.

I took them into the drawing room, which was filling up with people escaping the cold. I asked for cognac to be offered. I took a glass myself and drank it down. Then I fell asleep in a chair until someone came to tell me the guests wanted to have breakfast.

'What about a siesta?' asked Andrés, dunking a croissant in his coffee.

'All right,' I said. And I slept beside him for the first time since Carlos's death.

CHAPTER TWENTY-TWO

I wanted to frighten away my memories, but it was even more difficult now without Lili's noise around. I'd go from Puebla to Tonanzintla, from Carlos's grave to my garden, incapable of anything more than biting my nails, being grateful to my friends for their compassion, and spending the afternoons with Verania and Checo when they came home from school.

With the children it was all giving and seeming to be happy. I took them to the fair, up to the mountains or to look for frogs in the ponds near Mayorazgo, to rid my head of everything except games and easy solutions. Sometimes I thought I liked being with them. I insisted on constant affection and excitement, but my children had learned to do without me and after some time together it wasn't clear who was tolerating whom.

When I'd sit in the garden sucking bits of grass with my head bent between my crossed legs, they felt bad about coming up to me. They'd leave me alone, go away and find an excuse to call me.

The woman from Atencingo came. One afternoon the children ran up to tell me a lady was selling figs, and that I'd said I would buy them.

They brought her to my corner of the garden, basket and all. It was about five o'clock on a bright afternoon, and standing there in the sunlight with her basket on her arm, her fresh face and big toothy smile, she emanated security and charm.

She sat down beside me, put her basket on the ground and began talking to me as though we were friends and I'd been expecting her. Not once did she apologize for interrupting, ask if she was disturbing me or stop talking to see if my face showed approval.

Her name was Carmela, in case I hadn't remembered, her children were this and that age and, as she'd told me before, her husband was the man murdered at the mill in Atencingo. She'd saved up for a marble cross on his grave and often visited him to discuss how things were going at work and in the fields. I wasn't to know this but she and Fidel had always fought for what was just, that's why they'd helped Lola, that's why she'd joined the union in the factory in Atlixco. All her hate had flooded back when Medina and Carlos were murdered and she couldn't understand why I went on living with General Ascencio. She knew, I must know, everyone knew, what my general was. So in case I wanted, in case I'd ever thought of, just in case . . . she'd brought me some black lemon leaves for my headache and other pains. The tea from these leaves was fortifying but it was also habit-forming and you had to be careful because if you drank it every day it made you feel better temporarily but in the end it killed you. A lady in her village had died after drinking it for just a month, although the doctors never believed that was the cause. Her heart just stopped they said, and didn't know why, but Carmela was sure it was the leaves, because that's what the leaves did, they were good but treacherous. She'd brought them because at the wedding she'd heard me say I had a headache . . . and for anything else I might need them for. She was leaving the figs for me and was going now because it was late and she'd miss the bus back if she didn't.

I listened in silence, nodding sometimes, crying when she talked about Carlos as if she knew him, eating fig after fig while she recommended her herbal tea. She didn't seem to expect me to say anything. When she'd finished what she had to say, she got up and left.

Lucina was playing a game with the children. I could hear them shouting above Carmela's words, but they'd gone further away and then disappeared. Later they came back to eat figs and ask questions. I answered animatedly, talking rapidly, possessed by a sudden strange euphoria. We played, rolling around in the grass, and ended the day jumping on the beds and having a pillow fight. I didn't recognize myself.

Andrés's other daughters listened to our boisterous fun in surprise. The two who still lived in the house in Puebla were practically strangers. Marta was twenty and had a fiancé for whom she embroidered sheets, towels, tablecloths and napkins. They were getting married when he finished his studies and could keep her without having to ask Andrés for anything, not even his blessing. They spent the afternoons in the study. He would be the engineer, but for the time being it was she who drew the plans in Chinese ink. Marta and I never quarrelled, neither did we have much in common. She no longer needed me to hold her horse's tail, and she'd always known how to avoid making noise or allow anyone to bring noise into her life. I don't see her now; she went to live at the ranch she inherited in Orizaba. Her husband swapped engineering for agriculture and they hardly ever leave the place.

With Adriana, Lilia's twin, I didn't have much in common either. She never got on with her sister, whom she considered outrageously frivolous, and with me even less.

She joined 'Catholic Action' behind her father's back and her only act of defiance was to tell him this one night at dinner like someone confessing she's working in a brothel when everyone thinks she's at Mass. No one cared a hoot about her militancy. Even Andrés thought it might be a useful link with the mitre if the need arose. We let her go to church and dress like a nun without criticizing her.

Marta and Adriana weren't company for me, and I wasn't company for Checo and Verania, so I returned to Mexico City. ·

Andrés lived in the house in Las Lomas, at least officially, and so did Octavio and his gentle Marcela. My arrival didn't bother them. They almost thought of me as the matron of honour they would never have.

I started seeing Bibi. Gómez Soto's wife had been generous enough to die two years before and Bibi had passed from clandestine lover to worthy wife. The day of the wedding the general had put all the houses in her name and made a will with her as his sole heir. Everything was milk and honey in the new union. The newlyweds went to New York, then to Venice, and Bibi finally got a suntan outside her own garden. They travelled the country in the train the general had bought to visit his newspapers, and she showed off the international style she had cultivated within her four walls for so long.

One day she arrived at my house very early. I was in the garden in my dressing-gown. I'd felt like a pedicure and was soaking my feet in a basin. I hadn't put my make-up on.

Bibi came rushing in, in flat shoes, trousers and a checked shirt, practically a man. She looked pretty, but very odd. I don't remember if she said hallo; I think the first thing she did was ask me: 'Catalina, how did you manage to love one man and live with another?'

'I don't remember.'

'It's not twenty years ago.'

'It seems more. What's the matter? You look very peculiar.'

'I've fallen in love,' she said. 'I'm in love. I'm in love,' she repeated in different tones, as if talking to herself. 'I'm in love and I can't stand the smelly old fool I'm living with. Smelly, coarse, boring and dirty. Can you imagine, he does deals in the lavatory, he takes people into the train toilet and makes them talk business there. What can I do, married to a man like that? Kill him? I'm going to kill him, Cati, because I won't sleep another single night with him.'

She was unrecognizable. She'd taken her shoes off and sat on the grass with the soles of her feet together, thumping her knees on every third word.

'Who are you in love with?'

'A Colombian bullfighter. He's arriving tomorrow. He's coming to see me and doing a few fights at the same time. I met him in Madrid one afternoon while Odilón was seeing one of General Franco's ministers. I was in a café and he came in, "Can I sit here?" you know how it is. We made love twice.'

'And you fell in love after two times?'

'He's got a divine body. Like a teenager.'

'How old is he?'

'Twenty-five.'

'You're ten years older.'

'Seven.'

'Same thing.'

'Cati, if you're going to act like my mother, I'm going.'

'Sorry. Nice bum?'

'Nice everything.'

'Don't tell me. You want to exchange your general for a

nice foreskin? Has he got enough money to fill your pool with flowers?'

'Of course not, but I'm sick of pools. He's going to be a famous bullfighter; he's very good.'

'At twenty-five? If he's going to be famous he would be already.'

'He began late. It was his parents' fault. He had to study law before taking up bullfighting and leaving Colombia of course. Colombia must be like Puebla.'

'Does he know who your husband is?'

'He knows he owns newspapers.'

'And?' I asked. 'What are you going to do with Odilón?'

'I don't know. I didn't know what to do to get rid of Odi without being left without a bean, but yesterday he went to one of those measuring parties. You know, the ones where they invite whores and they all get undressed to see who's got the biggest prick. The masseuse told me one of her clients had told her. I went disguised as a whore and saw him being totally ridiculous – well he would be, wouldn't he? They were all old fogeys like him, of course they weren't going to measure up with teenagers, but it was really pathetic.'

'How did you get in?'

'The owner of the place took me; she's a client of Raquel's too.'

'That's my Bibi of old. I was afraid you'd gone soft in the head for ever.'

'What should I do? Can you think of anything?'

'Play the offended wife. So offended you're reduced to tears.'

'But I'm not you. I can't act.'

'Write him a letter, say you're leaving him for reasons which he is well aware of and which injure your honour.'

'Write it for me?'

'If you wait while Trini finishes my feet. She's a savage, she finds a tiny bit of skin by your big toenail and before you know it her scissors are half way up your shin.'

'Careful, Señora, or I won't tell you Doña Chofi's latest bit of gossip,' said Trini, who did Chofi too and was in her confidence.

'Can't be any good. My poor *comadre*'s so boring. For fifteen years we've been trying to get a good story out of her and have got nothing but her quarrels with the chauffeur and the cook.'

'And with Don Rodolfo now and again,' said Trini.

'Those are the most boring of all. They fight because Chofi doesn't hang the paintings where Fito tells her, or he loses the gold coins he gets given at his meetings. Silly things.'

'That's not all. I was just about to tell you that the gold coin turned up; the chauffeur had it, and when questioned he said that the Señora had given it to him in payment for a special favour but that he was a man of his word and wouldn't say what it was.'

'No. I don't believe you, Trinita.'

'True as I stand here. Don Rodolfo was furious. He threatened to use his gun.'

'But he didn't.'

'He was going to, but the chauffeur promised to tell all.'

'Fancy Chofi. Poor old Fattie. At her age.'

'You should have seen her. She turned tough. Hand on her hips, she went up to Don Rodolfo, took his gun from him and said: 'If someone has to, I'll tell you. René did me the favour of taking Zodiac to the beauty salon to have his hair cut and washed despite you saying that that's only for pansy dogs.'

'See, they have proper dramas,' I said. 'Not like yours,

Bibi. Big deal, falling in love with a bullfighter. Come on, I'll help you write the letter.'

'Only in rough,' said Bibi, 'because I want to send it on this special paper I bought in Switzerland and I've only got one page and one envelope left.'

'Why the special paper?'

'I know his tricks. If he doesn't like what I say he'll send the letter back in an identical envelope, sealed and everything, as though he hadn't opened it.

'"Letters, Bibi, letters," he says. "I see them all day, every day. If you have something to say I'm at your disposal, just tell me, my love," and he pretends he hasn't read my rebukes. That's why I want this envelope; I've only one left and you can't get them in Mexico. If he opens it, and he will, he'll have to react.'

'What shall we put, then?'

'Well, all about the orgy I saw.'

'Tell me exactly how it went. How did you get there?'

'Raquel helped me. The first thing I did when I came back from Spain all fat was go to see her, she asked me how I was and I told her about Tirsillo and that I wanted to leave Odi, etc. Anyway, it so happened that she also massages a lady who runs one of those "measuring" parlours, and she had told Raquel that my husband had hired it for a stag night for Governor Benítez's brother. You know him, don't you?'

'Yes, of course. And you saw all his too?'

'I saw everybody's everything. Brusca was wonderful. She disguised me as an invalid whore. Because she says they always like expensive attractions. She pretended I'd burned my body and bandaged me from top to toe. I sat in the midst of it all like a mummy. I had to stay like that the whole time. I could barely breathe.'

'You're making it up.'

'I swear. They all arrived together. It was their party. They didn't take any notice of the women. Just them and lots of booze. I got the most attention. "Poor little tart, what will you live off now?" I just lowered my eyes. Odilón didn't look at me much. He was cross I'd been put in the middle.

' "Take that misery away, she puts a damper on things," he said as he patted a little girl's bum. "What about the bridegroom? Let's see his tool." "I'll show you," he said, pulling a blonde girl in front of him. "D'you think it's scared, Blondie?" '

' "Show me, sweetie," she said.

'And the bridegroom took his trousers down. Everyone clapped.

' "Get it up, get it up," they shouted.

'The blonde girl began fondling the prick as though she were whipping chocolate.

' "Very good. Fantastic cutlass, dear brother-in-law," said Victoriano Velázquez, the brother of the bride.

' "Fan-tas-dick, fan-tas-dick," shouted the others. They were like schoolboys at break time.'

'And they all got undressed?'

'All of them. Even my poor husband, who is no longer a pretty sight.'

'And you were watching? How marvellous!'

'Not really. Too many pricks. One is exciting, but not a whole bunch of nude bodies. They were ridiculous. They were all feeling each other. They stood hip to hip to see whose thing was the longest. Really stupid. I didn't see how it ended because Odilón insisted I was pathetic and made Brusca take me out.'

'They made you leave? But what else did you see? Did they fuck the women in front of each other?'

'Not while I was there. They just had them there for

encouragement. The game is between them, they're the ones who are playing, seeing each others' willies; they just put the women there so no one will think they're fairies. That's what Brusca told me. Write me the letter.'

'All right. What do you want from Gómez?'

'The house, the servants, the chauffeurs and money – a lot of money,' she said and began singing, 'As soon as I saw him I told myself, he's my man.'

'That doesn't need too much thought. I think you should be short, sharp but meaty: "Odilón, I was the invalid tart the other night. I want a divorce and a lot of money. Bibi."'

'No, I need to move him, make him see I'm sad. But I'm so happy I can't think of anything dramatic. That's why I came to you, you're an expert in dramas. Don't tell me little messages like that are the best you can do.'

'I think they're the best. Let's be practical for once, Bibi. Why waste words?'

'Since when have you been practical?'

'In the nick of time.'

'Don't start wishing Carlos were alive again because it's impossible, Catín, accept it.'

'I do accept it,' I said, becoming sad.

'I beg you, don't start wailing. This is urgent.'

We spent the morning tearing up rough sketches. 'Odi, my heart is broken.' 'Odi, what I saw has disturbed me so much I don't know if I now feel hate or pity for you.' 'Odi, how can you seek happiness elsewhere and hurt me with behaviour so unworthy of you?' Etc., etc.

In the end, about two in the afternoon, we managed a sorrowful, sober letter. Bibi wrote it out afresh and went home delighted.

*

I didn't see her for three days. On the fourth day she came to the house, she was Señora Gómez Soto once again. She wore a hat with a veil, a grey suit, black stockings and very high heels.

We sat down to talk in the drawing room as befitted her outfit. She lifted her veil, crossed her legs, lit a cigarette and said in a solemn voice: 'I nearly got caught.'

I laughed. So did she. Then she told me the story.

The bullfighter arrived the afternoon she had sent her husband the letter. She went to meet him at the airport and installed him in the Hotel Del Prado. She wasn't too pleased that he'd brought a young gypsy-looking woman along as his assistant, but she wanted to fuck so much that she got each of them a room and pushed the bullfighter into one.

She was so deliriously happy and grateful afterwards that she began talking about the future and described the steps she'd taken to get a divorce as soon as possible. The bullfighter couldn't believe his ears. The woman of the world looking for an occasional lover whom she could thank in the form of various articles deployed in her husband's sports paper had become an enamoured adolescent ready for marriage and martyrdom.

Take on the general? How could Bibi be so naïve as to imagine he could fight in the bullrings of Mexico without backing from her husband's newspaper chain? Besides, *she* might want a divorce but *he* didn't and his assistant was his wife.

With all the dignity she could muster, Bibi got dressed and left the hotel. Despite her haste, she had time to retrieve from the management her authorization to pay the bullfighter's expenses.

At home she searched desperately for the servant she had

given the letter to. Unfortunately, the woman was so efficient she had gone to the lengths of handing it to the general personally.

Bibi locked herself in her room to regret bitterly the sudden impulse of irresponsibility and frivolity which had led to this moment. She hated me for not having warned her, for having been an accomplice in her suicide. She didn't know what to do. She didn't even cry; her tragedy didn't lend itself to anything as glamorous and comforting as tears.

The next day she went down for breakfast at a time her husband usually had his.

She found the general friendly but in a hurry, eating huge mouthfuls of scrambled egg and sausage between gulps of orange juice. When she came in he got up, held her chair and suggested she had the same breakfast as him and forget all about diets and boiled eggs. She agreed to a sausage, she would have agreed to anything. She didn't know whether to thank the general for ignoring the subject or tremble at the thought of the plans he'd be making in the back of his mind.

She opted for gratitude. She'd never been sweeter or prettier, never more suggestive. The breakfast ended with the general cancelling a very important meeting and the two of them going back to bed.

That night they had a dinner at the United States Embassy and when they got back she found the letter unopened on her dressing table. Hadn't her husband seen it? Or where had he found an identical envelope? She fell asleep with her questions, clutching the Swiss paper, still sealed, with her initials on the back.

She woke up in time to organize a romantic breakfast in

the garden by the pool. When the general came down she had put on a white organdy pinny and the smile of wife-cum-angel which had served her so well and which she never wanted to lose. She cooked the breakfast and served it. Then, with the same modesty, as though she were getting undressed, she took the pinny off and sat by the satisfied general.

They were finishing their coffee when the small, nervous assistant who always followed her husband around arrived to remind him of his appointments. Bibi asked him if he'd like some coffee and served him while Gómez Soto went to the bathroom before leaving. They'd become friends, and sometimes laughed about the general's obsessions.

'You've got bags under your eyes,' said Bibi.

'I still haven't recovered from my trip. I went to Switzerland and back in twenty-four hours. Just to buy envelopes, can you believe it?'

'Serve you right for fooling around with your daily bread,' I said when she'd finished.

'After all, it was funny,' she replied. 'If you fancy some fun, Alonso Quijano's showing his new film on Tuesday. He asked me to invite you.'

I talked it over with Palmita, who always seemed so sensible, and in the end I went with her. The film was terrible. But I fancied Quijano again, so much so that I went first to the cocktail party, then to his house and then to his bed without stopping to think for one second about Andrés. But when it started to get light I woke up sort of scared. I wrote a note, 'Thanks for the welcome', and left.

I got home as the sun was barely filtering through the trees in the garden. Just like the morning I had seen it come up with Carlos.

It was so long ago, yet I remember it as if it were yesterday. Scared of Andrés? Scared of what?

I made a lot of noise as I went in; I wanted to be noticed. But he hadn't got back either.

CHAPTER TWENTY-THREE

Without deciding to, I changed.

I asked Andrés for a Ferrari like Lilia's. He gave me one. I wanted him to put money in a personal bank account, enough for my needs, the children's and the house. I had a door made between our bedroom and the next and moved into it with the excuse that I needed more space. Sometimes I slept with the door shut. Andrés never asked me to open it. When it was open, he came to sleep in my bed. In time, we seemed like friends again.

I learned to look at him objectively. I studied the way he spoke, the things he did, the way he went about them. He slowly stopped seeming so unpredictable and arbitrary. I could almost guess what he'd decide to do about what, who he'd send to do which job, how he'd reply to such a minister, what he'd say in his speech of such-and-such a date.

I slept with Quijano many times. He moved to a house with two entrances, two façades, two gardens. One opened on to the street in front and the other behind. He would go in through one door and I the other, and we'd both arrive at exactly the same time in the same sunny, plant-filled room. Quijano was very serious. He would try to describe what he called 'our thing', and speechify about it as though he were rehearsing the screenplay for his next film. He'd go on about my freshness, my spontaneity, my charm. Listening to it all I'd fall asleep and totally relax until hours later.

Andrés bought a house in Acapulco which he never used because he thought the sea was a waste of time. I took it over. We often went at weekends. I'd invite other friends as a smokescreen, take the children, Lilia would come when she wanted a rest from Emilito, and of course Marcela and Octavio. My relationship with Quijano was more or less obvious to all of them, even Verania, who never said a word to her father but kicked Alonso's shins and intrigued with Checo whenever she could.

The house lay between Caleta and Caletilla, surrounded by sea, and the afternoons there passed like a dream. I could have spent every one sitting on the terrace looking out over the infinite like an old woman groping for her memories. For me the sea was Carlos Vives, ever since that time when we had slipped away to a deserted beach in Cozumel for three days. I looked out to sea trying to recapture something. What was best? We had had so much. Why not death, I asked myself, since even on days by the sea the subject inevitably came up.

'I'm going to die of love,' I'd said, laughing, as we strolled along one afternoon, paddling in the warm water.

I was always the one who died, it even seemed romantic to leave him missing me, dreaming of my good qualities, feeling a gap in his body, searching for me in the things we did together.

I often imagined Carlos weeping for me, killing Andrés, mad with grief. Never dead.

In Acapulco I spent hours looking out to sea, Alonso's hand on my leg, remembering Vives.

'Nobody dies of love, Catalina; we wouldn't even if we wanted to,' he had said.

I would have stayed there for good if, in order to have the place, I didn't have to go back to Mexico City and earn it by listening to Andrés's ravings against his *compadre*, his plans for becoming president which were frustrated every other day, his 'hero of the motherland' speeches requested by Puebla every so often.

On top of that, Fito was always calling to ask me to attend strange functions. One day I had to go with him to lay the foundation stone for what was going to be the 'Monument to Mothers'. He gave a speech about the immense joy of motherhood and things like that. Afterwards he invited me to lunch at Los Pinos.

Chofi, who had pleaded a migraine and avoided the sun and the crowd at the inauguration, asked me what I'd thought of Fito's speech. Instead of saying it was spot on or at least keeping quiet, I unfortunately spouted off about the discomfort, boredom and hair-raising re-sponsibilities of maternity. I came over like a real harpy. My love for Andrés's children had been pure invention then; how could I say I loved them if I wasn't even proud of being a mother to my own? But I had no apologies, I neither defended myself nor cared if they thought I was a shrew. I'd sometimes hated being a mother to my own children and other women's, and it was my right to say so.

We said goodbye after coffee, and I didn't hear from them for quite a while. Chofi finally called me when Porfirio Díaz's wife, Doña Carmen Romero Rubio, died. She wanted to know if I was going to the funeral and told me that unfortunately her husband had forbidden her to. She'd always thought poor Carmelita such a victim. This time I agreed with her.

'You're right, poor Carmelita,' I said, 'but where would you and I be if she hadn't got her come-uppance?'

She hung up, certain that her husband had been right to forbid her to go to the funeral.

Alonso, on the other hand, went. He did strange things. I never knew what was going on in his head. He'd go to Carmelita Romero Rubio's funeral for the same reason he'd stay up all night to celebrate the liberation of Paris or spend weeks with the anthropologists who discovered the Toltec sculptures in the city centre. Everything is cinema, he said in his defence.

Andrés was up to his neck in trouble at the time. A journalist had accused his friend the Minister of Finance of complicity with profiteers and of getting rich while ordinary people went hungry. The journalist was a friend of Fito's and Andrés thought his *compadre* was behind the article and that it was directed at him. I tried to persuade him that his theory was rather convoluted, but he was so convinced he wouldn't listen. A few days later the CTM organized a demonstration of 80,000 people to protest the rise in the cost of living, again putting the blame on Andrés's friend. And to cap it all, private enterprise demanded that the Finance Ministry's powers of control be reduced. This confirmed Andrés's theory that Fito was plotting his friend's resignation because, among other things, he was his candidate for the presidency. This time I didn't argue, because Fito signed a law which took away the ministry's power to control the production of cement, manufactured goods and heaven knows what else. Stripped of his authority, my general's candidate resigned.

Andrés spent the days cursing Fito, the Left and Maldonado, the leader he had chosen to get rid of Cordera. He was so furious he didn't even want to go to the president's annual 1 September speech. When the day came I had to persuade him to get dressed; fights with Rodolfo should be fought in private, I said.

We went to yet another of his *compadre*'s tedious speeches, and to our surprise enjoyed ourselves, because the deputy who replied to the speech spoke of a president's responsibility to God to save the motherland, criticized the way elections were held and, in passing, accused the Right of discrediting the Revolution and the Left of sowing immorality and anarchy. Nobody was pleased. When Fito left the Chamber, the other deputies attacked the speechmaker and removed him from office. Andrés nearly died laughing at the spectacle. He enjoyed the prospect of his *compadre* having problems and turning to him when he couldn't handle them alone. That's why he had been appointed adviser, to handle problems. But this time Fito decided not to need him.

After congratulations at the Government Palace there was to be a dinner with the cabinet. To his amazement, Andrés was not seated on his *compadre*'s left. The card with his name was placed on one side of the table, at the end of a string of ministers. Not first and foremost, where it usually was. On Fito's right was a very old general who was Secretary of Defence, and on his left Martín Cienfuegos.

Andrés hated Cienfuegos more than ever. Again he regretted having helped him when he was only a little shyster lawyer, again he was furious with his mother for having taken a shine to him and loving him like an adopted son.

He couldn't remember the exact moment Cienfuegos had ceased to be his ally and subaltern and decided to go it alone; perhaps it was the very morning Andrés introduced him to Rodolfo many years ago, or perhaps only when, as Governor of Tabasco, he had been first to support General

Campos's candidacy and later become his campaign manager, or any of the other things that now came flooding back, interrupted only to call him a bloody opportunist.

Throughout the meal Andrés studied Cienfuegos, seated on Rodolfo's left with a bigger smile and better coiffure than ever. He arrived home cursing his *compadre* because he was stupid enough to leave the presidency to that phoney bastard Martín Cienfuegos. His *compadre* was like that, he let himself be swayed, he was impressed by posh people, the fewer soldiers the better, the more elegant the person the more dazzled the fool was.

He began drinking and ranting and raving, still hoping that Fito would call him. But Fito didn't call. A few days later he got the leader of the Chamber to revoke the agreements of 1 September and reinstate the deputy who replied to the speech.

Andrés couldn't resist going to see Fito. He came back from Los Pinos vomiting bile and with a blinding headache. He couldn't stand light. He shut himself in a darkened room and told me over and over again how Fattie had praised the way Cienfuegos had helped solve his problem. What made him even more angry was his *compadre* saying he hadn't consulted Andrés because he hadn't wanted to bother him. He didn't want to believe that Fito could get by without his advice and help. He couldn't believe it, although it was clearer and clearer with every day that passed and more and more matters were settled or unsettled without anyone even so much as asking his opinion. It seemed as though Rodolfo alone was going to decide who would follow him as President, and it was increasingly obvious that his *compadre* was hindering him in this.

Andrés couldn't get rid of the headache he'd got on that last visit to Los Pinos. One day I offered him Carmela's tea. He drank it down while he pooh-poohed peasants' superstitions, but when the pain eased and he felt like going out and facing Rodolfo again, he gazed into his empty cup.

'I'm sure it's just a coincidence, but it won't hurt to drink it,' he said.

'Not at all,' I replied, pouring myself a cup.

It was a dark-green liquid that tasted of mint and *epazote*. After drinking it I went out to dinner with Alonso and was with him until dawn. I laughed a lot and wasn't sleepy at all. Carmela's tea did me good too but I didn't drink any the next morning. Andrés, however, wanted more, that morning and every morning until he reached the point when he had nothing for breakfast but that.

He would wake up cursing his *compadre*, Old Fattie Campos, and the time he'd wasted buttering him up, and lie on his bed chewing over the previous day's defeats and plotting some new attack on Martín Cienfuegos until I sweetened his green tea.

One day, after his tea, he asked his assistant for the newspapers because he'd had a premonition, or so he said. He must have known something about it, but he pretended to be surprised at the headlines. The attorney-general's office, in the guise of a lawyer named Rocha, a faithful servant of Cienfuegos's, had unearthed the case of the disappearance and death of a certain Señor Maynez in Puebla. According to the article, it had been requested by his daughter Magdalena, who swore that the author of the crime was the then Governor of Puebla, General Andrés Ascencio.

All the witnesses who years ago had been content to merely say their rosaries came out and described the car that kidnapped lawyer Maynez near the cinema, his voice calling for help through the window, the many successful cases he had fought that were contrary to the governor's interests. Magda described the morning we had met in

Cuernavaca. She said she had seen her father arguing with Andrés Ascencio and had asked him why. Her father had told her that the governor was interested in the Agua Clara hotel and recreation area and had forbidden him to plead the owners' case against the state embargo. Magda said that her father had not only refused but had also turned down the thirty per cent of the value of the land that the governor had offered him to lose the case. 'That,' she concluded, 'was when he threatened to kill him.'

Andrés got to his feet yelling and cursing. I still had the newspapers on my knees when his assistant came in with a summons from the attorney-general.

'They are bigger fools than bastards,' said Andrés. 'As if I didn't have something on all of them.'

He poured another cup of tea and went to the bathroom whistling. He came out of the shower delighted and pink. Naturally he didn't go to the attorney-general but to see Fito.

Who knows what they talked about, but the result was that the next day the papers published an interview with the attorney-general in which he exonerated Andrés from any responsibility and referred to him several times as the respected principal adviser to the president.

Apart from Magdalena, whom nobody ever heard of again, all the witnesses said they had been mistaken, and a few days later the guilty parties were established as being members of a gang of hired criminals who were unfortunately not able to give evidence because they had died in a shoot-out with the police who tried to arrest them.

At any rate, Andrés was hurt and didn't see Fattie again, but he didn't have to resign his post. He bought a cigarette factory and planned to make it the biggest in Mexico. He returned to his theme of real power lying in the hands of the rich and decided to become a banker so that in the future all the bastards who sat on the Eagle Throne, on which Zapata had wisely not wished to be photographed, would do his bidding.

I wasn't sorry to see him lose his power. Alonso and I socialized as if we were a couple. We dined at Ciro's almost every night. He took me to all the gala occasions and I spent hours with him on his film sets. One night, after a bottle of wine, he even kissed me in public.

I arrived home at dawn and didn't open my bedroom door for weeks. Just occasionally I'd have tea with Andrés in the mornings like someone visiting her grandmother.

I spent the whole of December in Acapulco without the slightest twinge of remorse. The children were on holiday, their father had always said that Christmas was a stupid invention, why should we spend it together?

However, a few days before New Year I called to ask him just as a formality to come and spend it with us. Imagine my surprise when he turned up on the morning of the 31st. He had lost about ten kilos and gained about ten years, but he still walked as straight as a ramrod and hadn't lost the ironic smile which had served him so well. Verania called to him from the terrace and ran down to kiss him. He had brought Marta and Adriana and their fiancés. Lilia was already there with her boring husband, so were Octavio and Marcela. The general's whole family.

Naturally Alonso was already installed and my other guests were Mónica and her children, Palma and Julia Guzmán. Bibi and Gómez Soto and Helen Heiss and her children were arriving that night. Octavio and Marcela had invited three couples and Lilia had brought Georgina Letona, her husband's ex-fiancée. She was trying to marry her off to my brother Marcos, as if she didn't know Milito was still fucking her, or perhaps because she did know.

Anyway, there were more than fifty of us for dinner. I

thought that with all those people Alonso wouldn't be noticed and I was as sweet as I could be to Andrés. I even apologized for filling the house with people when he was hoping for a family reunion. We spent the afternoon on the terrace drinking gin with lemon while Alonso walked happily with Verania along the beach and Checo was bent on killing crabs.

Andrés was silent for a long time and then said: 'The bull killed Armillita in San Luis Potosí, and Briones in El Toreo. Where will it get me?'

His voice was so gloomy I felt almost sorry for him. Apparently a clairvoyant had told him that when two bullfighters were killed within a fortnight of each other, his death would come within the year.

'Well, you're all right then because this year is over,' I said laughing. 'Unless you die tonight, by the time another two bullfighters are killed in the space of a fortnight you'll have outlived us all.'

'You're still my ray of sunshine,' he answered in an odd voice.

I didn't know if he was making fun of me or if the gin went to his head quicker than it used to. Either way it made me nervous and I kissed him.

CHAPTER TWENTY-FOUR

The year didn't begin well for Alonso. He found Andrés's presence in Acapulco unbearable. It was only natural. Despite his perfect body and fashion-magazine attire, despite his youthful face and pleasant manner, Andrés was a bigger presence than he was. He only had to walk into a room or go up to a group and everything revolved around him. He was a hero to his children, the centre of attention for my guests, the owner of the house and my husband to boot.

That afternoon I proposed a trip to Pie de la Cuesta to watch the sun go down. Quijano didn't want to come. On our return, Lucina told us that he'd been urgently called away to a film set. Later she gave me a brief note, saying,

I'm leaving. I suppose you understand why. In spite of everything, I love you. Alonso.

At dinner that night Andrés made more than twenty jokes about the 'pin-up boy' who'd been good enough to leave us alone *en famille*. His children laughed at all of them, me at some of them.

The first night I felt guilty about Alonso, the second I moved into Andrés's bedroom. The children never got a bigger surprise than the one we gave them that New Year, obviously reconciled, with kisses in public and little lovers' courtesies.

We went back to Mexico City well into January. I didn't ring Quijano. I was busy with Andrés's tantrums and helped him criticize Fattie and endure the imminent candidacy of Cienfuegos.

At the beginning of February we went to Puebla, where Andrés's choice for governor was taking office. In Puebla, Andrés was still the cacique, his power was intact and he loved all the honours and deferential treatment he received. He felt so comfortable and secure there that he forgot his job of presidential adviser. I had no wish to return to Mexico City either and shared that immense house with him, empty when Lucina accompanied the children back to their various schools.

He was getting old; one day his leg would hurt, another it would be his knee. He drank endless brandies through the afternoon and evening and his black lemon tea all morning. I'd have been moved to pity if the garden and room with the fern didn't constantly remind me of Carlos.

Lilia came to see me every day, told me the latest gossip and made me laugh. I saw my friends sometimes in the afternoons. Mónica worked so furiously hard that she only had time to drop in, say hallo and disappear. Pepa, on the other hand, stayed in the garden the whole afternoon and the tranquillity of her encounters in the market showed on her face and in her speech. I also made up for lost time with my sister Bárbara, my guardian angel, or better than an angel because she didn't judge me, she just died laughing or cried buckets and, like me, went from one to the other quite effortlessly. She was with me the afternoon Andrés came home feeling very ill. He'd been to Tehuacán where they'd been paying him some tribute – one of those functions he sometimes went to, surrounded by the state authorities who honoured him publicly and treated him like a boss. That particular day he'd gone with the new governor, the mayor of Puebla and of course the mayor of Tehuacán, where he had been the town's favourite son.

It was about five when we heard the cars draw up at the gates.

'What a bore, Bárbara,' I said, 'he's back. He'll make me listen to him recounting his glories.'

He'd spent breakfast reminding me of the unrest among the workers when he had become governor, and how under his administration roads had been improved, schools had been built and the discontent had disappeared.

'I'm going to tell them,' he said. '"I'm not here as your governor – that part of my life is over – I'm here as a son of the state of Puebla, a citizen, a man who gives you his heart." What d'you think? Tell me what you think, Catalina, what else are you here for?'

He'd become so crazy over the last few months that he'd made me his private secretary again and I'd gone along with it just for something to do. I handed him a sheet of paper with a speech I'd drafted and pointed to some paragraph or other. He read it aloud: '"I will serve this town as an official and a simple citizen, both here and when I'm away. I beg you to bury dissent, ignore difficulties and go on working together with enthusiasm, as brothers, as men who fought the Revolution for a specific social programme, one which I would fight alongside you to defend once again if the need arose. I bring no personal political ambition, because I have already done my duty as governor. I bring only the desire to protect the peace and progress of our beloved state."'

He finished reading and said, 'I was right about you,

bloody clever, like a man, that's why I forgive you your loose morals. I fucked with you better than anyone. You're the best woman, and the best man, I know, you bastard.'

Before leaving he sent for his tea and offered me a cup. I drank it slowly, waiting to be overtaken by the strange euphoria it produced.

Matilde was still in the room. She put the tea on the table, watched us drink it and said to Andrés: 'Forgive me interfering, General, but you drink this tea very often, and too much isn't good for you.'

'Ah, it does no harm. I'd already be dead if it weren't for the tea. It stops me feeling tired.'

'But in the long run it's bad for your health. I've noticed, you're getting worse.'

'Not because of the tea, Matilde. Don't tell me you believe in those things?' said Andrés, taking one last sip. 'Look how gorgeous the Señora is, and she drinks it too.'

CHAPTER TWENTY-FIVE

The mayor of Puebla came running into the room with the fern. 'Señora, the general seems to have got over-excited. Come quickly, he's not well.'

I went down to what used to be our bedroom. Andrés was lying on the bed, even paler than usual and having difficulty breathing.

'What's the matter? Didn't you feel well? Why didn't you stay for the dinner?'

'I was tired and didn't want to die in the street. Call Esparza and Téllez.'

'Don't go overboard about it. Everyone gets tired. You've been rushing around like a madman for months. You should go to Acapulco more often.'

'Acapulco. Only you can stand that ghastly place. And you do it to escape, so you can abandon me by pretending the sea does you good. What does you good is getting away from me.'

'Liar.'

'Don't play the innocent. We both know what the house in Acapulco is for.'

'You apparently don't know, you hardly ever go.'

'I haven't time to go paddling about, and I can't rest there. The sea bothers me, it's never quiet, like a woman. I fancy going to Zacatlán. You can rest in the mountains and the days are so long there's time for everything.'

'But there's nothing to do. What d'you need time for?' I said.

'Always criticizing my town, you rootless old bag,' he said, trying to get his boot off.

'I'll get Tulio to help you, don't strain yourself, you really are tired.'

'I told you to phone Téllez, but you want me to die without help.'

'We call Téllez every time you sneeze; it's pitiful.'

'Pity is the last thing you feel. Phone him. Now I'm really going to set you up. I'm dying. Call him as a witness so they can't say you poisoned me.'

I sat on the edge of the bed and massaged his leg. He went on talking with a calmness I'd glimpsed just a couple of times before. He was strange.

'I fucked your life up, didn't I?' he said. 'The others got what they wanted. But what do you want? I've never figured out what you want. Not that I gave it much thought, but I'm not a total fool, I know there are many women inside you and I only knew a few of them.'

He had slowly been growing old. Over the last few weeks he'd got thin and bent, but that afternoon he grew older by the minute. Suddenly his jacket swamped him. His shoulders were shrivelled and his face wizened, his chin was lost in the stiff collar of his military tunic and the braid seemed more rigid than usual.

'Take that off,' I said. 'I'll help you.'

I began undoing that hard shell, wrestling with gold buttons which were always bigger than the buttonholes. I pulled one sleeve off and turned him over to pull the other. I kissed his neck.

'Do you really want to die?' I asked.

'Why should I want to die? I don't want to, but I'm dying, can't you see?'

Esparza and Téllez – our most prestigious local doctors, who treated Andrés for his sporadic colds and diarrhoea, and all the major illnesses he invented every three days – entered the room with their usual phlegm, convinced that the matter would be dealt with in the usual way, by giving the general the same aspirins but a new colour. Last month we'd called them whenever my husband had nothing to do or wanted someone to talk to. He was desperate to have people around, listening to him, revering him, and since we'd taken most of his usual cronies with us to Mexico City, in Puebla he always ended up phoning Esparza or Téllez or both, and Judge Cabañas for good measure, so the consultation would turn into a poker game.

'What are you dying of today, General?' asked Téllez, going through the usual ritual with Esparza. They listened to his heart, took his pulse, made him breathe in and out slowly. The only thing that was different was Andrés's comments. Usually while they gave him his check-up he'd relate all his many and conflicting aches and pains. This hurt him, that hurt him and there where the doctor had his hand, that was painful too. That afternoon he did not complain at all.

'Go through the motions, you bastards,' he said, 'I'm going to die anyway. I hope you'll mourn me a while at least, in memory of all you've got out of me. I hope you'll mourn me because this old bag who pretends to be my wife is already celebrating. Just look at her, she can't wait to run off with whoever lets her. There'll be lots of them because she's still fanciable, in fact, even more than when I met her all those bloody years ago. How many, Catalina? You were a child. Lovely hard bum, and head, you were so hardheaded. It hasn't softened over the years. Your bum yes, but your head, not a bit. Luckily Rodolfo will be there to check up on her. My *compadre* Rodolfo, so stupid, poor thing.'

'You need rest,' said Téllez. 'Did you take any kind of stimulant? It looks as though you were overcome by the emotion of the tribute. Just rest, General. We'll give you some pills to help you relax. You're only tired, you'll be a different man tomorrow.'

'Of course I will, you bastards, stiff and cold. More rested too, naturally. You don't realize how much I'll be missed; the country needs men like me. You'll see when you're left in the hands of Fito and his stupid candidate. Me? Tired? Fattie's the one who's tired, he can't even think straight. Fancy making Cienfuegos his candidate!'

'Are you sure it's Cienfuegos? Who told you?'

'No one told me, I just know. I know a lot of things, and I know my *compadre*, he'll give his arse to the first person who asks for it. Martín asked in a thousand ways, most of them deceitful. He even made him believe he was intelligent.'

Cienfuegos was Andrés's worst enemy because he was untouchable. Not because he had once been Andrés's protégé, nor because he was Fito's favourite minister, but because he was a professional charmer who had won Doña Herminia over in an afternoon, and since Andrés was her only son she was obsessed by trying to find him brothers. When he was little she'd made Fito into a brother for him, and when he was older she'd fallen for the smile and flattery of the boy from the Caribbean coast, Martín Cienfuegos.

'Martín will be like another son to me, he'll be the one who died. And he'll be like a brother to you, understand, Andrés Ascencio?' said Doña Herminia.

From then on Andrés began distrusting Cienfuegos's charm and turned him into the rival he inevitably became.

'I'm giving you another brother,' said his mother. 'Look after him, Andrés, because he even reminds me of your father. Would you like to be my son?' she asked Martín, who was listening to her more attentively than the Chamber of Deputies.

'It will be an honour, Señora,' he said, bending over the rocking-chair to kiss Doña Herminia's forehead, then hugging her, caressing her cheek and finally, on his knees, kissing her hands.

I can't remember a better staged scene of filial love. He even cried tears of gratitude. Not even Andrés who idolized the old woman could have done anything like it. He came back from Zacatlán livid. He spent the whole return journey calling him a fucking phoney bastard. Apparently in jest, but that's where it stayed.

'What kind of brothers did that mother of mine give me?' he began, sitting on his bed. 'Not a single one who understands anything. First she took a shine to Fattie Campos, and then that phoney bastard Martín. My mother is a fool, an ignorant woman who wants to mother anyone who smiles at her and kisses her. At least I didn't inherit her stupidity. But she adopted Campos and he inherited it. You should see him. The idiot thinks he can do it all, showing off and pretending to be so refined and upright. As if he could achieve anything with laws and compliments. He has laws for everything. What about the one making every Mexican teach another to read and write? That, according to him, solves the problem. Soon there won't be a single Indian who can't write his name, the name of the country and naturally the name of the worthy president. Fattie is a genius, you only have to look at his face. And his 'brother' Martín, his little candidate, will bugger up what's left of the country. That bastard is even capable of selling hope to the highest bidder. Soon he'll be putting the sighs of 3,000 unemployed in tins and selling them to the *gringos* for when they want to feel depressed. He'll sell the Independence Angel, the Juárez Monument and Church of Guadalupe if you're not careful. Souvenirs from Mexico: waves from Acapulco, bits of La Quebrada as relics and pieces of women's bums wrapped in cellophane. Everything very modern, very American, so you don't notice the peasants, the pigs, the idiots, the untouchables. The other Mexico. Shame I'm going to die, because with me alive only guns would get that bastard the presidency, and I can outgun him, him and all the other prissy little bastards who apparently support him. And may my blessed mother forgive me, but I'd rid that fucking phoney bastard of his mothers for good. Both of them, the whore who bore him and the idiot who adopted him.'

'Stop all that now you're dying,' I said. 'Why don't you do what Dr Téllez says, take your pills and play some poker before going to bed?'

'I am in bed, but not how I like it, looking at the ceiling with nobody on top of me.'

'We're leaving,' said Esparza.

'Not before time, you bastards,' replied Andrés.

'Get some rest, General, no coffee, no brandy, no stimulants. I'll be round tomorrow to thrash you at poker.'

They left me alone with him. I sat on the edge of the bed.

'Like some more tea?' I said, pouring it out.

He sat up to drink it and asked me again: 'What do you want, Catalina? Are you going to flirt with Cienfuegos? Who is Efraín Huerta? And how does he know that between your breasts drops a tear of tenderness?'

'Where did you find his poems?' I asked.

'Locks are no good in my house.'

'What is any good?'

'He was a friend of Vives's, wasn't he? He doesn't know you very well, you don't have tears between your breasts or anywhere. And tenderness, Catalina? How naïve of him! He's not in the Communist Party for nothing.'

I went over to the window. Go on, die, I murmured as he rambled on until he fell asleep. I lay down beside him.

He woke up shortly afterwards, put a hand on my legs and caressed me. I opened my eyes, winked at him and wrinkled my nose.

'Why don't you get up and ring Cabañas?' he said. 'My leg aches.'

'Not Téllez?'

'Cabañas, Catalina, there's no time to lose.'

When Cabañas arrived, both his legs were stiff and he was speaking slowly.

'Did you bring the second one, Cabañas?' he said with difficulty.

'Yes, General, I brought all of them.'

'Give me the second one.'

'What's the second one?' I asked.

He didn't answer. He signed with his eternal fountain pen with the green ink.

A moment later he was dead.

CHAPTER TWENTY-SIX

I called his children. Someone told Rodolfo and he arrived at about eleven that night. He turned up with his paunch, his languor and his wealth, and wanted to organize everything.

'We'll take him to Zacatlán.'

'As you wish,' I replied.

'That's what he wanted.'

'Yes, Señor President, we'll take him to Zacatlán.'

'Thank you for everything. I know about the will.'

'No need to thank me. I'll try to do it well.'

'If you've any problems, you can count on me.'

'I'm counting on you to stop me having any,' I replied.

'I don't understand; he was like a brother to me, you're his wife, what d'you want me to do?'

'Don't interfere, don't help me, don't make agreements with the other widows. They'll all get their share, but they'll have to come to me for it.'

'Who are the other widows?'

'*Compadre*, you're not talking to your wife, you know. I know perfectly well who the other widows are and how many of his children were not living with us. I know which farms and houses are for which. I know which property, which money, even down to the last watch and cufflinks, is for which.'

He said nothing, nodded his head and went to stand beside the grey coffin. He tried on an expression of grief but only managed the one of boredom he took with him everywhere.

People flooded into the house. They elbowed their way through to Rodolfo. The men embraced him and patted him on the back and the women squeezed his hand.

I stood on the other side of the coffin; I didn't want to sit down. I spent the whole night shaking hands and receiving embraces. I did not cry. I talked continuously. With each one I spoke of him, remembering where they had met and when we'd seen each other last. Fito went to bed at about two in the morning. Lucina brought me a tea. I sat down for a minute. In the chair next to me was Checo. He seemed so young.

'How are you, Mama?' he asked.

'Fine, my love, and you?'

'I'm fine too.'

We didn't speak again. Verania had gone to bed earlier. The doctor had come to check up on Marta because she'd felt faint.

'I see your boyfriend hasn't come to give you his condolences,' said Adriana when we were alone.

'Don't talk like that,' I told her.

'Don't try and teach me manners now. It's a bit late,' she replied. 'Besides, everyone knows about Alonso. I'm sure half the people here have come to see him arrive with a "I was a friend of the dead man" expression.'

She was right. And she was resentful. How well directed her hate was. Lilia, Marcela and Octavio stayed with me till dawn.

The procession of mourners went on all night. I didn't move from my widow's place.

'I admire your fortitude, Señora,' said Bermúdez, who acted as master of ceremonies when Andrés was governor.

'Congratulations, Doña Catalina,' said the mayor's wife.

There was a bit of everything. I think I enjoyed myself that night.

I was the centre of attention and I liked that. All eyes were on me as they came in, almost everybody wanted to hug me and whisper little things, but the best was what Josefita Rojas said to me. She came in with the same hurried steps and upright bearing with which she walked the streets of the city, as though she wanted to wear them out. She never went in a car, she walked everywhere. She lived on the hillside in Loreto and would walk down to the centre, to Santiago, or wherever she was invited, with those purposeful steps which kept her still young. Josefita hugged me hard, then took me by the shoulders and looked me straight in the eye.

'I'm happy for you,' she said. 'Widowhood is the ideal state for women. You bury your dead husband, you honour his memory whenever necessary, and then get on with all the things you couldn't do when he was alive. Let me tell you from experience, there's nothing better than being a widow. Especially at your age. As long as you don't make the mistake of getting another man too soon, your life will change for the better. Don't let anyone hear me, but it's true. I hope the poor corpse forgives me saying so.'

At about six in the morning I thought I should change my clothes and wash. There was almost no one in the drawing room at that hour. I went up to the open coffin and saw Andrés's dead face. I looked for some trace of sweetness in his face, one of those complicitous winks he sometimes gave me, but I only found the stiff expression he had when he was angry, when he went days without talking to me because something was worrying him and he couldn't even interrupt his train of thought to say good-night.

'Goodbye, Andrés,' I said. 'They're coming to take you to Zacatlán. You wanted to go there to rest and Fito is determined to please you. Now he'll give you whatever you want, ask him whatever you want. How ugly you are. That expression frightens me. That particular expression always has. Show it to someone else, I've enough problems without having to deal with reproachful looks from you. You didn't expect me to kill myself out of grief, did you? You heard what Josefita said, I'm going to be much better off without you. I don't want to go to your funeral; they're bound to want to put me in Rodolfo's car and I'll have to put up with him all the way to Zacatlán. You'll be in your coffin, away from it all, and I'll have to put up with him. Will it always be like that? When will I get him off my back? He'd better not try and get on my front. You yes, because you were charming and you caught me young. How you amused me, how you frightened me! When you looked like that you frightened me. That was the look you had when I shouted at you for having killed Lola. What's it got to do with you, you said. So you're leaving everything for me to share out. What you want is to make trouble, as usual. D'you want me to see how difficult it is? Who gets what? D'you want me to guess, to think of you while the ghast-liness of giving everyone their due lasts? D'you want to see if I keep everything? Who d'you think you are? Won't you ever leave me in peace, are you going to torment me all my life, even when you're dead will you dominate my thoughts, think I'm going to look after your children and your wives? You'd like that, to keep on being a burden. Who gets what, I'll be the judge? Think I'm going to keep wagging tongues happy by keeping everything myself? So that they can say they were right, that they always knew I was just an opportunist. Or d'you think I'm going to go begging Fito for charity? No, Andrés, I'm going to make them toss for it, to see which wife wins this ugly old house, who the ranches in the mountains, who Santa Julia, who La Mandarina, who the business with Heiss, who the bootleg alcohol stills, who the bullring, who the cinemas, who the shares in the race-course, who the big house in Mexico City and who the smaller ones. Heads or tails, Andrés, and whoever is hidden away somewhere, let her stay there, I won't throw Olga out of the Veracruz farm or Cande out of the house in Teziutlán. I wouldn't be crazy enough to want someone else's house. I want a smaller house, by the sea, near the waves, my own house where nobody asks me to do things, orders me about or criticizes me. A house where I can enjoy remembering the good things. Your smile some afternoon or other, the games we played on horseback, the day we tried out our new Ford convertible and drove like crazy to Mexico City for the first time. That night you said, "Let me undress you," and you took my clothes off slowly, and I was still until I stood there naked, looking at you. I always looked at you with gratitude in those days. I began trembling with cold and I felt ashamed, naked in the middle of the room. You pursed your lips and took a step backwards, "You're so lovely," you said, as though you were seeing me for the first time and I wasn't yet yours. I didn't want to go on standing there, I said, "Stop it, Andrés, don't look at me like that," and got quickly under the sheets. You came to me and put your finger in my belly button. "What do you keep in this little hole?" you asked, and I said, "A secret." You searched for that secret the whole night, remember? I want to sleep, to lie in a bed all to myself, without your legs crossing mine at midnight, without your snoring. I'd go to bed now but I have to go to Zacatlán. I hate that rainy place, full of chicken markets, but I want to see the people standing in their doorways watching us go by with you a corpse, finally. The peasants who sow your crops and tend your cattle will look sad, but they'll really be delighted and that night they'll drink cherry brandy and laugh at us. "There goes the widow," they'll say. "She's a crafty one, she almost paid him back in the same coin. Dirty old man, bastard, thief, murderer." "Charming," someone will say. "Crazy," your mother's friend Doña Rafa will murmur. A hundred years old, she'll watch you pass from her wooden rocking-chair. "Crazy," she'll say, "I always told Herminia that boy had turned out half crazy." "A go-getter," your mother would reply, "that's what I like about him." That's what I liked about you too. But how could I have fancied someone so ugly? Had I imagined you like this the afternoon we met, I'd never have got mixed in so much mess, I wouldn't be here alone watching the sun come up, with no desire at all to go and bury you. But I have to. I'm going to get dressed. What shall I put on? Not widow's weeds. You used to give me good ideas sometimes. Remember when I bought the red silk dress in that shop in New York? I didn't want it, you chose it, and I like wearing it. A widow in red wouldn't look good but in that dress I could play to the gallery much better. Rodolfo would be nice to me. I remember when I wore it for Independence Day last year. Late in the evening, after a lot of toasts, his presidential sash askew, he had pulled me towards the balcony, and made me go out onto it over a square that was slowly emptying. "In that dress you look like part of the flag. I haven't been able to keep my eyes off you, I had to restrain myself from shouting after the Long Live Mexico, Long Live Independence, 'Long live my *comadre* who is as beautiful as Mexico.'" He lunged at me, and I shot off to find you. He followed me, "I was just telling your wife how lovely she looks, you don't mind, do you?" he said, as though he were afraid I'd tell. He didn't know you, he didn't know that you'd be on his side, that you'd have said I was vain if I'd told you about his ridiculous behaviour. It's very late, I haven't left much time for getting changed, I can't go looking like this. There will be photographers, and Martín Cienfuegos will be there.'

I put on a black wool dress and an astrakhan coat. I couldn't find any flat shoes. I had about ninety pairs of shoes and couldn't find a single comfortable black pair. I only dressed in black for parties. I couldn't even find a court shoe, and only Chofi would wear open-toed shoes in this cold and with this coat. I put very little make-up on, mascara on my eyelashes and cream on my lips, no rouge. My hair was scraped back in a bun. Andrés would have said I was a splendid widow.

We left at nine. A caravan of about forty cars. Close friends, apparently. I wanted to go with Checo and my chauffeur Juan. I made the most of Fito's decision to carry the coffin out to the waiting hearse with the governor, Martín Cienfuegos and a union leader.

'You and I'll go in the Packard,' I said to Checo. 'Call Juan.'

We got in and Juan slotted in after Fito's car, which was behind the hearse. I thought it better not to drive all the way looking at it.

We sat in the back seat, just the two of us. I stretched my legs and kissed my son. We were just getting comfortable when Rodolfo's secretary came to tell me the president had said I should go with him in the other car.

'Thank him, but I'm fine here; I don't want to leave the boy alone.'

He went away and came back more forcefully: 'He says bring the boy.'

I was going to give another excuse when Fito appeared. His secretary opened the door and without more ado he got into our car.

'Forgive me, Catalina,' he said, 'I didn't know you were already settled. I don't want you to go alone. You and I must travel together behind the hearse. You don't have to follow my car, at a moment like this we're just family. I'm not the president today.'

Without that pose what's left of you, I wanted to say, but I just smiled a sad smile as though I were thanking him for his concern although my grief prevented me from expressing it in words.

I moved over so he could sit beside us. That car was huge, five people could fit in the back easily. Between the back seat and the chauffeur was a pane of glass which I never closed. I liked talking to Juan and listening to him singing. The first thing Rodolfo did was try and close it. It was stiff, but his secretary struggled with it until the handle turned and the glass moved upwards. I felt bad for Juan, he wasn't used to such rudeness. Checo noticed it. He was a good friend of Juan's. Juan had been his father and mother for a long period. He said he wanted to sit in the front so he could see; he got out and was sitting beside Juan in a trice. He turned to look at me. Bloody kid, he left me with Rodolfo and his secretary.

'Tell Regino to move the car in front. You go with him,' ordered Fito, and we were alone. I put my head in my hands and sighed. The president was unbearable.

The cars moved off slowly as if we were just going over to the French Cemetery.

'It'll take two days to get there at this speed,' I said to Rodolfo when we finally left the city. He looked back. You couldn't even see the end of the line of cars following us.

'You're right,' he replied, and lowered the glass to tell Juan to call to the driver of the hearse in which Andrés was riding to his final tribute. He would have been delighted by so many people. The driver of the hearse led the cortège at a less funereal speed.

'Is that better?' asked Fito, stroking my gloved hand.

We drove through grey, dusty towns. The towns are all like that before you reach the mountains, little greenery grows, only grey earth and dusty peasants. In some, the governor had organized groups of Party faithfuls to stand by the roadside with flowers. We stopped when we saw them, and the most important of them came up to the car and shook hands. The others put the flowers on the hearse and then stood nearby with their sombreros in their hands.

I felt incredibly sleepy. I made a valiant effort not to nod off, but my eyes started to close.

'Get comfortable and sleep,' said Fito.

I was wide awake at the very suggestion. I couldn't bear the thought of him seeing me asleep, perhaps babbling unawares. What humiliation. I preferred talking to him. About himself, Andrés, our children, the country, the war.

We had never talked for so long. He was not as stupid as I'd imagined. And less boring. Or perhaps it just seemed like that because we ended up talking about the succession and what he thought of each of the candidates. I managed to get out of him that Cienfuegos was his choice. He talked about him until we reached Zacatlán at about five.

The streets were filled with onlookers. 'All those seeing me are eyes,' said a lorry that overtook us on the road. I thought of it like that. Arseholes, Andrés would say, all those watching me and criticizing are arseholes.

266

We went to the main square to pick up Doña Herminia. Fito hugged her.

There in the street, clinging on to Rodolfo, she seemed older and more fragile than ever, but as soon as she got in the car she recovered her strong, detached self. Not a tear or a word. Ninety-four years old.

Several specches were made at the cemetery. I thought we'd never leave. Verania and Sergio stood by me the whole time as though we were rehearsing the film of the family united in grief. Verania even let me hug her, and Checo squeezed my hand like a boyfriend.

When the grave-diggers were about to shovel the earth in over their father I told the children to get a handful of earth and throw it in. I bent down at the same time and threw the earth against the coffin at the bottom of a dark pit. The children did the same. I wanted to remember Andrés's face. I couldn't. I wanted to feel the grief of never seeing him again. I couldn't. I felt free. I was afraid.

I wanted to sit on the ground. I wished people were not watching me. I wanted not to care if I cried like Lilia with her dirty face and sobbing noises, like Marcela leaning against Octavio, like Verania hiccupping from shock and abandon.

I thought of Carlos, whose funeral I went to forcibly holding back my tears. I could remember him. I remembered his exact smile and hands, taken away so suddenly. At that point, as was fitting for a widow, I began to cry more than my children.

Checo kept clutching my hand, Verania tried to comfort me; it started to rain. That was Zacatlán for you, always raining. But I didn't care what happened to that town, I wasn't ever coming back. I stopped crying at the thought. There were so many things I would never have to do again. I was myself, nobody could order me about. So many things I could do, I thought laughing to myself in the pouring rain. Sitting on the ground, playing with the wet earth around Andrés's grave. Delighted with my future, almost happy.

400357

400357

F
MAS

Mastretta, Angeles,
1949-

Mexican bolero

$19.95

DATE DUE			